Portrait of Amy

a novel by

Dorothy
Saltwell Kimmings

Lovemore Books

Portrait of Amy

First published in Great Britain in paperback in August 2014 by Lovemore Books,
28 Quintin Gurney House, Keswick Hall, Keswick, Norwich NR4 6RP
Tel: 01603 454636 email: anthony.grey@virgin.net

ISBN Paperback 978-1-906749-28-6

A CIP catalogue record for this book is available from the British Library

Front cover and text designed by Graham Watering
Printed by The Really Useful Print Company, Unit 15,
Bessemer Road, Norwich NR4 6DQ
Tel: 01603 629796

Lovemore Books

First Reviews of
PORTRAIT OF AMY

'The gradual unfolding of the past and Amy's part within it, is fascinating... The background is terrifically convincing... Amy's character makes the book, and our interest in her keeps us turning the pages... The final scene had me in tears. Lovely, and very romantic!'

Susan Sallis, bestselling author of the romantic novels *Come Rain or Shine, Choices,* and *Sea of Dreams*

'In describing the life of central character Amy, and her friends and family across more than seven decades of the 20th century and through two world wars, Dorothy Kimmings displays a maturity and confidence of style rare in a first novel. She skilfully interweaves suburban and rural Essex with London's sophisticated West End and the glittering fashion salons of Paris, creating a captivating narrative that artfully draws the engrossed reader through to its poignant climax.'

Anthony Grey, bestselling author of the historical novels *Saigon, Peking,* and *Tokyo Bay*

'All the characters in this fine, romantic, historical novel, are cleverly and economically drawn -- and what's most important, Dorothy Kimmings succeeds in making us care about all of them unremittingly right up to her very last page... It would not be difficult to imagine this story turning into a hugely successful televison drama series'

Sonja Haggett, author of *After Harvest.*

period fashion sketches by the author

CHAPTER ONE

The bar in the hotel was a long room, furnished in a style reminiscent of the 1920's, shades of pink and grey. Large windows looking on to a river were open on this warm June evening. The clink of bottles and tinkle of glasses, soft lights and music gave a romantic ambience to the room.

Small tables and grey upholstered chairs were arranged, not too closely, to give a degree of privacy to guests enjoying their pre-dinner drinks. At one of these tables sat a well dressed middle aged couple, sipping their aperitifs. The woman with hair and make-up too bright for her years, a bored expression, never exchanging a word with her companion. He, with immaculate hair, manicured fingers selecting nuts from a small dish on the table and looking, maybe with envy, at a group of men towards the centre of the room who were joking, tossing peanuts into their mouths and enjoying themselves loudly.

Amy looked to her right, there they were Margot and her family. six people, very much at ease, chairs and tables re-arranged to suit themselves. They sat easily and relaxed, enjoying their drinks, elegantly nibbling at crisps and olives. There was an abundance of light laughter and conversation. Margot and Tom with their pretty daughters and sons-in-law. Margot was as usual very vivacious and used her hands effectively to display her bracelets and rings which gleamed and sparkled in the glow from the softly shaded lamps. The evening breeze from the open windows wafted her expensive scent to the middle-aged man who had now turned his attention from the boisterous men to this animated group.

Amy moved back to the foyer, they hadn't seen her, she would wait here for Becky, they would make their entrance together. She found a chair which looked higher and more comfortable than the low, soft cushioned seating placed between banks of exotic plants. Thankfully Amy lowered her body on to the seat. She studied the plants and remembered the popular house plant of long ago. The Aspidistra, tapering broad leaves, dark green in a large round cachepot. Mother had had one, on a table in the window of the parlour. Every house seemed to have one, lace curtains too and a brown china tea-pot. Such lovely memories. Amy, as though watching an old film saw her life unfolding, slowly at first, dimly, then as memories came back it all became quite clear. It had really all started with that day in 1914 ...

* * * * *

"Mother, Mother, where are you?" called Amy. Distressed and out of breath she flung her coat on the floor and kicked off her heavy shoes.

Louise came to the back door and picked up her daughter's discarded clothing. "How many times must I tell you Amy, hang your coat on the hook and put shoes tidily under the stool", then more kindly, "Now what is the matter? Come in by the fire, the kettle's boiling".

Mother and daughter moved into the kitchen, a kettle was singing on top of the well polished black range. One end of the long table was laid with a white cloth and two cups and saucers.

"Tell me about it" said Louise as she warmed the brown pot and measured out the tea.

"Miss Chignall says I can't be a fairy in the Christmas Play" sobbed Amy. "It's not fair, she said I look like a gipsy and who ever saw a fairy with hair as black as mine".

"Whoever saw a fairy" remarked Louise, more to herself than her woebegone child. "I'm sure she'll find you another part, don't worry about it".

"But I want to be a fairy, in a white dress, carrying a wand with a silver star on the top. Oh! I wish I was like Sarah, fair and pretty. Oh I do, I do".

"Shush child, drink your tea, don't take on so".

Amy became calmer, she loved this time of the day, just Mother sitting opposite, both sipping the hot tea. The soft light from the oil lamp was kind to the room and the shabby chairs looked not old and worn but comfortable. The rag rug in front of the fire still looked fresh from the good shake Louise had given it that morning. The fire was bright and the fender and fire irons glowed in its light. Another hour and a large saucepan of potatoes would be put on the hot stove, then cabbage. Soon the room would be pervaded by the odour and steam of the family's evening meal. Amy dreamed of a time when she would have her own house and a separate dining room, a time when she didn't have to live in this old, shabby cottage.

Soon father would be home. He washed in the washhouse at the back of the cottage and then Harry would follow him. Both men worked on the farm, her father horse-man and brother Harry a labourer. Supper was always welcome, a hot stew or a bacon pudding, plenty of vegetables from father's garden. Tonight though, Amy was aware of an appetizing smell of meat roasting; strange, this was a weekday.......... Breaking in on her thoughts Louise said, "When you've finished your daydreaming child go upstairs and wash, put your Sunday dress on and your best slippers".

"Why? It isn't Sunday".

"Sarah's coming home to supper and bringing Hugh. Hurry now and you can lay the table".

Amy took the can of hot water from her mother and went into the hall. Under the door to the parlour there showed a faint glow, she opened the door and there, unbelievably, was a bright fire burning in the grate. Flowers in a glass vase in the centre of the round polished table. "It's beautiful, really beautiful" observed Amy, she was mystified, they never used this room except at Christmas and when, on the rare occasion, visitors were thought important enough to be entertained there. It was not anyone's birthday, Sarah was not a visitor, in a way she supposed Hugh could be classed as such but he was almost family.

The little girl made her way upstairs to her small bedroom. It was cold, cold and cheerless. The flame from the tiny oil lamp hardly gave enough light to assist her in her ablutions. Amy removed the large china jug from its matching basin and poured the hot water from the can she had carried so carefully up the stairs. It was not enough, for the basin was large and the coldness of the china soon chilled the water. She took pleasure however from washing with the remains of a bar of scented soap. Soap given to her last birthday by Sarah, treasured and kept for 'special' occasions.

At ten years old Amy was too thin, shy and awkward, she was a dreamer, her nose always in a book. Still anxious about the fire in the parlour she pulled on her Sunday dress tugging at the sleeves now too short for her long skinny arms. A line low on the skirt was evidence that a tuck had been taken out to lengthen the grey woollen dress which did not flatter the child's sallow complexion.

Amy bent her head and brushed and brushed her long black hair, the hair that she so despised. It crackled and shone in the lamplight. Her disappointment concerning the school play was forgotten in the excitement of seeing Hugh again.

Hugh had been walking out with Sarah for a year now. They both worked up at the Hall. Sarah parlourmaid and Hugh, chauffeur to Major Lambert, sometimes he was allowed to use the car on his days off. Amy loved to see her sister sitting beside him, like a Queen, wearing a dust coat to protect her blouse and skirt, a veil tied over her large hat. Perhaps one day Hugh might take her for a ride, dreamed Amy and then .... "Amy, come down and help me, what are you doing?".

"Coming Mother, I'm coming".

In the parlour a large starched cloth, snowy white had been arranged on the round table and a jumble of glass and cutlery rested in the middle. Amy liked setting a table, to create something attractive out of an assortment of objects. She carefully sorted out the knives and forks, not any of them matched having been collected over the years when Louise was in service, presents from her wealthy employers. Amy was responsible for cleaning the silver and it did her justice this evening. The glasses just needed a polish with a clean cloth, the flowers rearranged to her liking and the table was finished.

As she walked into the kitchen Amy could now definitely smell roast beef. This was an important occasion! "There you are at last" said her mother, "I expect you have laid the table perfectly. At least I can rely on you for that. While you're here give that batter a stir, there's a good girl".

"I'm dying to know mother, why all the fuss?"

Louise, her face flushed from opening and closing doors in the hot range, straightened up and wiping her hands on her apron replied. "Hugh has asked Father's permission to marry Sarah and tonight we are celebrating their engagement".

"Will Sarah have a ring, will I be a bridesmaid, when's the wedding, do you know, do you know?"

"Don't get so excited child, you'll hear everything in good time, don't worry".

The door opened and William Clayden walked in. His tall, rather heavy figure was tonight looking at its best. A starched cotton shirt open at the neck, his weathered skin looked tanned and healthy against the pale shirt. No collar or tie but he had deigned to wear tonight his best grey serge trousers and waistcoat. Amy thought her father looked very handsome. She was glad he was not wearing a spotted cotton neckerchief, because after all this was a very special occasion. William bent down to kiss his wife, Amy felt a happy glow when she saw her mother react with a smile and a loving look in her dark eyes. Father could be strict, his stern looks and gruff voice were off putting and Amy never felt she was very close to him. To see him actually kiss mother was indeed a rare sight and it added to the excitement of the evening.

"Harry nearly ready?" enquired Louise.

"Yes, he'll only be a few minutes. Amy, you look very smart, almost grown-up".

Praise from her father was scarce and Amy blushed with pleasure, she watched as he prepared a tray with glasses and a bottle of home-made wine.

Louise enquired if William had chosen Rhubarb or Parsnip wine and was satisfied that her husband had chosen what she considered the better Rhubarb to drink their daughter's health. "Another half an hour and they should be here" she announced.

Harry burst into the room, collar undone, hair awry. He informed his family, "I think they're here, heard the click of the gate. Mother help me with this collar, quickly please, they're coming". His dark eyes flashed, his voice loud as usual.

During the next few minutes Amy saw her mother fix the collar, remove her apron, pat her dark hair. Louise was flustered that the guests had arrived early. William opened the window to let out some of the steam and Harry was sent to open the front door. A door rarely used, this was indeed a special evening observed Amy.

Harry was too late. Hugh and Sarah had pushed their cycles round to the back of the house and came in at the back door. Sarah's voice and Hugh's could be heard saying "Hello's" and "Nice to see you's".

Amy's eyes went at once to Hugh, tall and fair, he .... stood there holding a parcel and some flowers. "For you Mrs. Clayden" he said, bending slightly to kiss his future Mother-in-law. She accepted the bouquet with a smile and pink cheeks. The little girl had her eyes on the parcel. Who was that for? It was put on a chair with Hugh's coat, a package the size of a shoe-box.

The beef was succulent, tender and Louise was congratulated on the well risen Yorkshire pudding. Father stood, glass in hand. "Best of luck and good health to Hugh and Sarah". he said. "I'm sure James wishes them the same".

James, the younger son was in Devon serving an apprenticeship with Louise's brother Walter in his Cabinet Makers Business. Amy missed Jim, Berrycombe was a long way from this Essex village of Shearfield, visits would be rare.

"Thank you, father", said Sarah. "A wonderful meal Mother and we are both so happy. Can you imagine, I shall soon be Mrs. Lodge?".

Sarah was glowing, her deep gold hair dressed high on her head. Her figure shown off admirably by the white, pintucked blouse. 'What a tiny waist' observed Amy. 'How fair her skin'. Oh to be eighteen and beautiful and to be engaged to Hugh. She saw the look in Hugh's eyes as he smiled at her sister.

Conversation around the table was of James and Devon. The War of course came under discussion and then Amy's attention wandered. She watched the shadows flickering on the parlour walls as the flames danced in the grate. She listened to Hugh's voice, deep and attractive without the Essex drawl she was used to hearing all around her.

The little girl looked shyly at her hero as he teased Harry about some village girl they both knew. His cheeks creased so attractively when he smiled. Amy loved his face and his voice. Hugh was perfect, Sarah so lucky to be grown-up. It wasn't fair.

Louise began to clear the table. Father lit his pipe and Harry became restless. He pushed back his chair noisily, wiped his mouth with the back of his hand. "Time for me to meet the lads in the Nag's Head. Thanks for the supper Ma, me belly's full to bursting" and he was gone.

"I'll help you with the dishes mother" said Sarah. She removed the ring she had so proudly displayed to her family, a small diamond set in a plain gold band. "Here Amy, you can wear it until I've finished". Amy was thrilled to place the ring on her finger. She sat next to Hugh, he put his arm around her and she pretended it was she who was Hugh's fiancee.

"There's a present for you in the kitchen, with my coat" he said, "Go and get it and bring it in here to open".

Amy was out of the parlour and back in a flash with the box. "Now Amy it is not new, Miss Lambert was turning out the nursery and thought you may like to have it. Afraid over the years it has been damaged slightly".

The paper and string were torn off, the lid lifted and there, lying in the cardboard box, trimmed with a narrow strip of white paper made to look like lace, lay a china doll. Dark hair, brown eyes that opened and closed.

Amy took her out carefully and gazed with wonder, the doll was dressed as a bride. The dress and veil were exquisitely fashioned of silk, lace and tulle. A minature wreath of orange blossom crowned the dark wavy hair. "She's lovely, beautiful" breathed Amy.

"And she's broken" laughed Hugh as he raised the dress to reveal one perfect leg complete with a white satin slipper and one broken stump.

"She was made in France" explained Hugh, "made in 1890 and her real name is Therese. Miss Lambert always called her Tessie though and she hopes you will keep her name and look after her".

"Oh I will, I will", said the excited little girl. "For always and always. Thank the lady for me Hugh" .

"Write a letter Amy, Miss Lambert would be pleased with that".

Later that evening Hugh and Sarah learned of the disappointment Amy had suffered over the school concert. "It's not fair" said Sarah. "Hugh you know Miss Chignall don't you? We'll go and see her, you can think of something surely".

Hugh came up with a wonderful idea. The next day he saw the schoolteacher and it was decided Amy could be a fairy. Silver dust sprinkled in her hair, her arms, rubbed with vaseline, would also be dusted with this sparkling dust and she should make a perfect fairy.

Sarah and Amy hugged him when Hugh told of his success. It really wasn't surprising that as young as she was, Amy Clayden fell in love with the handsome Hugh Lodge that day in 1914.

* * * * *

The school concert was a success. The tiny hall was crowded with parents. Miss Parish played the piano which badly needed tuning. The stage was much too small and the 'make-do' curtains never did meet in the middle. Miss Chignall presented her fairies and as Amy appeared in her much coveted white dress, hair and skin sparkling with silver dust, a long drawn out 'Ooooh' emitted from the delighted onlookers. Amy sang off key but she did dance well and waved her wand with her friends. She was a happy little girl. Even happier that night when Father of all people said "Amy, you were the loveliest fairy of them all".

* * * * *

Christmas came and went, not the usual jolly time with James away in Devon. He and Amy had always loved their stockings; filled with an orange, a pencil, sugar mouse and maybe a book and a tin toy. Mother, as usual, cooked the large joint of beef, an annual present from Farmer Yeldham to all his men. There was jelly and Christmas cake, nuts and fruit. Sarah had to work of course and Hugh was required to help the rest of the staff to look after the many guests staying at the Hall.

Amy spent the day enjoying the festive food and playing with Tessie. Her father remarked, "You're getting too big a girl to be playing with dolls, you must start learning to cook and clean. Another year or two and we must look for a place for you" Amy said nothing, she had dreams of a grander life. Hadn't Hugh told her she had hands and nails like a lady and that she must always take care of them. She was not going into service if she could help it.

The war news was worrying. The Germans had used gas on the Canadian troops fighting north of Ypres. The French had sustained heavy losses, the British also in the battles taking place. Harry having responded to Kitchener's call after seeing a poster in Epping one evening, was now in the army on the muddy Western Front. Worrying times.

In Shearfield however there was an exciting plan afoot for the summer of 1915. William was to have a week's holiday before harvest time and the family were going to visit James in Devon. Chelmsford, Epping and Ongar were regular jaunts. A few years before, William had been in The London Hospital at Whitechapel, Louise had once visited a cousin who lived in Bow and that was the extent of their travels.

Amy could think of nothing else. Dinah, her pretty best friend, was subjected to the details of the impending journey almost daily. "Do you know Dinah?" she said, "Major Lambert has offered to let Hugh use his car to drive us to Ongar station. His car! Us in a car can you believe it? We shall leave early in the morning and go to Liverpool Street and then underground to Paddington. The train for Newton Abbot leaves at midday and we shall take sandwiches and cold tea as we shall be travelling for hours and hours".

She danced her way home from school. Past the baker's and the blacksmith's forge, her shoes with their steel tipped heels and toes ringing on the rough road.

Dinah could picture the whole exciting journey. "I do wish I were coming too Amy" she said wistfully.

At the begining of July a visit was made to Ashdown's store in Ongar and Louise and Amy came home with light summer dresses, shoes and straw hats. Father had been treated to three new shirts and although he grumbled at the sight of the bills he was secretly pleased that he and his wife would make a good impression on Louise's brother Walter who was doing so well in his business.

The sun was shining and the garden was fragrant even so early in the morning. Eight o'clock and Amy stood by the gate looking for the car. It was warm with the promise of a hot day. She had insisted on wearing, with one of her new summer dresses, an old black and white fur tippet and was feeling extremely smart. Tessie was propped up on her good leg looking out of the parlour window. Cases stood by the front door, full to bursting. Mother and Father making the last rounds of the cottage seeing all was well. A little argument was taking place. Amy could hear it. Father wanted to wear his overcoat, grey and heavy, it sported a navy blue velvet collar and pocket flaps. The coat had been worn for his wedding and had been so fashionable then. Mother objected, the weather would be hot, the coat was old fashioned. No-one argued with Father but he compromised by carrying his prized possession over his arm, just in case it was needed.

Shining and beautiful the car arrived. Hugh looking unfamiliar in his immaculate uniform. He climbed down from his high seat and helped with the cases. Amy felt shy, this was not the Hugh she knew, the peaked hat, the navy coat with the double row of buttons, the leather gauntlet gloves, how smart he was, how handsome. The little girl sat beside him, Mother and Father behind. The open car went slowly through the village, Dinah's mother, Mrs. Rayne, stood at her door to wave as they passed. At the black boarded cottages Miss Saville and Mrs. Thurley waved their dusters and ceased their morning gossip to call out "Have a lovely time, remember us to young James". And then they were away, riding in style along the dusty road to the nearest railway station, Ongar, the terminus for the Liverpool Street-Ongar line.

A breeze played with the old fur of Amy's tippet as she held on to her new straw hat. Something tickled her nose and she saw to her horror a flurry of white hairs drifting across from her precious fur to land on Hugh's immaculate jacket. There was nothing she could do about it so she gave herself up to the pleasure of her very first ride in a motor car.

Amy became a grand lady of twenty five, sitting beside her handsome husband Hugh. They were off on their honeymoon, Italy or Switzerland maybe. Her blonde hair was piled high on her head and she was dressed in the latest Parisian fashion. The car stopped and Amy was once again ten years old, thin and gipsy dark, sitting beside a chauffeur who was her sister's fiancé. They had arrived at the station and were causing a stir. A car was still a rare sight in this quiet town and a group of locals were staring. 'Perhaps they think we are Royalty' mused Amy as Hugh helped down from their high seat, Louise and William, dressed in their country best. Someone in the group recognised her father and called out the Essex greeting, "Whoop Bill, moind how yer goo".

The train journey to Liverpool Street was not as comfortable as their ride in the car had been. Hard seats but the changing views from the windows kept the family turning their heads this way and that, not wanting to miss a thing. Epping, green fields and sheep under the trees. Woodford, houses with pretty gardens. washing blowing in the morning breeze. On to Stratford and Bow where father pulled up the window by the leather strap to shut out the smell of the soap factory. The backs of the houses here were grey, tiny yards for gardens where flowers and grass struggled to reach the light between high walls. Old Ford, "This is where we came to visit Cousin Annie" said Louise straining to see if she could pick out the house from the dozens that all looked identical as the train rumbled past.

Then they were at Liverpool Street. The noise and the crowds confused the Claydens. Soldiers and sailors carrying their kit bags jostled with the travellers. Carrying their heavy cases they asked for help to find the underground train to take them to Paddington. No-one mentioned it, but they were each very apprehensive about this journey under the streets of London. Paddington, it was so big. Amy stood with her mouth open, the noise, the bustle, so many people all hurrying somewhere. She stood close to Mother and was glad when Father took her little hand in his large, strong fingers.

The midday train was waiting in the platform and William found a carriage towards the middle of the train as instructed by Louise's brother Walter. Two men and a woman were already seated and nodded pleasantly to this little family so obviously 'up from the country' and continued to read their newspapers.

The journey began, it was not long before London and its buildings were left behind and green fields once more rushed past the windows. One of the occupants of the carriage began his lunch. A white linen napkin was unfolded and placed on his knee. Sandwiches, thinly cut bread, the slices cut through once to make a triangle, were eaten slowly and tidily. The woman also decided to eat and Amy watched fascinated as a dainty lace trimmed napkin was laid on her blue serge lap and sandwiches so small they could have been swallowed in a mouthful were daintily consumed. Louise, to distract her daughter who was so rudely staring, began to unpack their own vitals. Amy blushed, a large piece of crusty bread and a chunk of cheese for Father and thickly cut beef sandwiches for Louise and Amy. This followed by a lemonade bottle filled with cold tea to pass round the three of them. Amy refused a drink, she was mortified by the picnic, aware also of the sly looks and smiles that passed between the other occupants.

Things were better when the remains of the meal were put away and attention could once again be given to the ever changing views from the windows. It was hot and after a while heads began to nod. Amy tried not to doze but the monotonous rythmn of the wheels had its effect and she slept.

"Exeter, Exeter" shouted a porter and Amy opened her eyes. Mother and Father nodded 'Goodbye' to their travelling companions as they alighted from the train. The platform was busy, friends meeting, couples kissing, laughing and talking as they walked towards the exit. Porters handled the luggage, pocketed tips with a smile, doors slammed, a whistle blew and they were off again.

It was not long before the sea was sighted, the afternoon sun sparkled on the waves, the cliffs were red and William marvelled at the pinky redness of the soil as they passed through Dawlish and on to Teignmouth. Newton Abbot would be the next stop. Uncle Walter was to meet them there in his pony and trap. James, hopefully, would be with him and then a mile or two toward Torquay and journey's end.

Cases gathered up, hats put on and Amy had to succumb to having her face scrubbed by Louise who had hastily dampened a handkerchief with spit for the operation. They all stood waiting, waiting to open the carriage door the moment the train came to a halt.

"There he is, look, there", shouted the usually quietly spoken Louise as she caught sight of her brother. She almost fell out of the carriage in her excitement and the two small, dark people embraced each other fondly. Where was James?

"He's minding the pony and trap" explained Uncle Walter, a case in each hand his short sturdy legs led them up steps, across the bridge, down steps and out into the forecourt.

More greetings. James looked tanned, healthy and older somehow. Amy was quiet, her brother was almost a man, would he still play pranks and could they still laugh at the grown-ups? She hoped so, she had missed James at home and the fun they had shared.

Amy needn't have worried, they giggled all the way to Berrycombe, along narrow, dusty lanes. Fuschia hedges lined the lane, red blossoms hanging like lanterns, the sky a deep blue above their heads. The pony stopped outside a low, stone house, this then was where Uncle Walter lived with his 'Devonshire Dumpling' as he called his plump, pretty wife Anne.

More kisses and hugs. Louise and Amy were asked if they would like to "Wash your faces off?" which set the two young people giggling again. Supper was a lively affair. Aunt Anne provided a good supper. An immense steak and onion pie stood steaming in the middle of the long table and vegetables, that Uncle Walter assured them were only this morning still enjoying the red Devon soil in his garden. To follow there was junket and cream, cream of a colour and consistency that the visitors had never seen before. Amy took a spoonful of the junket, expecting it to taste like blancmagne. Ugh! She thought it horrible, she couldn't possibly swallow the stuff. Louise who was keeping an eye on her daughter's table manners signalled that she must eat it, all of it and poor Amy obliged.

"I think the poor l'il maid didn't like our local delicacy", observed Aunt Anne. "Jim, there's a dish of fresh raspberries in the larder, be a good boy and bring them in for your sister". So the meal went on, more cream and a cheddar cheese with homemade oat biscuits. Amy decided that if she could eat like this for a week she stood a better chance of attaining the plumpness she so admired in Sarah and Dinah.

An early night was requested by Louise and they retired to their small bedrooms under the eaves. Amy, looking out of her window before getting into bed found it difficult to believe that the moon she was looking at was the very same moon that was shining down on Tessie. She missed the doll, she should have brought her but Tessie was propped up on her one good leg in the parlour window all those miles away in Essex.

In the area around Torquay there was much to see, a week was not long enough. The Claydens were up early each morning and out exploring in the trap. William happily driving the willing pony who seemed to know his way to all the beauty spots. The carefree family would picnic by a river, trot through the fragrant lanes and visit the tiny villages with their thatched cottages. A memorable day was spent on Dartmoor. Amy loved the ponies, the wild bleakness around Hay Tor. William was interested in the dry stone walls and also the rough cider he was able to drink at an inn at Widecombe-in-the-Moor.

Each evening they would come back to a warm welcome and a huge supper. Amy listened to the conversation around the table and tried to keep awake. She did not want to miss a minute, not a second of this exciting holiday.

The workshop at the back of the house had the sweet smell of wood. Planks of elm, ash and mahogany were stacked against the walls waiting to be transformed into tables, chairs, chests of drawers or whatever was commissioned. There was a glue pot on the fire and tools were arranged neatly above the two work benches. Various pieces of furniture stood awaiting polishing or for brass handles to be fixed.

James was working on an oak side table under the watchful eye of his craftsman Uncle. Louise and William proudly watched their young son, glad he had chosen to learn a trade. Hopefully when his apprenticeship was completed James would return to Essex and find work in Chelmsford. Louise prayed that the war would be over soon. She did not want to see another son in Khaki uniform. Everyone was saying that by Christmas the Germans would be beaten, she hoped they were right. It would be wonderful to have Harry back again, to suffer his teasing and loud voice.

The drive back to Newton Abbot station was a quiet one. They were all sad the holiday was at an end. Secretly though William would be glad to see his horses again, the two shires Daisy and Betsy would have missed him. A busy time was ahead with the harvest. Such a lot to tell Dinah, thought Amy. She had missed her friend and looked forward to seeing her round face, surrounded by the chestnut curls of which she was secretly envious.

The train journey seemed to take all day and it was a tired looking little group that Hugh picked up at Ongar station. He patiently listened to all the Claydens news then he told them his. "I'm joining up, sorry to be leaving the Major, but I must do my bit".

Amy felt her heart almost stop, Hugh couldn't leave them. What about Sarah, what would they all do without him, his kind visits, his help and funny stories?

At the end of September news came that Harry had been killed during the offensive in Flanders. Amy had come home from school, no tablecloth or cups and saucers, no kettle singing on the hob. No mother to welcome her. From upstairs there came a muffled sobbing and Amy guessed, guessed the horrible truth. Harry, the lovable rascal of a brother, he was dead, another name to add to the growing list of men and boys this little village had lost. They would never see the Essex cornfields again, no more Harvest Suppers. Harry would never again drink too much at the Nag's Head and come home on unsteady feet.

Hugh, on leave early in October, stayed for a few days with William and Louise that he may see Sarah on her days off and make arrangements for their wedding. A date in April 1916 was decided upon, surely this war would be over by then.

The weather was wonderful that October, golden days, warm sunshine. Hugh found Amy sitting on a broken tombstone in the churchyard. She had been there a long time, she had been crying, crying at last for Harry. He would never sit here looking down over the farm. In front, over the road, was the Chase leading to their cottage. Amy could see the dairy, the cows, black and white against the green of the fields. A peaceful scene but the little girl imagined the muddy battlefield which was Harry's grave. He should have been buried here, sleeping beside Grandmother, Grandfather, surrounded by trees, hedges and birdsong.

When Hugh had come upon her, the little girl had stopped crying but he could see how sad she was. They talked and Hugh somehow managed to lift her out of her depression.

They sat there in the autumn sunlight, a little girl and a young soldier enjoying the quietness. Amy felt a twinge of jealousy when she thought of Hugh and Sarah sitting together like this. If only she were eighteen or even sixteen maybe ....but no, she was only an eleven year old schoolgirl and Sarah's sister at that.

Hugh, appreciating the peacefulness of this Essex churchyard lay back, closed his eyes and pushed away thoughts of trenches, mud and gunfire to which, all too soon, he was forced to return. Amy looked at his soft fair hair, falling over his forehead. Dark lashes, long and curled lay on his cheek. She wanted so much to touch that cheek. Was his skin as soft as it looked? He was a man but surely his skin was finer and softer than father's weatherbeaten face. Yes she must touch him, very lightly, with just one finger, just to make sure. Amy raised her hand and Hugh, sensing a movement, opened his grey eyes and smiled into her face. The precious moment was lost.

He sat up. "Amy, I've been thinking. Promise me you will not go into service at the Hall or the Rectory. Life is changing for women. You can have a career, break away, go out and do something with your life. Fight your father if necessary, I know he will be difficult but try, for my sake".

"I promise, I don't want to stay here for ever anyway. I'll work hard, earn a lot of money and come back to this church to be married. Dressed like Tessie in real silk and lace".

"But with two good legs we hope", said Hugh as he rose and dragged Amy up with him. "Race you home for some bread and cheese". They ran down the hill from the church, over the road and down the Chase arriving red faced and breathless.

Sarah waited for Hugh to get leave for the wedding. She had chosen the hymns. Amy had learned the duties of a bridesmaid and a perfect wedding dress was ready to be worn. Spring 1916 passed into summer and the wedding dress, covered with a white sheet hung in Louise's wardrobe.

Amy dawdled along the village street arm in arm with Dinah. It was July and the schoolroom had been hot and stuffy. It was wonderful to be released into the sunny afternoon. The village had a sleepy air, the blacksmith was taking a rest, his head down on his chest, his large hands dropped at his sides. The two friends stopped to look through the window of the village shop. No customers to disturb Mrs. Shepherd and she was taking advantage of this by having forty winks behind the counter. Her white apron was over her face to protect her from the flies. Dinah and Amy pressed their noses against the glass and made faces at the sleeping woman.

"What a sleepy place" said Amy. "There won't be time to sleep in the shop I am going to work in".

"You, work in a shop?".

"Yes, I shall work in a big shop, in London. Serve Duchesses, smell nice and wear real silk underclothes".

Dinah, practical as always enquired as to how she would acquire such a position. Amy, not knowing the answer said, "You wait and see".

Dinah's mother was at her gate looking for them. Mrs. Rayne's face looked a bit odd Amy thought as she said to her "Where have you both been, I've looked up the road for ages. Run along home now Amy, run, quickly now".

Amy picked up her pinafore and her dress in her grubby hands and ran down the Chase. She knew what it was, she knew! Hugh was home at last, he had come to visit them. Mother wanted her to run up to the Hall to let Sarah know. The wedding would take place, she would wear the pink bridesmaid's dress. Amy pushed aside the little thought that came unbidden. Hugh would soon belong entirely to Sarah. Her heart was racing with anticipation of seeing him again.

She nearly fell over a bicycle, Sarah's bicycle, it was lying on Father's vegetable garden. Not like Sarah to be so careless, Amy jumped over it. So, Sarah was already home, they would all be in the kitchen drinking tea, laughing, talking, waiting for her. She burst into the kitchen. Amy took in the scene, her lovely sister was in mother's arms, sobbing, tears running down her cheeks as she cried. "I want to die"

She tore at her blouse, her fingers dug into mother's arms. "Mother, Hugh can't be dead, he mustn't be dead, I'll die without him!".

The shocked Amy had a fleeting vision of Hugh's face as it had been that sunny autumn morning. If only, oh if only she had touched his face then. Now it was gone forever. Hugh was dead. Not here to be married, not here to see Sarah in that dress that had hung for so long waiting under a white sheet.

"Amy dear, make some strong tea, there's a good girl".

Amy picked up the kettle. Hugh was dead, just one of the thousands of casualties of this horrible war. His body was somewhere in the mud, the mud of the battlefields of France. Hugh was not here in the kitchen waiting for Amy to make a strong cup of tea. Perhaps it was a dream, it was so warm today, maybe she had fallen asleep at her desk and was dreaming all of this. Amy pinched herself, it hurt but not as much as the knife that appeared to have pierced her heart. She didn't wake up. Amy knew it had really happened, she looked at Sarah in Mother's arms, heard the heartrending sobs of the sister she had so envied. The little girl had a momentary feeling of anger. Anyone else could be killed, she didn't care but not Hugh, she needed him. God should have not let it happen, anyone else but not Hugh Lodge. Disbelief, anger and all the time the pain in her chest; but Amy could not shed tears.

Sarah's grief was more obvious and terrible to witness. She stayed at home not able to carry out her duties at the Hall. The bedroom where once Harry had slept peacefully and to which he now would never return was made over to Sarah. Amy was glad she did not have to share her own tiny room with this girl she hardly recognised. Sarah's face was swollen with crying, the lovely golden hair lank and lifeless.

William and Louise suffered in a quieter way. Their eldest son had gone forever and now their hearts were full of sadness for the beautiful Sarah. No-one spared a thought for the plain little girl who had lost her lively brother and now was mourning her sister's fiance.

CHAPTER TWO

One afternoon in August, Louise asked Amy to pick some flowers for the parlour. "Miss Lambert is coming to see Sarah. I expect she is wanting her to go back to work. We'll have tea and some of my madeira cake in the parlour about four o'clock. Don't be shy of Miss Lambert, she's very nice, come in and see her".

"Yes mother, I'd like to see her. I wonder if she will wear one of her tea-gowns that Sarah has described to me. Real silk or chiffon, pleated, trimmed with ribbon and lace".

"Can you think of nothing else child but finery and frippery? Now would a lady visit a cottage of all places wearing such a thing? Get out in that garden and pick some flowers, do".

When Miss Lambert arrived Amy was rather disappointed to see, when she stepped down from the governess cart, that it was one of the new, shapeless, loose fitting coats that the young lady was wearing. Amy was however, fascinated by the length of the garment. Miss Lambert was showing her ankles and even an inch or two of shapely leg. Dinah would be interested in this snippet of information.

Imogen Lambert enjoyed her afternoon tea. She remarked on the lightness of the madeira and Louise blushed with pleasure. Sarah was looking and feeling better and it was agreed that she would recommence her duties at the Hall in a day or two.

Plucking up courage Amy asked "Please Miss, would you like to see Tessie?"

“I certainly would Amy, it was so kind of you to write and thank me when I gave her to you. I did appreciate that so much. From what you said in your letter I knew my doll had found the right home”.

Amy brought Tessie down from her bedroom. The wedding dress and veil were still spotless and Amy showed the dolls’ former mistress how she had recently made another leg out of calico stuffed with horsehair. It was an improvement on the broken stump.

Watching the little girl, Imogen could see how she admired the fine materials and workmanship of the doll’s clothes. “I can see you and I have something in common” smiled the young lady from the Hall. “What are you going to do when you leave school Amy?”

“Father says I must go into service Miss. Don’t want to but he says I have to”.

“Amy, don’t worry Miss Lambert with that. Quiet now, little girls should be seen and not heard”.

Imogen Lambert rose gracefully to her feet, fastened her coat and picked up her kid gloves. Amy thought her very beautiful with her red hair pulled back in a chignon, little wispy curls escaping to rest on her forehead. Were her eyes really green? Sarah had said they were ‘green as emeralds’. Amy had not liked to look into them to find out.

* * * * *

Amy’s reverie was interrupted. Becky, late as usual, stepped out of the hotel lift and walked briskly toward her. “Wake up Ma, I’m here, no time to daydream. Margot will be wondering what has happened to us. Come on, I’ll help you up”.

Amy rose from her seat unaided, annoyed at being treated like an old woman. She refrained from pointing out to her daughter that she, Amy, had been waiting for Becky. Best not to start the evening on a wrong note. Eyes followed Amy as she walked across the room with her daughter. Tall, dignified, her silver hair shining and beautifully dressed. The brilliance of those large dark eyes was undiminished by the years. Tonight Amy was wearing a silk jersey dress, an expensive dress, draped at the right hip. A lovely shade of mid-blue and the long rope of creamy pearls with their silver and turquoise clasp gleaming in the soft light.

Kisses and hugs all round, everyone telling everyone else how well they looked. Amy always felt a twinge of sadness at these occasions. Margot had become so like Dinah, if only Jim and Dinah could also have been here to celebrate her eightieth birthday. The meal was artistically presented, the service quiet and efficient. Amy toyed with her salmon, studied the rim of her plate. It seemed a pity to disturb the pattern the chef had made with the courgettes and beans. The vegetables could have been cooked a little more. 'Nouvelle cuisine' it was called, she knew that but....

Amy did not join in the conversation, these days people did mumble so, difficult to hear. Her thoughts returned to meals and conversations of yesteryear. 1918 ....

* * * * *

Dinah and Amy had left school. Over the supper table she would try to persuade Father to let her do something other than go into service at one of the big houses. Mother was on her side but Father would say, "I'll not have you moving above your station Amy. It does not make for happiness to move out of your class" or sometimes "What was good enough for your mother and for Sarah is good enough for you my girl. Into service you will go. Anyway it is good training for marriage and running a home".

No argument could win him over. Amy wished that Hugh was sitting in the cottage and could speak up for her. She was falling into the trap of which he had warned.

Amy, at the suggestion of Sarah, applied for the position of housemaid at the Hall. Imogen Lambert was glad to take on the younger sister of her parlourmaid of whom she could not speak too highly. With reluctance Amy took up her duties. There were compensations though, she enjoyed living in the old house, loved the elegant furniture, the many pictures that hung on the faded wallpaper, the magazines that found their way to the servants' hall.

On several occasions Amy had to be reprimanded by Miss Lambert when she was found reading in the library or rearranging furniture to her liking. Once Imogen caught her posing in front of a mirror wearing one of her fashionable coats. Sarah was shocked at her young sister's behaviour but Miss Lambert was amused by the audacity of the housemaid and was lenient with her.

* * * * *

Tom was asking "Coffee for you too Amy?". She made an effort after that to join in the conversation around the table. "Ma and I have lovely rooms, overlooking the river" said Becky. "We'll drive out to Widecombe tomorrow for lunch and then I'm afraid it's back to London for me".

'She looks tired' thought Amy, she really needed a longer break. Just then, the middle aged man with the manicured hands passed their table with his bored looking companion. Amy noticed he paused momentarily at the table, Becky stiffened but he continued on his way. There was no sign of recognition between them. It happened so swiftly that Amy wondered if she had imagined the incident. A slight flush appearing on Becky's neck confirmed she had not been mistaken. Who was he? One of Becky's discarded lovers maybe. It was with a tiny trace of bitterness that Amy knew Becky would not confide in her.

Amy chatted to Margot's girls, they were so kind and spoke clearly to her. She had a soft spot for Susan and Anne, both so like their father, dear brother Jim. The same dark eyes and hair. They look as though they should be my daughters, Becky is not a bit like me she mused. She studied her daughter, smart blonde hair cut, rather severe black suit, an air of authority. Strange to think that both Becky and Margot were now in their fifties. Neither cousin looked her age, both glamorous women but with very different personalities.

Tom and Margot stood up. "Come on boys and girls," instructed Margot, "we must let Aunt Amy get to bed. It has been a busy day for her".

She bent down to kiss Amy and the hug they exchanged was a warm reassurance of the love they had for each other. "See you next week" whispered Margot. "You look so elegant as always. People have been looking at you all the evening, they probably see you as an Italian Contessa. It has been fun, I love it when we are all together. Enjoy tomorrow with Becky".

Becky went to see her cousins and family into their cars and to wave 'goodbye'. Amy gathered up the gifts and flowers she had received. Margot's present was Guerlains's 'Jicky'. What memories that evoked. Amy had used Guerlain perfumes nearly all her life and still could not make up her mind which was her favourite.

"Sleep well, Ma", said Becky as they parted outside their respective bedrooms. Amy guessed she would not sleep until the small hours but she could while away the darkness with memories of youth. A pleasant pastime in which she seemed to indulge frequently these days.

The bed was comfortable and Amy, her head resting on soft pillows, cast her mind back to the Hall at Shearfield, over sixty years ago.

* * * * *

Imogen Lambert, dressed in black, looked out of the Library window. The house seemed quiet now that the last of the mourners had departed. Father would have approved of his funeral thought Imogen. Not a hitch, the vicar gave the Major a 'good send off' and family and friends had gathered at the Hall afterwards to drink sherry and eat tiny inadequate sandwiches before making their way home. Only Imogen and her brother Charles left now to eat at the long polished table in the dining room. Imogen sighed and walked out of this room where her father had spent so many hours during his latter years.

Amy scuttled across the hall carrying a flower arrangement for the dining table. Imogen smiled, poor Amy, a sixteen year old housemaid now. Still thin and awkward, her thick black hair put up in a 'bun' was forever escaping from the many pins designed to hold it in place. Sarah was training her young sister to take her place as parlourmaid as she was soon to leave the Hall to marry. Her heart was now given to Jack Shepherd the village baker. The couple would live over the village shop with Jack's widowed mother. Imogen, remembering Sarah's grief on the death of Hugh Lodge told herself again that 'time was a great healer'. She and Charles would come to terms with the loss of their father just as they had when their mother had passed away when they were children.

Amy stood back and surveyed the table. The lace mats set on the dark polished wood, the crystal, the shining silver. Yes, everything was in order. Sarah had taught her well, the glasses for water and wine, the folded napkins each in its rightful place. Tonight as only Miss Imogen and Master Charles were here to dine, cook had arranged a simple meal and Sarah had suggested that Amy wait on table.

Maybe Father was right, perhaps this was where she belonged. Answering bells, polishing furniture, dusting, making up fires. Amy grimaced, she had tried so hard to avoid all this but all her cajoling had had no effect on William who saw his daughter only as a domestic servant. "What was good enough for your mother and for Sarah is good enough for you my girl" he would say and here she was at the Hall.

Dinah was working for Dr. Blair. The Lindens was a busy, happy house, full of children. An untidy house but no one worried about that. Food was the most important feature of life here and Dinah was learning to cook under an excellent teacher. Mrs. Cross had been with the Doctor's mother and father and took great pride in the meals sent up to the dining room. Dinah was very happy and a willing pupil. Dinah, much to Amy's surprise was corresponding with Jim. Many letters were posted to Berrycombe and Dinah treasured the replies she received from the young man. Jim was now out of his apprenticeship and almost running the business for Uncle Walter who was semi-retired. There was no longer any talk of returning to Essex and finding employment in Chelmsford.

Jim came to Shearfield for a short holiday each year and it was on one of these visits that he discovered his sister's friend had grown into a most attractive young woman. Dinah had a warm, lively disposition. When she visited the Claydens she would keep the family enthralled with tales of the boisterous Blair children. James listened, but he also was fascinated by her dancing hazel eyes, the chestnut curls and the pretty hands she used to give emphasis to the anecdotes.

Jim fell in love and that was how the correspondence began.

CHAPTER THREE

"Amy, Amy, where are you?" Cook's voice broke in on Amy's thoughts. She hurried back to the kitchen. This was Cook's domain, spacious and warm. Mrs. Bush was proud of the well scrubbed deal topped table, the shining black-leaded range, the dresser arrayed with a collection of blue and white china. She had worked for the Lamberts for nearly fifty years and was ready to retire. The death of the Major would mean change, of that she was sure. Her dream of a warm cottage with herself sitting with slippered feet on a stool in front of a fire did not now seem impossible. Mrs. Bush had already hinted to Miss Imogen that the time was coming when the Hall would have to manage without her services.

"The table is laid Cook, I have remembered everything", said Amy.

"Half an hour and you can sound the gong Amy. For goodness sake tidy that hair of yours before then. Don't forget to serve from the left and Miss Imogen first of course. Move quietly and when you leave don't let me hear that door slam or you'll be for it?".

"I know, I know", replied Amy impatiently. "Don't worry, Sarah has instructed me and I have practiced with her. I'll be alright".

Cook sniffed and stirred the chicken soup. Sixteen, only sixteen and she thought she knew it all. Now when she was a girl....but she had to admit, Amy was a good girl. Her heart was not really in her job but she never complained and was helpful and pleasant. A good family the Claydens, well mannered and respected in the village.

Charles began to whistle. 'It's a long way to Tipperary' as he descended the wide oak staircase but remembered just in time that this was a solemn day and completed his descent in silence. He was a tall slim young man, his Army service was responsible for the look of maturity out of keeping with his twenty two years. Imogen was in the hall, taking a pink carnation from a vase of flowers. She tucked it into the neckline of her black dress and looked up at her brother. "That's better don't you think? Unrelieved black does not suit me. Come and have a sherry before the gong sounds for dinner".

Amy managed perfectly, just as she said she would. She was of course used to Miss Imogen but was in awe of Mr. Charles who rarely visited the Hall. Charles' green eyes followed her every movement and Amy was very much aware of the attractive young man. Whilst serving him vegetables she was filled with pleasure at the scent of his cologne as she bent over him. She noticed his slim hands as he cut his meat, the long fingers holding the silver she had cleaned that morning. The brother and sister talked together as though they were alone. Amy was quiet in her movements, unobtrusive as instructed and she closed the door gently and hurried back to the kitchen with her loaded tray.

"Where did you find the gipsy?".

"Oh Charles, don't call her that, she would be so hurt. Amy is Sarah's sister and is training to be a parlourmaid. She doesn't look a bit like Sarah does she? I found it difficult not to laugh when I saw all that hair threatening yet again to tumble down her back".

Charles smiled, toying with his glass of port. "You know Imogen, I should love to paint her, she has wonderful bones and colouring".

"Saw you studying her Charles, poor girl she was so embarrassed. Enough of this, we have important things to discuss, might as well get it over with before you go back to London".

They sat for a long time in the drawing room over their coffee. The talk was of their future, Mrs. Bush was ready to retire, Sarah was leaving when she married. The Hall was too big for just Imogen to live in, Charles would not consider living in Shearfield, he had his studio in Chelsea and was happy there. The Major had not taken his children into his confidence regarding his financial affairs and they had both been shocked to discover that the

Major's capital had for some time been depleting. Interest on his stocks and shares was not as high as they had imagined. There would be only a small income for Imogen.

"Yes, you are right Charles", agreed Imogen. "It is the most sensible thing to do, with the imminent changes in the staff, now is the time to sell. I shall go into partnership with Dolly Wise, her shop is doing well and she has been on at me for ages to join her".

"Good for you, I know your passion for clothes", smiled Charles. "Will you buy a house in London, near me possibly?".

"No", replied Imogen. "I shall look for a house in Leytonstone or Ilford. There are some very nice new properties on the market. Fairly large houses but if can persuade Amy to come with me we should manage very well".

What a battle Amy had with her father. William at first refused to even listen. Louise tried to reason with him. Jim wrote from Berrycombe. Even Dinah became involved. Father was determined his daughter was on the downhill path!

"Two young women, living together on the outskirts of London? I just cannot agree Amy. No, you find yourself another situation my girl. Let Miss Imogen Lambert find someone else to run her house".

It was Sarah who finally settled the dispute. A long talk with father with much praise for the 'kind, sensible Miss Lambert'. Praise too for the way Amy had behaved at the Hall. William learned that his younger daughter was obedient, hardworking, conscientious and unlikely, most unlikely, to get into any trouble at all.

He gave in, tired of the whole business.

The Hall was put on the market, a tiny cottage bought for Mrs. Bush who agreed to stay and cook until the Hall was sold. Sarah's wedding day drew nearer. Amy just could not understand how Sarah could have forgotten Hugh in such a short time. How could she think of marrying Jack Shepherd. Not after being engaged to Hugh. They were not a bit alike, the only similarity that Amy was aware of was the ability to drive. Jack delivered the bread he made in a van, an unusual sight in the surrounding countryside where tradesman were still using their horse and cart to call on their customers. Jack didn't even look like Hugh, his hair was not soft and fair falling over his forehead. Jack slicked his dark hair back from his broad ruddy face and greeted all and sundry with a cheerful smile.

Amy felt sad and gave Tessie a hug as she made her bed in the narrow attic room at the Hall. Tessie sat on the white cotton counterpane, her orange blossom head dress askew. "Oh Tessie, you are the only thing I have to remind me of Hugh. He was so pleased to bring you to me that night and now he is gone, gone forever, forgotton by Sarah but I shall always remember him".

Imogen had been too helpful over the wedding. Magazines were studied by Sarah, Amy and Imogen and when decisions had been made, Imogen ordered and paid for the wedding and bridesmaid dresses. Sarah's dress was of white silk, a fashionable tubular shape with a low waist and gathered skirt to just below the knee. The chiffon veil with its embroidered edge was delicate and beautiful, white stockings and white pointed-toe Louis-heeled kid shoes completed the ensemble. Amy was to wear an almost identical outfit in the palest pink and pale grey stockings and shoes.

It was a lovely wedding, everybody agreed on that. The day fine, the bride beautiful and the reception in the village hall simple but extremely enjoyable. Jim came up from Devon and he and Dinah were as happy as the bridal pair, just to be together for a few hours. Amy found almost against her will that she was happy. Life would soon take her away from Shearfield, away from the sleepy village and its people she had known all her life. It surely must be more exciting to live in a town, she would no longer be 'little Amy, the Claydens youngest' but a young lady who would visit her parents in their cottage for holidays. Before long there would probably be a young man to show off on these visits. Yes, life was about to begin.

Imogen was busy with preparations for the move. She looked at several houses before deciding on a four-bedroomed terraced house in a select area of Ilford. An Essex town but near enough to London to make travelling to business an easy matter.

Dolly Wise, a smart, attractive Jewish woman was delighted when Imogen took up her offer to become a partner in her business. Dolly owned a fashionable dress shop in Kensington. Women now were leaving their dressmakers and buying 'ready to wear'. Imogen and Dolly had been at boarding school together and looked forward to once again spending most of their days with each other.

Amy was just longing to see her new home, the days dragged as she helped Mrs. Bush pack china, books and ornaments in preparation for the move.

* * * * *

The effort of recalling these details from so many years ago had tired the eighty year old Amy and she slipped down into the comfortable bed from her sitting position and drifted into a deep sleep. She awoke next morning from a dream where she was once again a housemaid, her uniform adorned by a long row of expensive pearls. The man with the well manicured hands was attempting to buy them from her. Imogen Lambert floated above her near the ceiling, looked down and gently shook her head. 'No, no', she seemed to say. Becky, so smart in a 1930's chiffon dress stood next to the man looking extremely cross. Amy, for some reason felt fear, fear of the unknown man. She was glad to awaken safe in the comfortable hotel bedroom.

Breakfasting together in the bay window, looking out over Torbay the mother and daughter talked over the pleasant evening they had spent with Margot and family. Amy mentioned her dream and Becky, her fork poised in mid-air looked for some reason embarrassed. Amy thought she was going to make some comment but the moment passed and Becky continued with her breakfast.

They spent a lazy morning, a stroll along the front, back to the hotel for coffee. Cases placed in the boot of Becky's car, the two then set off for a drive over Dartmoor to Widecombe and a light lunch at a pub before Amy was driven back to her Georgian house near Buckfastleigh.

Amy unlocked the front door, Becky carried in her mother's overnight case and set it down in the attractive white painted hall. "Mother, do please think over what I said to you Friday night. There are so many very good Residential Homes in the Torquay area. You are foolhardy to live on your own in this large house. You need company, someone to look after you at your age".

"Becky, it doesn't matter how many times you try to persuade me, I intend to stay put. Mrs. Monk comes in each day, her husband keeps the garden going. Margot or one-of the girls visit at least twice a week. You have to admit I am in very good health so why should I have all the upheaval of a move?".

In spite of her grumpy expression, Becky answered quite pleasantly. "O.K. Mother, stay here, I just hope you don't come face to face with some vicious thug one night. Take care, you are very precious to us all you know".

Amy knew her daughter was anxious to start the journey back to London and was not offended when Becky declined to stay for tea. They kissed and said 'goodbye', Amy waving until the car was out of sight.

Amy was touched at the family's concern for her safety but she was so happy in this lovely house. She wandered into various rooms; just one night away but as always on her return Amy wished to look at her treasures, touch the antique boxes and vases. pick up leather bound books. Smell the pot-pourri in the beautiful porcelain dishes. How could she ever leave this house she had furnished with such care? Even widowhood was made more bearable surrounded by objects they had chosen together. A Residential Home indeed!

Looking out of her sitting room window Amy thought of the pleasure she derived from her belongings. Was it wrong she wondered as she lovingly studied the patina of a small table made for her by her brother Jim over forty years ago. A copy of a William and Mary lowboy in walnut. Moving over to the window Amy ran her fingers lightly over the rich fold of the velvet curtains and as she looked out of the window she remembered her first sight of another house in another time.

CHAPTER FOUR

Imogen Lambert had described the house to Amy and she was prepared for the sight of the long, tree lined road with double fronted, red brick houses, each one identical to its neighbour. How very different to Shearfield Hall set in its own grounds. Number 34 had a gravel drive, double gates on the left hand and a single on the right. As they approached the green front door Amy noticed that the brass needed cleaning and that the two steps were of marble, dusty and dirty.

Imogen took a key from her bag and inserted it in the dull keyhole. The heavy door swung back easily and they were in a hall flooded with light. The rays from the afternoon sun were shining through the coloured glass in a door at the rear of the hall. A large window on the first landing of the staircase in front of the young women also allowed the sun to shine through. The front door was partially glazed and this together with a panel of patterned glass above it added to the brilliance.

"It has a pleasant feel to it, don't you think Amy?".

"Oh Miss, it's lovely, it really is", breathed Amy, anxious to see more.

A panelled door to the right opened into the dining room, spacious, square, with a bay window. An attractive white marble fireplace flanked by shelved alcoves.

"I can display my collection of china to good advantage there Amy, I can see it already", said Imogen her green eyes alight with excitement.

Down the hall to the left, a door was open, it gave a view of the drawing room. A long room, again filled with light there being a bay window in the front and french doors at the rear. Amy had a momentary glimpse of a rather overgrown garden before she was called to inspect the rest of the ground floor. The morning room was behind the dining room, square and pleasant with a view of the garden but somewhat darker than the other rooms. A large dresser took up almost one wall. Cupboards either side of a small fireplace. A tiny kitchen adjoined and Amy saw she would still have some blackleading to do as an old range stood opposite the usual Butler sink. A door led into the garden and there was an outside lavatory for her use.

"May I see my bedroom, please Miss?".

"Of course Amy, run up the stairs and you will see a door on your right, I think that is the room you would like". Amy ran up the first flight of stairs, paused on the landing to look once again at the untidy garden, then up the five stairs to open the door. Her room, not a small dark room as in the cottage, not a long narrow attic room as she had at the Hall,· but a good sized square sunny room. A large window looked over the garden and Amy pushed up one of the sashes. How strange to look out over neighbours gardens. Was Miss Lambert going to like this after the fine house and garden she was used to?

Imogen had by this time also climbed the stairs and invited Amy to see her own large, front bedroom. Two windows, a marble fireplace and as in all the rooms in this house the cornice was of a very good quality decorative plaster. Amy could imagine Miss Imogen's brass bedstead with the muslin drapes in this room. Together with the dressing table Amy so admired with its crystal bottles and their silver tops, the heavy silver brushes and hand mirror.

The second front bedroom was similar, there was a bathroom, quite up to date with black and white tiles. Next to this was the tiny back bedroom usually reserved for the maid. Amy turned up her nose at the sight of it.

"I thought you would be happier in the larger room Amy" , said Imogen. "I am sure we can make it very comfortable for you. I know I have two small armchairs and I think there is a small table all just the right size.

Imogen and Amy moved into 34 Welbeck Gardens on the 23rd May 1920. Ready to begin a new life in an exciting new era.

The remainder of that year was a busy one. Imogen wanted the whole house decorated and it seemed to Amy she spent most of her time making tea for painters and moving furniture from one room to another as the army of workmen progressed. Imogen, aware of the interest Amy appeared to have in fabrics, furniture and colours was not above asking her maid's opinion. Amy of course was in her element and once or twice had to be reminded by Imogen of her position.

Louise spent a few days before Christmas at the house to teach Amy to prepare and cook the sort of meals Miss Imogen might wish to serve should she entertain. Amy had been taught by her mother the basic skills before she had left school and found the more fancy cooking much more to her artistic taste.

On her return to Shearfield, William had to hear, in detail, a description of the fine Edwardian house, built in 1905 on the site of an orchard. He heard how the garden still contained some of the old apple trees. He learned of the large windows letting in so much light, the lovely staircase, of Miss Lambert's collection of china displayed so well in the dining room alcoves. William, seated in his shabby old chair beside his own fire, couldn't care less. He shook the pages of that week's West Essex Gazette and continued reading. He did mutter however, "As long as Amy is happy and behaving herself it doesn't matter how the house looks. Glad you went though Louise, it's set your mind at rest I know".

By the New Year a routine had been established. Imogen left the house each weekday about 8.30 a.m., to travel to Kensington. Amy then cleaned the door steps and the brass. Various chores took up the morning and when Amy sat down to her lunch of bread and cheese she would look around the morning room with contentment. The house was immaculate and was easy to keep that way. The afternoon was taken up with ironing, mending etc. Imogen would usually return about 6.30 p.m., to a meal prepared by a willing Amy.

Imogen was generous in the time off that she allowed Amy. There were plenty of shops to enjoy in Ilford and Amy loved to window gaze. At times, Ivy, the maid from number 36 would accompany Amy on her trips to the shops and their afternoon would end with tea at one of the many little tea shops in the town.

Worldly Ivy, so full of confidence, would order tea, toast and cakes and was not afraid to complain if everything was not to her satisfaction.

It took Amy several weeks to summon up the courage to enter a tea shop on her own and order for herself. One afternoon at the end of the winter, Amy took the plunge. She chose a shop opposite the Railway Station, found a table in the window and sat down to enjoy her tea and to study the passers by.

She lingered over a third cup of tea and slowly savoured the delicious sponge cake filled with jam and cream. Soon the trains would arrive from Liverpool Street, packed with passengers returning from their work in the City. Amy found pleasure in watching the people hurrying to their homes. She picked out the latest fashions. How short the skirts were worn now, girls were showing their calves. Many had followed the latest craze and 'bobbed' their hair. Amy thought that this new hairstyle complimented the present boyish fashion in clothes. Yes, they were right to 'bob their hair'.

Amy had considered doing the same but she did not think Father would approve. She must write to Dinah and bring her up to date with what was being worn in town ....and then she saw him. Standing taller than the girls, hurrying out of the station exit. Fair, soft hair falling over his forehead. Shoulders back, stiff white collar and a dark immaculate overcoat. He held a rolled umbrella in his hand and looking to his left and right he dashed across the road toward the shop. Amy's heart jumped, it was Hugh, he had seen her, was coming into the shop. She stood up pressing money into the hand of the surprised waitress. The young man held up his free hand and jumped on the bus that had slowed down for him and then he had gone.

Amy gathered up her scarf and bag, rushed to the door in time to see another red 'bus lumbering along in the same direction. Amy was on the platform the moment it stopped. The conductor stood in front of her as she sat down "Where to love?".

"Where are you going?", breathed Amy.

"Barking" snapped the conductor and gave her a ticket.

It was dark now and Amy peered out at the streets. streets she did not know. She had never been this far out of Ilford, where was she? She realised now that she had probably made a mistake, it couldn't have been Hugh, but somehow she was not sure, it was so much like him. If only it wasn't so dark then maybe she could see if he had alighted from the 'bus in front and was walking along the pavement. If she could only see him once more she would know for sure.

After a while the 'bus in front made a turn to the right and Amy to her dismay saw that the conveyance that was carrying her was turning to the left and there was no sign of it stopping. It had been such a foolish thing to do, to follow a stranger, not knowing where she was going. Amy knew that now.

A dejected girl got off at the next stop. She was in a road that was badly lit. No shops here to shed a light from their windows on the to narrow pavement, only small, dark houses. Amy felt frightened and lonely, she realized she did not even know the number of the 'bus that would take her back to Ilford. She crossed the road and began to walk back in the direction she had come. There would be a 'bus stop soon, there must be. She seemed to have been walking for a long time, her thin coat not warm enough to keep out the chilly night air, her hands were deep in the pockets in the effort to warm them. Then she saw a dark, stocky, overcoated figure approaching her. Should she ask her way?

"Please", said Amy in a timid voice, "can you tell me how I find the stop for the Ilford 'bus?".

His voice was reassuring, quiet and low. "Of course, don't look so worried. I'll walk back with you, it is quite a way and it's a bit lonely on your own".

As they passed a lamp post Amy looked up at her escort, he at the same time glanced at her and said.

"Why, I know you, let's see it's number 32, no number 34, Welbeck isn't it?".

"Yes, I live there", replied Amy.

"Don't you recognise me? I'm George the milkman. See you cleaning the step sometime if I'm late. What's your name?".

"Amy Clayden".

Amy was relieved, he almost seemed like an old friend at that moment. She told him of her impulsiveness and the consequent panic on finding herself alone in strange surroundings.

"You may have been right I suppose", said George. "I'm inclined to think though that you saw something in the man that reminded you of your friend and because you wanted it to be him you convinced yourself it was him".

"Maybe", said Amy. "He did seem to me to be Hugh, I just don't know".

"Here's your 'bus Amy. Got money for your fare?".

Amy thanked the boy. When she was sitting down and feeling safe again she relived her adventure and couldn't wait to get home to relate it in detail to Miss Imogen.

Imogen listened with sympathy. "Oh Amy, I fear you have made a mistake, it couldn't have been Hugh Lodge. He was reported 'Killed in action' you know, not 'Missing'. I should forget about it dear".

The next morning when Amy took in the milk, under one of the bottles was a note.

'Dear Amy', it read, 'I hope you got home safe. Are you out on Sunday, if so would you like to walk in the Park? Let me know tomorrow. George'. Amy was delighted, at last, a young man asking her out. She had begun to think it would never happen. It was a pleasant if not an exciting friendship.

For the first time Amy visited the cinema, she saw Rudolph Valentino in 'The Four Horseman of the Apocalypse' and was fascinated by the Italian actor with his dark good looks and flashing eyes. George also took her to see Charlie Chaplin in 'The Kid' but this did not appeal to Amy's romantic nature.

Imogen was pleased for her maid. George was a pleasant, well mannered young man and he was meticulous about bringing Amy right back to the door after an evening out. Imogen felt responsible for Amy who was not yet seventeen. The relationship between the two young women was changing gradually, Amy still had respect for her employer but living in close proximity she was not now in awe of Imogen Lambert.

When they had first moved into Ilford, Imogen ate alone at the walnut table in the dining room, Amy quietly moving backwards and forwards serving her mistress. The arrangement was now discontinued. Imogen on returning from Kensington preferred to dine with Amy in the cosy morning room. She would relate the events of her day at 'Theodora' the smart shop she now partly owned. They sat facing each other over the small table, Amy devouring every word, her large dark eyes fixed on the 'business woman' she envied.

Amy would have liked to talk to Imogen about George's kisses, but she refrained. George, when seeing her home, would now stop at the top of the road and sheltered somewhat by a large cherry tree he would put his arms around her and press his lips to hers. The first time this had happened Amy had expected, well, she didn't quite know what she expected. A thrill of some kind, a thudding of her heart, a tingling excitement as their lips met. It was supposed to be like that, she had read about it. She was disappointed, it was quite a nice feeling, George's face, warm, so close to hers. His breath was fresh, he smelt of soap, clean and wholesome. There was no magic, no bells ringing, perhaps it only happened in books. Could Miss Imogen have told her?

George on the other hand was very happy. He always whistled on his morning rounds but now when he came up the path of number 34 he would be singing! Singing 'If You Were The Only Girl In the World' or more embarrassingly his verion of 'K-K-Katy, Wonderful K-Katy' with the name A-Amy substituted.

Amy welcomed the time she could spend in her own room. Curtains and bedcover were in a pretty cotton print, rosebuds and violets scattered on a white ground. Imogen, as she had promised, had supplied two armchairs and a small round table. Louise at Amy's request had found some deep pink, heavy cotton and made for her daughter, frilled cushions and tablecloth. A cupboard to the right of the small fireplace acted as a wardrobe, hanging inside was the dress Amy had worn for Sarah's wedding, a navy blue Melton coat which had once belonged to Sarah. Two afternoon dresses made by Louise hung next to Amy's uniform of blue cotton morning and black sateen afternoon dresses. Shoes, hats and gloves were stored on the top shelf. To the left of the fireplace were shelves. Tessie sat on the top shelf her eyes staring, black lashes painted on to the china face. The replacement leg had gone and her one leg was covered modestly by her wedding dress. Next to the doll was a photograph in an oval wooden frame, a family group. Taken when Amy was a little girl there were Mother and Father side by side. Amy sitting in front of them, Jim next to her. Harry, poor Harry stood smiling beside the lovely Sarah and next to her, tall, upright and so handsome was Hugh. That had been a happy day remembered Amy, cousin Will had been visiting and it had been a great thrill to be photographed. They all looked a bit scared by the unusual event as they posed in the garden of the cottage at Shearfield.

Amy was chatting to Tessie as she often did. "Do you know Tessie, George and Ivy too, are always teasing me about they way I speak. Well, I wouldn't want to sound like them but I would very much like to speak as Miss Imogen does. I have decided I am going to listen to her voice most carefully. Each evening I shall practice on you until I get it right". She gave the doll a quick kiss on her cold little china nose before getting into bed.

For several weeks after the sighting of the man who looked like Hugh, Amy haunted Ilford station between five and six o'clock in the evenings whenever she was able. She scanned the figures as they came up the steps from the platform but never again saw that tall, fair figure. If she did see him again and it was Hugh, what would happen? Sarah was married to Jack now and was happily running the village shop with Jack's mother. Sarah was happy, did she ever even spare a thought for her dead sweetheart Amy wondered?

Before Christmas Amy went to stay for a few days with her mother and father. She had not realized just how much she had missed the village and the people. She had been so anxious to get away. Dinah asked so many questions about George and Amy was aware that Dinah and Jim shared a much closer relationship than she had with the kind considerate milkman. A special meal was put on, William opened a bottle of wine that was not home-made and Louise excelled herself with the food she produced. Sarah and Jack came, they were expecting their first baby and the family raised their glasses in honour of the baby. Amy was reminded of another celebration back in 1914 when other faces had been around the table. Sitting in the parlour Amy looked around and remembered how as a child she had thought this room so beautiful and how she had planned to have one such as this when she grew up. After living at Shearfield Hall and now Welbeck Gardens, Amy's aspirations had changed somewhat.

Christmas drew near. Charles was going to spend the holiday with Imogen. He sometimes came at weekends for a meal and would occasionally use the second front bedroom for the night. Amy was still a little shy of the good looking younger brother of her employer.

Imogen and Amy decorated the hall and the drawing room. A tall tree was placed in the front bay, decorated with gold and silver baubles. It glittered magnificently. Mistletoe was hung over the dining room door and a holly wreath welcomed callers.

Charles arrived on Christmas Eve. He seemed to fill the hall when Amy opened the door to him. His face was vivid with his wide smile and laughing green eyes. Breathless from the walk up the hill from the station, he dropped various parcels and bags on the floor. The cold air had come in with him, he unwound the long scarf that was around his neck and Amy helped him out of his warm overcoat. She felt a thrill of excitement, Christmas had begun, the house had come alive.

"Imogen, Imogen. I'm here. What about a drink for your little brother". Imogen came running down the stairs looking much younger than her twenty eight years. Amy approved of Imogen's short skirted jumper suit, belted low on the hips. She decided, there and then, to buy something similar to wear at Easter.

Dinner that evening was taken by the brother and sister in the dining room and Amy ate alone at the small table in the morning room. Charles remarked to his sister how Amy had changed. "She is not the 'country girl' I first met Imogen. She is no longer gauche and appears to have lost completely her broad Essex accent".

"She has certainly lost her awkwardness and is not shy with me anymore", Imogen thought for a moment. "I really hadn't noticed her speech, but you are right. I expect living so closely to me Amy has unconsciously picked up my manner of speaking".

Charles replied, "I have noticed you two have formed a relationship that is unusual between a mistress and maid. Whatever would father have said I wonder".

"You are as bad as Amy", said Imogen. "She is always saying 'Father wouldn't like it or I don't know what Father would say'. I know we both loved Dad but he did stop me from doing so many things. I so wanted to drive an ambulance in the war or to nurse. He kept me at home at his beck and call. I can tell you from now on I shall do whatever I please".

As if to prove her point, Imogen produced a long ebony holder and inserted one of the cigarettes of which she knew Charles disapproved.

Charles thought it wise to change the subject and said, "I still want to paint the girl you know".

"Why don't you ask her over the holiday. Be careful though Charles, don't frighten her, she is still shy of you. She might think you mean to paint her in the nude and I don't want her running back to Shearfield".

During the evening the brother and sister arranged the presents under the tree and drank quite an amount of the sherry that Amy had left on a silver salver together with nuts and fruit.

Sitting on the hearth rug, cracking a brazil nut Charles looked around the drawing room with admiration. "You know you have created a lovely, harmonious room Imogen". he said. "What a clever idea to paint the ceiling in that particular pale blue, so delicate and the white cornice is now shown off to advantage. I was hardly aware of it before. I like the way in which the furniture is arranged and how lovely that turquoise velvet chair looks against the Chinese screen. The colour draws attention to the turquoise of the flowers and birds feathers beautifully. The lamps and china are just right for this room, well done".

"You must give some of the credit to Amy", smiled Imogen. "She suggested the colour scheme and the treatment of the ceiling. I came home one day and she had rearranged everything. Brought in lamps and vases from the hall and dining room, put those from here in other rooms. I was cross with her at first, eventually I could see she was right. She has an eye for such things you might say".

Meanwhile, Amy had called on Ivy at number 36 to wish her 'A Happy Christmas' and to give her a small gift of 'Parma Violet' soap.

"You seeing George over Christmas?" asked Ivy wiping her hands on an apron that looked as though it should by now be in the dirty linen basket not tied around Ivy's ample hips.

"Boxing Day" said Amy with a smile. "I've been given permission to have him in the morning room for tea and supper. Shall get him to help with some washing up. Miss Imogen's invited friends for the evening and I have to serve food and drinks".

"Lucky you", said Ivy grumpily. "You should see the size of the turkey I am trying to stuff. We have people staying, mountains of food for me to cook and no extra help. I'd like to be in Bow with me mum and dad, but no such luck".

Amy commiserated and went back to her warm chair by the morning room fire.

*   *   *   *   *

It was a busy and happy Christmas Day. After a splendid and satisfying lunch Amy carried a tray of coffee into the drawing room.

"Bring a cup and saucer in for yourself Amy!" instructed Imogen. She was sitting gracefully in one of the armchairs. Wearing a dress of pale blue silk Imogen had, as was the vogue, made up her face with pencilled brows and bright lipstick. "Have your coffee with us today, much more festive in here. Besides, we have presents to open".

Charles went to the tree and handed out the packages. Imogen was soon surrounded with tissue paper and ribbons. Amy gazed in awe at the pale blue satin mules and the dressing gown trimmed with white swansdown that her mistress had received. A lace trimmed handkerchief and Eau-de-cologne were also unwrapped before Imogen said, "Look Amy, there are two parcels beside you".

"Yes, let's see what Father Christmas has brought for you", laughed Charles.

The label said 'To Amy, with thanks and admiration for all the help you have given. Imogen Lambert'.

Amy carefully removed the paper to reveal a white box with the name THEODORA printed in black across the lid. Tissue paper had to be lifted before she glimpsed the contents. Her shaking hands lifted out an ivory Crepe-de-Chine nightgown, the yoke trimmed with hand-made lace. Exquisitely feminine. Palest pink ribbons threaded through the bodice and cuffs. Amy looked down, the box was not empty. Another layer of tissue was removed and out came a negligee to match the gown.

Amy, for a moment or two was speechless. She had never owned anything so pretty, had never imagined anything so soft and beautifully worked could belong to her.

At last, aware that Imogen was waiting for her thanks Amy spoke. "1 just don't know how to thank you Miss, I really don't. They are so lovely. Thank you, thank you so much".

"You are very welcome my dear", smiled Imogen. "It has not gone unnoticed you know, your love of beautiful things. I thought it time you had some of your own. Why not put the lingerie in your 'bottom drawer'? suppose you have started one by now!".

Amy thought of George and blushed.

"Open mine" instructed Charles, bending his knees and sitting on his heels to watch her.

The package was large, rectangular and' fairly heavy. Taking off the wrapping Amy found a box covered in a gold silk brocade, a bright red ribbon tied across the lid. She lifted the lid and an exquisite aroma arose. Chocolate, expensive dark chocolate, hand made. Layer upon layer of succulent looking chocolates, each in its own little brown paper case with crinkled edges. Different shapes, round, square, oval. Some wrapped in gold paper, some topped with nuts or crystallized violets. Amy had never received a box of chocolates in her life. She had often admired such boxes in confectioners when she was buying Raspberry Ruffles or Sugared Almonds and now, in her hands was a 4lb box of her very own.

Charles smiled at her obvious delight and accepted her shy thanks. Amy passed the box to Imogen and Charles for them to take their pick. There was so much deliberation from them both that Amy thought she would never ever get to taste one of the delicious looking confections.

Before Christmas Imogen had ordered from Harrods, a gramophone. It stood in a corner of the drawing room, an attractive piece of mahogany furniture. The turntable was under a hinged lid and the lower part of the cabinet was racked to store the records. At the moment the number of records was very small and they had been played over and over again. Amy was instructed this Christmas afternoon to change out of her uniform and to be one of the family. "Charles is going to teach us the latest dances", said Imogen.

Amy wound the gramophone by the handle sticking out of the side of the cabinet. Charles taught the girls to dance the Tango, still considered rather daring and Imogen in return danced 'The Black Bottom'. Christmas Day had been a great success. Charles and Imogen even helped with the washing up that evening. Amy was happy, very happy. This was the way life should be, she belonged with the dancing, the laughing, and people like Imogen and Charles. Father was wrong to have insisted she be a domestic servant.

When Amy finally went to her bedroom she had come to a decision. She no longer wanted to work for Miss Imogen. It was time to spread her wings and it was only fair to tell her kind employer as soon as possible. Amy looked at the presents, how could she say she wanted to leave. The truth was, she wanted to live here, be with Imogen enjoy her companionship. Not as a servant though, not any longer.

Before she went to bed Amy tried on the new nightgown and studied herself in the cheval mirror. Staring back at her was a fairly tall young woman. Dishevelled black hair, thick and glossy. The olive complexion tonight had an attractive glow, resulting no doubt from the festive wines Amy had been imbibing since the afternoon. Above her large, lustrous black eyes, the dark brows almost met as she frowned at the narrow face with it's straight nose just a shade too large. Her mouth was attractive, not too small, full with well shaped lips above a well modelled chin. It was a strong face and did not please Amy who longed for the pretty features of Sarah or Dinah.

She removed the nightgown, folded it and wrapped it with the negligee in the tissue paper. The bottom drawer of her chest was empty and recalling Imogen's words the Christmas present was laid inside.

The moment Amy awoke on Boxing Day she knew her resolution of last evening had been a mistake. She looked around the comfortable room, she couldn't leave this and unless she continued to work in the house another home would have to be found. It must have been the wine that Charles had been so generous with that had given her the idea of handing in her notice. As Amy put her feet on the floor and stretched her arms she told herself that another month or two and then she would summon up the courage.

During the morning Amy, in the dining room, could hear Imogen and Charles upstairs, calling to each other from their bedrooms. Charles teasing his sister, Imogen quick with her replies. Amy smiled, she liked the atmosphere of the house when Charles was here, he was so full of life. She heard him running down the stairs, whistling a popular tune as usual.

Amy was just leaving the room, carrying a tray of china when Charles called out to her. "Stop Amy, don't move, stand right there".

The young man took a step or two toward her and in the doorway bent and kissed her lightly on the lips. A pleasant shock went through the startled girl. A warmth engulfed her. Amy's impulse was to throw her arms around the young man's neck, to pull him close that he may repeat the kiss. He had been so close, the lemony scent of his cologne and the feel of his face against hers had been so fleeting. Charles had kissed her. So this then was how she would feel when one day someone like Hugh would take her in his arms and kiss her. She had known that there was more to kissing than the lukewarm response she gave to George. Amy stood transfixed, blushing, unable to meet those laughing green eyes.

"There Amy, caught you under the Mistletoe" laughed the young man to whom the kiss had meant nothing. He took the tray of china from Amy as it looked as though it was in danger of being dropped and carried it down the hall into the morning room.

Charles put the tray on the table and said to Amy, "Sit down, I want to talk to you. Imogen will be here in a moment".

Trying to compose herself Amy sat on the edge of a Windsor chair and waited for Imogen's appearance. What had she done wrong?

Imogen came in, sat down and elbows on the table she smiled at Amy and said. "Charles has something to put to you Amy. We both hope you will agree to his suggestion".

"You know don't you Amy that I have a house and studio in Chelsea", began Charles. "Well I would very much like you to sit for me that I may paint your portrait. It would mean you coming to Chelsea several times and I would of course pay you for your trouble. Please say you will do it" .

Amy looked at him and then at Imogen. She cleared her throat, clapsed and unclasped her hands. "But Miss Imogen, what about my work here?".

"Amy dear, don't worry about that. I'm certainly not going to worry about a little dust on the furniture or complain if the brass is not cleaned every day. Please say you will sit for Charles. Please sit for him. You could travel up with me in the mornings and come to the shop when Charles finishes for the day. I would love you to see the 'salon' as Dolly now calls it and I want her to meet you".

"I don't know what Father will say about it", said Amy rather shamefacedly. She knew Imogen considered her old fashioned in the way she was always concerned about father's reactions.

"You make me cross Amy", said Imogen. "Why should you even tell your father. You must live your own life, he doesn't own you you know. If my father was alive today I know he would be horrified to see me earning my living and would probably have tried to stop me, so although I am irritated I can also understand".

Amy looked at Charles, that kiss had not meant a thing to him. Just something that happened when mistletoe was hung up at Christmas. He was looking at her now, his green eyes searching her face for an answer.

"Yes, I'll sit for you Mr. Charles ..."

After lunch Charles and Imogen prepared for the small party they were giving that evening. Amy cut turkey sandwiches and arranged the sausage rolls she had made, on an elaborate oval dish. She was proud of those sausage rolls, even Dinah couldn't have done better. Dinah would not be a cook much longer though, she and Jim were to be married at Easter. Amy's schoolfriend would then live in Berrycombe. Devon was a long way away but Amy suddenly realized it would solve the question of where to spend her annual holiday next summer.

George arrived at four o'clock, he felt rather nervous drinking tea in the morning room with Imogen dashing in and out with glasses, plates and food. George surreptitiously studied Amy's mistress. How lovely she was with her bobbed auburn curls held in place with a silk band low on her forehead. He approved of the cream chiffon dress, the skirt hem uneven, falling in handkerchief points above slim legs and gold strapped sandals. Amy would look nice in something like that. Amy was a little flustered, it seemed strange George sitting there looking at her. Amy straightened her white cap and was glad she was wearing the crisp Broderie Anglaise apron that mother had sent for Christmas. George was probably thinking how smart she looked in the black sateen dress.

Imogen's friends arrived and George and Amy could soon hear music and laughter emerging from the drawing room.

Later in the evening, his face flushed with the consumption of sausage rolls, mincepies, cake and several glasses of sherry, Geroge held out his arms and said, "Give us a kiss Amy, a proper kiss". The young man came toward her, manouvered her into a corner and tried to press his lips on her unwilling mouth. Amy averted her face. For the first time she noticed how George had rather pudgy hands and he was now moving them over the bodice of her afternoon dress. She looked again at his hands, the skin chapped and split from his deliveries on the cold, frosty mornings.

Amy had a sudden vision of the nightgown lying in her bottom drawer. A vision of George touching her in that gown, of his rough skin snagging the silk crepe-de-chine. In that moment Amy knew, George would not be the one to see her in the treasure hidden in the bottom drawer.

Amy felt ashamed, he was such a nice boy, they had spent some happy times together. How could she be so unkind but she pushed him away.

"No George, someone might come in. I feel uncomfortable. I know Miss Imogen said you could spend this evening with me, but..."

George interuppted. "But you are my girl aren't you Amy and we are walking out?". Amy straightened her dress and mumbled that they would talk about it next week.

The remainder of the Boxing Day evening passed quickly. Amy was kept busy and George made himself useful by taking over the washing up. Amy did mention to her subdued friend the impending visits to Chelsea. George nodded and kept his thoughts to himself.

CHAPTER FIVE

There was some sad news at the end of January. Amy received a letter from Louise, written hurriedly, explaining that Sarah had lost the baby. Amy, her eyes filled with tears, looked out of her bedroom window, visualizing Sarah as she had last seen her. Sarah radiant, smiling up at Jack, drinking to the expected baby's health. Tessie, the bride doll looked back at Amy, her face as usual expressionless.

"Oh Tessie, it's so sad, so sad. Poor Sarah, why does everything go wrong for her".

Amy pulled at the doll's yellowing veil roughly, remembering the occasion when Hugh had arrived with the doll. Sarah's engagement, they had all been so happy then. Oh, life was unfair.

George had been let down gently. It was not in Amy's nature to be unkind and it had worried her that she must tell George that her feelings did not match his own. For a few weeks the young man was subdued, he did not sing as he delivered his bottles to no. 34. After a while his whistling could be heard again and Ivy from No. 36 was only too happy to take Amy's place at the 'pictures' or a walk in Valentine's Park.

The telephone, newly installed, rang one evening. Imogen when she had finished the conversation, replaced the receiver and said to Amy, "You are summoned to the palace".

Laughing at Amy's expression she enlightened her.

"Charles is ready to start the portrait. You had better catch the 8.30 with me tomorrow and I can explain how you get to Chelsea from Liverpool Street".

Amy had trouble with her hair the next morning, she had washed it the night before and the heavy mass was too soft for the pins to grip. She wore one of the flowered dresses her mother had made, cornflower blue. It looked well with a hat she had recently purchased. Blue felt, the brim was turned up at the front and down at the back. Unfortunately the hat did not sit comfortably on the abundant hair. Her only coat, a navy blue Melton cloth was rather too warm for the sunny April morning but Amy was pleased with her new shoes, fashionable with their Louis heels and three narrow straps across the instep. Imogen had passed on a beige leather pochette which matched the shoes perfectly.

Imogen, titivating in the hall mirror, awaited Amy's descent from her bedroom. She looked askance at her maid's heavy navy coat, much too warm for the springlike morning. On an impulse Imogen suggested that Amy may like to accept a blue tweed cardigan suit she no longer wore. "Have you a cream blouse to wear with it?".

"Yes Miss, I do have a shantung blouse, I haven't worn it very much", answered the grateful Amy.

They set off together down the hill, Amy almost danced along; she knew she looked as smart as most of the young women making their way to the station that morning. Amy wondered if she would see the match-seller outside the station at this early hour. She felt so sorry for the thin, poorly dressed young man, he would stand, on crutches, a tray of matches hanging from his shoulders. A cardboard notice stating 'Ex-serviceman. Wife and family to support'. Yes, he was there and Amy was pleased to see that already there were quite a few coppers in his tray.

Her ticket purchased, seats found on the crowded train and Amy was soon at Liverpool Street. She said 'goodbye' to Imogen who told her over and over again the route she must take to Chelsea.

Amy was very early for her 10.30 appointment and spent the time in Sloane Square looking at the window displays in the smart shops. A reflection stared back at her. The shoes of which she was so proud looked right with the blue and cream suit, the blouse with its embroidered collar was to her liking. The hair, that was what was wrong, Amy studied it, too much of it, the wrong shape for the modish outfit she was wearing. Then she saw it, a Ladies Hairdresser. The window dressed attractively, brushes combs and various bottles arranged on a crumpled satin base. Pictures of the latest hair styles were displayed. The 'Bob' was the rage and the 'Shingle' just introduced. A 'Permanent Wave' could be given here for the cost of four guineas.

Amy pushed open the glass door and walked in. An assistant in a smart white coat and with a haughty air came forward. "How much would it be to 'bob' my hair?".

"We would charge Modom four shillings and sixpence", came the reply.

It had to be done, she must be brave. "Can you do it now?" asked Amy breathlessly.

After consulting a book on a glass topped counter the girl looked up and said "Mr Charik is free in ten minutes. May I take your hat and coat?".

And so it was done. That long, glossy, blue-black hair lay on the floor. Amy looked down, there was so much of it lying carelessly in a heap on the black and white tiled floor. The black shoes of the hairdresser trampling it underfoot. She looked in the mirror, was that really Amy Clayden, the same face she had seen in her mirror this morning before she left home? A straight 'Bob' a heavy fringe above her large eyes, the smooth shining hair ended level with the lobes of her ears. The charming Mr. Charik held a mirror that she may admire his work from all angles.

"Thank you" , said Amy and rose, bemused from the leather chair. The gown was removed, more black hair floated down to join Amy's discarded, sad looking 'crowning glory'. What had she done? She rescued one glossy lock of hair from the floor. Wrapped in a handkerchief, hidden in the leather pochette it would be another treasure to place in the empty chocolate box, along with special letters and mementos.

The assistant smiled as she took the two halfcrowns and gave Amy sixpence change. "You look different, it is very smart you know".

"It is very short", said Amy ruefully.

"But so chic, so modern". The smile had disappeared. Complaints were not encouraged.

A young girl was sweeping the discarded hair into a heap.

That's the end of the old me, decided Amy. When Samson had his hair cut off he lost his strength, but I shall be the opposite, the 'country mouse' is no more.

She left the shop, a modern young thing, short skirted, long legged with a head that felt incredibly light. Amy felt so confident, she was now as good as the smartly dressed women about their business in Sloane Square that bright April morning. She carried her hat in her hand, the straight bob shone in the sun. How different the people looked in London decided Amy. Uniformed Nannies pushed immaculate perambulators. Young ladies window shopped and sometimes giggled at the sight of a self-conscious man walking by in trousers of the latest fashion, Oxford Bags, the immensely wide legs flapping. Amy thought them ugly and how uncomfortable they must be to wear.

It was not difficult to find the house, one of several around a small square. Tall and narrow with a black and white tiled path leading up to a white painted door. Amy rang the bell at exactly 10.30 a.m.

The door was opened by an elderly woman, her face lined but round and soft, broke into a welcoming smile. "Why, you must be Amy, do come in my dear".

"Master Charles, she's here", called the housekeeper and Charles appeared in a doorway at the end of the hall.

"Thank you Mrs. Gurney, hello Amy, do ------" Charles stopped, stared at Amy in disbelief. "Good God Amy, what have you done? You fool, you silly fool!" shouted Charles, his face contorted with anger, a deep red mounting his cheeks. "You knew I wanted to paint you and you come to me looking like this. You stupid, stupid creature". Charles eyes flashed with anger. "Oh go away, get out of my sight".

The Amy who had left Welbeck Gardens earlier that morning would have dissolved into tears at this tirade. Before she knew it, "Don't you dare to speak to me like that, ever again", came from Amy's lips. Her legs were shaking, the palms of her hands were damp but Amy's voice was steady.

Charles, in an effort to regain his composure, turned his back on her. Closed his eyes, unclenched his hands and relaxed his tense muscles.

Mrs. Gurney took control, she smiled gently and ushered Amy into a huge room at the end of the hall. "Sit down, I'll make some coffee. Don't mind Master Charles, just one of his paddies. He'll be right as rain in a minute or two. Please try not to get upset".

Amy was looking at a book when Charles came into the room a few minutes later. Rubbing the side of his nose in embarrassment he said, "Amy, that was unforgivable, I am so sorry, I really am. I was so disappointed because I knew exactly how I was to paint the portrait. I had composed it in my mind. Your lovely hair loose about your face, a crimson shawl covering your shoulders. A Gypsy caravan in the background. Now, well I see before me a completely different person".

"I'm sorry, really sorry Mr. Charles but I had no idea. I just thought you were going to paint my face", said a contrite Amy.

Charles, good humoured once again, gave a wry smile and said, "Mrs Gurney will give me a wigging for that outburst but she will produce some good coffee and home made cake first".

He was right about the coffee and Amy felt better after eating and drinking. She had been too excited for breakfast that morning.

The studio was built on to the back of the narrow house. Light and airy it took up most of the paved courtyard. The smell of oil paint and turpentine was in the room and then Amy became aware of the large wooden easel, the long table with its untidy jumble of jars holding brushes. Rags, dirty with paint stains, a palette lay next to a half empty cup of tea. Pictures finished and unfinished were propped against the walls. At one end under a large glass skylight was a wooden dais on which stood a chaise longue. A beautiful piece of furniture, the back and scrolled head in carved walnut. The upholstery was of dark green velvet, deeply buttoned. Amy gazed in awe at the elegance, she would have loved to examine the carving but was too shy.

Draped over a nearby chair was a crimson shawl, fringed with gold silk, embroidered with gold thread. Charles picked it up, spread it out to display it's splendour to Amy. He said ruefully, "Won't be needing this now. I shall have to revise the composition".

Charles came over to Amy and turned her face to the light. "Take your jacket off Amy and go and sit on the couch. I am going to spend some time sketching your head from various angles".

The remainder of the morning passed quickly, Amy loving the novel experience of just sitting, with plenty of time to daydream. She also studied the artist at work. This was not the Charles she knew. He was serious, his eyes searching her face, measuring, his pencil held upright at arm's length, one eye closed, not speaking much. The odd instruction was given to raise her chin or to turn slightly to the left or right.

Mrs. Gurney appeared to suggest surely it was time to have a rest. Charles agreed and he led Amy into the courtyard to test the temperature. Yes, it was warm enough to sit outside and eat the sandwiches the housekeeper brought on a tray. There was beer for Charles and home made lemonade for Amy.

"What a tall house," said Amy craning her neck. to look upwards. "Tall and narrow, do you use all the rooms?".

Charles, amused by Amy's curiosity, described his home. "In the basement there is a kitchen, scullery, a large pantry and coal-house", he began. "The ground floor has the dining room in the front and the drawing room that you have seen. The lovely curving staircase you must have noticed as you came in leads up to the first floor where I have two bedrooms and my bathroom. The next floor I have rented to friends of mine, Stefan and

Sasha, they come and go, no doubt you will meet them one day. Three small bedrooms and another bathroom in the attics".

"Poor Mrs. Gurney has many stairs to climb at the end of the day" stated Amy, sympathetically, guessing correctly that the housekeeper would sleep in one of the attic bedrooms as she had done at Shearfield Hall.

"Has Mrs. Gurney worked for you for long?", enquired Amy.

"This was my grandparents home as you know Amy. Mr. & Mrs. Gurney came here almost fifty years ago. When father was in India, Imogen and I spent our holidays here. I was in the basement most of the time and Mrs. Gurney seems almost a mother to me. Her husband died years ago and she has no children. I believe the dear old soul looks upon me as a son. She certainly spoils me!".

They went back to the studio, Charles was by now his usual cheerful self and whistled one of the latest dance tunes as he sorted through his canvases to show the best works to Amy. "I've sold a few but am not well known yet. In September I intend to hold an exhibition of my work in a small gallery that my friend Sasha owns, just off Bond Street. Your portrait, I hope, will be one of the important exhibits" Charles smiled and restacked the paintings.

Amy once again composed herself on the chaise longue and Charles studied her skin tones and hair.

"You know Amy", he said, "I have to admit the hair style does suit you. Thank God you did not have one of those awful Permanent Waves. The weight of your hair and the straight lines of the 'Bob' suit your strong features. You are a striking looking young woman and my portrait must do justice to the 'new' you".

He came closer to Amy, took her chin between his thumb and forefinger and turned her face that he may study her profile.

Amy again smelt his lemony cologne, this time mingled with the smell of paint and there was a very faint yeasty aroma of the beer he had drunk with his lunch. She moved, not her face but just her eyes that she may see the face so close to hers. His dark eyebrows were drawn together with concentration, his cheekbones were high, the mouth generous. Amy noticed that Charles wore his hair slightly longer than was fashionable. The reddish brown hair curled at the nape of his neck, Amy felt an urge to touch the hair, to feel the smooth skin. She felt a tenderness toward him. Charles was only a few years older than she, young to be without parents. Was he lonely she wondered with only Imogen to care for him.

Amy pulled herself together, thinking of her father's reaction if he had known that his daughter was having such thoughts about her employer's brother. Moving out of her class was how he would put it.

Charles moved away, unaware of Amy's thoughts. "I think we have done enough for today" he said. "You are going to Kensington aren't you? Well, I'll come with you, want to see Imogen about lending us a dress for the portrait. I'll only be a minute or two, have to wash and change. Wander around, go and see the dining room. I know you appreciate furnishings and china, you'll love it".

Amy put on her jacket, ran a comb through her hair and was startled when the comb went from the centre parting to the tip of the short bob so quickly. She did it again, what a strange feeling. She shook her head and felt the heavy hair swing against her cheek. She looked for a mirror, stood in front of it and admired the unfamiliar reflection. Amy had no regrets.

The dining room was rather dark, she noted a large gilt mirror lining one wall, this had the effect of doubling the true width of the room. The furniture was large and heavy, carved mahagony table and chairs. The massive sideboard held a silver tray on which reposed in splendour, an engraved silver tea service.

The table top shone like a still, dark lake, reflecting perfectly the porcelain dishes and silver candle sticks displayed thereon. A silver-gilt basket held a wonderful assortment of fruit. Amy did not like to touch but she felt that the fruit, maybe, was made of wax. From the lofty ceiling hung a magificent chandelier. It was an impressive grand room.

Amy could imagine Imogen and Charles as children, sitting here with their grandparents, behaving correctly at dinner. A nanny upstairs in a nursery, preparing for the children's bedtime. How the passing years had changed this family's life. Imogen working for her living, just one maid in her house. Charles renting out part of this elegant house left to him by his grandparents.

Charles was ready too soon for Amy, no time to revisit the drawing room. They left the house together. "Just around that corner" said Charles, "Alfred Munnings has a house and studio. I often see horses ridden into the rear garden to be painted by the great man. I shall never be able to paint like him Amy. I know that".

"Have you every met Augustus John?" enquired Amy. Charles looked at her in surprise. "No, I haven't, why do you ask?".

"When he was living at Matching Green for a while my great-uncle John was painted by him. My uncle was quite friendly with the various artists and friends living together in a house on the Green. Uncle John used to paint, watercolours. He would let me paint too when we visited".

"Now that is interesting Amy", remarked Charles. "I knew the Johns were at Matching and it would have been so easy to go over from Shearfield but at the time I was abroad".

Dolly Wise was dressing the window when she saw Charles. She called out to Imogen, "Charles is coming down the road. He's got a very fashionable girl with him today. It isn't Jane Forbes or Barbara Wickes this time".

"Another girl" , said Imogen. "Really where does he find them".

"This one walks beautifully", observed Dolly. "She is carrying her hat and she's wearing, no she can't be, but it looks like your ....".

Before she could finish, the door opened and Charles and Amy stood adjusting their eyes to the dim salon after the bright sunshine outside.

Imogen stared, she looked at Amy, then Charles and back to Amy again. "Oh Amy, your hair! Whatever will your father say?"

The two women looked at each other and burst into laughter, Charles joined in and Dolly asked them to share the joke. Imogen explained about Amy"s concern as to what her father would say or think whenever she did something unusual.

Amy liked Dolly Wise immediately, the tiny birdlike woman was as dark as herself, she also possessed large brown eyes and her nose was best described as 'important'. Dolly was 'chic' she was wearing a very simple black dress, straight, no collar or belt. A long, narrow, multi-coloured silk scarf added a vivid touch tied loosely at the neck, hanging to below the waist. The lipstick on her large mouth was very dark and matched the varnish on her long, perfect nails.

"Ruth will make us some tea", smiled Dolly as she tucked one of her thin hands under Charles' arm. Ruth came forward and looked Amy up and down, no smile on her hard face.

"Do you take sugar?", she asked as she disappeared through a door at the rear of the salon.

Amy's new hairstyle came under discussion. "It really does suit you", said Imogen. "We are seeing a new Amy Clayden today", turning to Charles she asked, "What did you think when first you saw her?".

"Better not talk about that" said Charles, winking at the embarrassed Amy.

Dolly, quick to sense Amy's discomfort took her on a tour of the shop or Salon as she liked to describe it. Dove grey walls, a thick pale green carpet. Spacious cubicles curtained with patterned chintz of grey, pink and green. The stock was hanging behind sliding doors the whole length of one wall. Two glass topped tables held the latest fashion magazines, a Vogue open at a page showing a haughty model wearing a dress embroidered with metal beads. There was a telephone, note pad and pens. At the back of the salon was a work room. An elderly woman sat at a sewing machine surrounded by dresses hanging from the picture rail, scraps of material, scissors and threads, altogether so much untidiness that Amy wondered how the harrased looking woman could concentrate on her work.

Ruth was in the minute kitchen arranging cups on a tray. "You stay here with Ruth", said Dolly. "Get to know each other. I'll take the tray with these three cups. If Mrs. Berg wants a drink she must come in here, don't risk a cup of tea in the work room Ruth".

Rose Berg was friendly. She chatted with Amy easily but Ruth hardly exchanged a word. Her longest sentence was, "That costume you are wearing belonged to Miss Lambert, I recognise it. It's too short for you, you know".

Amy blushed and carefully returned her cup to the small table. Mrs. Berg, her spectacles pushed up on to her forehead, rubbed her tired eyes and said, "Yes it is short, but what nice legs Amy has, they are worth showing".

Ruth just rattled the cups and saucers in the sink and did not reply.

Amy returned to the main salon and Dolly showed her the expensive garments hiding behind the sliding doors. Charles discussed with Imogen future visits Amy was to make to his studio and requested that a suitable dress be loaned for the portrait. Then it was time to join the crowds in the exodus from shops and offices.

Liverpool Street was noisy, men and women running for trains, pushing past ticket collectors. The engines like huge black beasts eager for their escape from the city to the counryside of Woodford, Epping, Ilford and Southend.

Amy was weary after the exciting day and glad to sink into a seat opposite Imogen, too tired for small talk. She closed her eyes but sensed that someone was watching her. Amy opened her eyes and standing over her, holding on to the luggage rack to steady himself, was the fair man she had followed last autumn. She could see now, that of course he was not Hugh, but how like him he was. He boldly smiled at her, his face creasing attractively as she remembered Hugh's had done. The man returned to reading his newspaper, swaying with the motion of the train. Amy felt her heart thumping. She stole another look at him from half closed eyes. He was tall, fair, well dressed. Long lashes rested on his cheeks as he read. He, like several of the men in the compartment, was hatless and his soft hair was so like that of the young soldier Amy had loved. Amy wondered, would his voice by like Hugh's, soft and gentle? The train stopped, here they were at Ilford and the standing passengers were the first on the platform. By the time Amy and Imogen alighted he had disappeared.

CHAPTER SIX

Amy's life was begining to go in the direction she desired. The dull routine of housework was no more. Most weekday mornings that April Amy travelled with Imogen, left her at Liverpool Street and then made her way to Chelsea.

Charles had decided on the pose Amy was to adopt. Wearing a pale sea-green dress of silk, a vivid pink satin sash low on the bodice, satin shoes to match the sash, Amy took up her position. She had to sit with one arm along the back of the chaise-longue, her hand relaxed at the wrist that her long fingers with their almond shaped nails be shown to advantage. The other hand was resting in her lap, the fingers lightly touching the long string of pearls that Charles had taken from a black velvet box. A turquoise, set in silver, formed the clasp which felt heavy on the nape of Amy's neck. Charles instructed his model to hold her head down slightly but to look up at him, thus making a feature of Amy's large, lustrous eyes.

The position of Amy's feet was marked in white chalk on the wooden platform, a lamp was placed to throw light on her face, the front of her dress, the pearls and her hair. Each morning the inexperienced model had to take up exactly the same pose and at first had found it almost impossible to keep as still as Charles demanded.

To pass the time as she sat, for Charles hardly spoke as he worked, Amy daydreamed. There were two dreams, one in which, the portrait finished, Amy would still travel up to town, but now to work in a large department store, Marshall and Snelgrove or maybe Liberty's. Amy could see herself, dressed in black, first assistant in the Gown Department. Going home to Welbeck Gardens at the end of the day to supper cooked by the little maid who had replaced her. The other dream concerned the man on the train. They travelled on the train together, he took her to theatres. He told her she was "beautiful" and she told him she was a famous artist's model. In her dream he held her hand and she looked forward to their first kiss. It was just like being with Hugh, but now she was grown up and this man didn't belong to her sister.

After a morning in Charles' studio and a light lunch with him, Amy was supposed to go straight back to Ilford and catch up with some housework. Occasionally Amy would have permission to spend the afternoon exploring London which she loved. Amy took advantage of her mistress's laxness and did not always return to the housework and spent far more time window shopping and exploring than Imogen realized.

At five o'clock Amy would be at Liverpool Street station in time to see the first of the office workers returning home. She hung around the platform, she walked up and down looking in carriages to no avail. The tall fair man was elusive.

One evening, later than usual having spent too much time in a Lyons tea shop, Amy ran to catch a train due to leave. She opened a door and almost fell into a compartment. An arm came out to steady her and it was him! They looked at each other and he smiled. Because she knew him so well from her daydreaming, Amy said quite naturally, "Hello, I'm glad you saved me, I nearly fell didn't I?".

His name was Douglas, he worked in an Insurance office and he kept Amy amused with his conversation. "I'll be on the same train tomorrow", he said as they parted outside Ilford station. "wait for me at the barrier and we won't miss each other".

Amy walked up the hill on air. She knew that tomorrow she must come home and clean, she was way way behind with her chores, but....

Imogen came home rather grumpy and complained about the meal Amy had hurriedly concocted.

"I've had a rotten day," she told Amy after apologizing for her brusque manner. "Dolly and I are not happy with Ruth. Again today she upset one of our very good customers. She was really quite rude to Mrs. Russell-Arnott".

"What does Ruth do in the salon?" asked Amy.

"She helps Mrs. Berg with hems and simple sewing on any dresses we may be making. Our trade is half ready to wear and half custom made. Ruth also runs errands for us, delivers clothes, welcomes and makes tea for customers. Should Dolly or myself not be at the shop we let her attend to a client, but her manner needs to improve".

"She does not smile very much does she", stated Amy.

Amy had by now made several visits to the salon and Ruth had never made her feel welcome. She would toss her blonde head when Amy arrived and forget to bring a cup for Amy when she made the tea.

Amy couldn't sleep, tomorrow she was to see Douglas again. She would come straight home after sitting and hurry through some housework. At 4 o'clock she would catch a train back to Liverpool Street and wait at the barrier for her new friend as arranged.

So it began, Amy was in love, every minute spent in the company of Douglas was heaven. She told him absolutely everything about herself. The train journey was much too short and he only lingered for a minute or two before hurrying to his home at Barking. Amy longed to hear the details of his life, but Douglas was not very forthcoming. Amy waited in vain for an invitation to the cinema or a walk in the park.

Charles was the first one to notice the change in Amy. One day he put down his palette and brush, wiped his fingers on the rag he kept in his pocket and remarked, "For goodness sake Amy, what is wrong? You can't sit still a minute, you're making it impossible for me to capture your expression. You keep smiling, spoiling the shadow on your cheek I am trying so hard to capture. Not laughing at me I hope?".

“No. no Charles”. He was no longer Mister Charles to her. “I am just so happy, can’t help smiling. Life’s wonderful isn’t it?”.

Charles waited for more but Amy stood up and asked to see the portrait. The last time she had looked at it she had not known quite what to say. The shape was right, the straight bobbed hair, the long slim legs. Dark shadows filled the eye sockets, dark brown umber at the side of her neck, one side of the dress shadowed in the dark paint. She had looked up at him a question in her eyes.

“Don’t worry Amy”, he had said. “That is the way I paint, I get the darks in first, you will see it all come to life in the next few sittings”.

Today Amy could see Charles had spoken the truth for the canvas was coming to life. She could see the texture of the silk, see the blue sheen on her black hair where the lamp light shone down. She marvelled at Charles’ skill, how had he made that sash look just like the satin it was? Amy put out her hand to touch the pink sash on the canvas.

“Don’t touch Amy, please don’t touch it, the paint is still wet”, exclaimed the alarmed Charles.

He stood back and examined his work. “I think we will leave this now until the begining of May. I have one or two small paintings to finish and no doubt you would welcome a break”.

“Dinah and Jim get married on the 29th of this month”, said Amy. “I hope to be at home in Shearfield for a few days. After that I can come whenever you wish”.

As she usually did these days, Amy went up the curving staircase to the second bedroom to change into her own clothes. As she reached the landing and was about to open the bedroom door, she heard footsteps above her and glimpsed a young man, broadshouldered, his face almost hidden by a blonde beard and moustache. He came down the stairs on to the landing, towering above Amy. He smiled, showing strong white teeth.

"Good morning", he said in a deep voice, bowing slightly and then he was gone, bounding down the last flight of stairs and out of the front door.

Stefan, that was Stefan then, like a blonde giant thought Amy.

There were several more meetings on the train before Douglas asked Amy to go to the 'pictures' with him. Amy was thrilled, at last he had asked her out. She had another boy-friend at last.

She described the young man to Imogen. "He is so nice Miss Imogen, very much like Hugh Lodge. I think I am with Hugh sometimes it's so exciting".

"Where does he live, how old is he?", enquired Imogen.

"I think he lives in Barking, he hasn't told me. I don't really know how old he is but he is quite a few years older than me, older than Charles I imagine, could be about thirty".

Imogen looked serious, she did not want to say it but she had to. "Amy, I do hope he is not a married man".

"Oh no. no", replied Amy, shocked that Imogen could have thought such a thing. "Douglas can't be married, he wouldn't have asked me out would he?".

Imogen shook her head at Amy's naivety and hoped her fears were unfounded.

* * * * *

Saturday, the 29th was a typical April day, the sun and the showers struggling for supremacy. Dinah made a lovely bride, her dress simple, her chestnut curls subdued by a circlet of orange blossom. Amy wore once again the dress she had worn as bridesmaid to Sarah. The little church was almost full and Mrs. Rayne gave a reception in her cottage. The table groaned under the weight of homemade pies, fruit tarts and cakes. Guests sat on the stairs, on the floor and in the porch. Mrs. Rayne was very brave but Louise guessed at the underlying sadness there must be with Dinah leaving to live in Berrycombe.

When Amy had arrived home on Friday she had made a great impact on her mother and father. William, the moment he saw his daughter said, "Very sensible thing to do Amy, to have all that hair cut off. It suits you, very smart and tidy my dear". He gave the surprised Amy a bear-hug before returning to his newspaper.

Louise smiled her approval and fingered the fine wool of Amy's jumper suit. Was her daughter warm enough she wondered. She looked at William and knew he too was impressed by the new found elegance of their daughter.

Jim and Dinah did not go away for a honeymoon but spent a few days with Dinah's mother. One afternoon they all came to tea, Sarah came too as it was early closing day in the village. Amy could see how very happy her mother was to have all the family sitting around the table. William and Louise had always wished that Jim had returned to Essex but it was not to be and they both looked forward to and enjoyed his annual visits. As Louise poured yet more tea she thought how young Dinah was, to be going so far from home. When was Amy going to bring a young man home she wondered as she listened to their chatter.

Jim and Sarah gave their mother a hand with the bedroom allowing Amy and Dinah the opportunity for a private talk. Amy had not told her parents about the plan she had for her future but she now confided in Dinah.

"I remember once on our way home from school you said your ambition was to work in a shop in London", said Dinah. "How will you tell Miss Lambert, won't she be cross with you, wanting to leave her?".

"I'm sure she will understand", said Amy, full of confidence now she was far away from Welbeck Gardens. "A daily woman could easily cope with the work, the house is not that big. Not a bit like Shearfield Hall you know".

"We are both going to have a change, imagine me a housewife, no-one to order me about any more".

Amy smiled and said: "I shall be keeping my promise to Hugh, no longer a domestic servant".

Then it was time to describe Douglas to her friend, Amy's eyes shone as she spoke about the young man who looked so much like Hugh.

Dinah listened and did not like to share her thoughts. Had Amy fallen in love with Douglas or the memory of the chauffeur who had become the handsome soldier to die in France?

CHAPTER SEVEN

Charles was ready to continue with the portrait and Amy again travelled up to London with Imogen. So many times it was on the tip of her tongue to suggest that the time had come to make the change from domestic to shop work, but somehow Amy could not bring herself to say the words. Her heart beat faster, her face became flushed whenever she nearly blurted it out, she knew that if she spoke her voice would shake. Amy was ashamed of herself, what had happened to the 'New' Amy. She was still the same shy country girl, unsure of herself, frightened that Imogen would not agree to her suggestion and insist that if Amy was no longer her maid then she must find other accommodation.

The weather was wonderful that May. Douglas sometimes met Amy in Kensington Gardens and they would spend the evening sitting close on a bench. His arm about her Douglas would relate his many adventures to Amy, who marvelled at his skills. He had driven fast cars and motor cycles. He could ride the most spirited horse, he would one day learn to fly. Amy snuggled close, enjoying the contact with his warm body. Douglas was doing extremely well with his insurance company, promotion came easily to the young man. Amy listened enthralled and believed every word.

Amy assumed Douglas was living with his parents in Barking and was disappointed that he was unable to see her at weekends. He said he had to visit a relative in hospital on Saturdays and Sundays and that it would be unkind to discontinue these visits.

Douglas did not walk her home as George had done, but would kiss her goodbye in some dark shop doorway. His kisses stirred her emotions, he was passionate, demanding. Amy responded, hating the moment when he would break away and leave her to get his transport to Barking. She would tidy her hair, straighten her jacket and hope no one had seen their embraces. Amy would walk home up the hill feeling slightly ashamed of her behaviour, but where could they go?

Imogen repeatedly invited Amy to bring Douglas to the house. Amy made excuses, for Douglas refused to meet her employer.

On the warm spring evenings Amy would push up the sash window in her bedroom and leaning out, taking in the scented air, indulge in romantic, impossible dreams.

She dreamed of the time Douglas would ask her to marry him, she wouldn't keep him dallying, he would have his answer straight away. They would live in a tiny villa near the station. Amy would have to leave the shop. (For by then surely she would have a position in marshall and Snelgroves). Soon she would become a mother, Douglas a manager. They would buy a car, Amy each month to buy the luxuries she knew they could not afford. It was all going to be so wonderful.

Charles had heard from his sister of the reluctance of Douglas to show himself. He agreed with Imogen that something had to be wrong.

"I'll speak to Amy", said Charles. "She's so unworldly isn't she? I can tell she has really fallen for the fellow, those huge eyes of hers shining, anxious to get away from the studio to meet him".

"How's the portrait going?".

"Fine, just fine. I'm pleased with things so far. The dress we borrowed from you is exactly right for Amy. She sits beautifully now, learned to sit perfectly still".

Amy sat, right arm resting along the carved back of the chaise-longue, hand relaxed. She knew the pose exactly by now, chin down, eyes open wide. She watched Charles mixing paint on his palette. "What are you working on today?".

"Your mouth, I'm mixing Venetian Red and Burnt Sienna for your upper lip and then it will be Cadmium Red with white for the lower lip. I have just put a dark, greenish shadow under your lower lip. Any more questions?", Charles smiled, pleased that Amy took such an interest.

"No, it all seems so complicated to me", said Amy. "I should just use red, white, black and a little pink if I should be painting my face".

"Don't speak for a little Amy, I am studying your lips".

Amy thought of Douglas, he had told her how lovely her mouth was. Told her he longed to possess her completely as he kissed her mouth, her eyelids, her neck. It was an unsatisfactory love affair, Amy knew that. Her idea of walking out was different to Douglas's. Amy wanted to be invited to his home, to meet his parents. She wanted to be able to take him to meet Mother and Father. She wanted a ring on her finger, it need not be a large one but Amy did want a ring.

"Amy, you have turned down the corners of your mouth. How can I get this right if you will keep changing your expression. Only another half an hour and I'll let you go".

The time passed and Amy, given permission to cease posing, rose gladly and stretched her arms, flexed her fingers. She moved over to the easel and studied the canvas. Almost finished now, details of the dress to be painted in, highlights on the fingernails, nose and lips. The eye sockets were as yet unfinished, Charles preferred to leave the detailed work of the iris and pupil until the last. Amy could see that once the eyes were completed the portrait would be an incredible likeness.

They drank lemonade in the courtyard, there was cold chicken and salad laid ready for them. Mrs. Gurney came out to them bearing strawberries and cream like a happy mother giving her children a treat.

Charles looked at Amy, her face was turned up to the sun. He wiped his lips on a paint stained rag and said, "I've an idea, on Thursday evening Imogen and I have arranged to have dinner at a little restaurant in the

Brompton Road. How about you and your friend Douglas joining us as my guests?".

Amy turned her head and squinted at him, did he mean it? Yes, he looked serious. She sat up straight in her chair. "I don't know, I mean, thank you Charles but I am not sure if Douglas will come. I'll ask him".

"If you are serious about this young man Amy, it is time Imogen and I met him. We feel responsible for you, you know".

Douglas, to Amy's surprise, accepted the invitation and arranged to meet them at the restaurant. Amy spent Wednesday afternoon looking for a dress to wear and was pleased with the jade green tunic dress she eventually bought.

Imogen and Charles, eager to meet the elusive Douglas, were chatting to Amy, endeavouring to make her feel at ease in unfamiliar surroundings when Douglas arrived. He was older than they had imagined, quite old in fact. Well older than Imogen they decided. Too confident they felt. Imogen had been prepared for the fact that he closely remembled their late chauffeur, he did but Douglas did not have Hugh's quiet unassuming manner. Throughout the evening Douglas led the conversation. Amy felt she was seeing him for the first time and felt embarrassed for him. Tonight with Charles and Imogen sitting there his stories did not quite ring true. Why had she believed everything he had told her in the past? Whatever did Charles and Imogen think of him she wondered?

Imogen kept her thoughts to herself and in the following week tried to think of how she might enable Amy to see for herself that Douglas was not all he pretended to be. At least she and Charles were convinced that was the case.

The difficult situation was resolved when, one summer evening, Imogen and a friend were taking a walk in Valentine's Park. They wished to look at the houses being built in what was to be called the Ilford Garden Suburb. Imogen met Douglas. He was arm in arm with a young woman and holding the hand of a little boy of about four years of age. Douglas met Imogen's stony stare and had the grace to blush as he removed his hold on the boy to raise his hat.

Amy did not want to believe what Imogen told her, although she knew that in her heart she had known but would not accept that it was possible Douglas was married. There was no sick relative to be visited each weekend but a wife and child demanding his attention. Amy shut herself in her bedroom to cry into her pillow. She had been so happy just to see him for a few hours each week. Now the days and evenings would be empty. How could he have lied to her, Hugh would never have done such a thing. Then Amy thought of George, poor George, he had been so kind and she had rejected him. Amy cried even more. Love was so cruel.

Life was miserable, food unappetising, her hair lost it's shine. Amy even declined to return to the studio and Charles was anxious to finish the portrait. He begged Imogen to intervene and somehow persuade Amy to pose again.

Sitting opposite Amy one evening, eating a lamb chop, watching her maid toying with the food on her plate, Imogen asked if there was anything, anything at all she could do to make Amy feel better.

"Yes, there is something Miss Imogen", began Amy, "I don't know quite how to put it. I've wanted to tell you for some time, I don't know what you will think".

"Do go on Amy, I'm not going to eat you, I am your friend you know".

"For years, even before I came to work for you at the Hall, I wanted to work in a shop, possibly a Department Store. I never wanted to go into domestic service but Father insisted. The trouble is, I don't want to leave you, I am so happy here it has become my home. My lovely bedroom, the view from my window since the garden has been taken care of. Remember how neglected it was when we first moved here?".

This was a long speech for Amy, Imogen nodded and waited for more.

"What I am trying to say is, would it be possible for me to find myself a position in a shop in London but still live here. A daily woman could easily cope with the work in this house. I would continue to wash, mend and iron for you. The cooking I could manage too. The idea has been in my head for weeks, please say I can do it".

Imogen put down her knife and fork, Amy had caught her unawares. She promised to think about it, even discuss it with her brother but begged Amy to do nothing until she had carefully thought it over.

Amy agreed, feeling better for having spoken to Imogen about her ambition, she announced that Charles could expect her at the studio once more.

* * * * *

The eyes were almost finished. Charles worked carefully, slowly, concentrating on the iris, the upper part darker where the shadow was cast by the upper lid. He painted in the black of the pupil, put some reflected lights in the iris. With bold strokes Amy's dark, straight brows were portrayed. Selecting a Sable Round from his many brushes Charles put in the final highlights, in the corners where the eyes met the bridge of the nose and at the edge where the pupil ran into the iris. The artist stood back and surveyed his work, satisfied he had done justice to those magnificent eyes.

Still studying the nearly completed portrait, his head on one side he spoke.

"I am pleased with the composition of the picture Amy, it has worked well. I painted the sash in that vivid pink for a reason, it represents your determination to be different. There is something in your personality that makes you long to be noticed and yet you are shy. The shyness I have tried to capture in the way your head is held slightly down, your eyes wide open and looking up shows an eagerness to know and see more of life. The pearls were to add interest to the simple dress but I have just remembered that pearls signify tears. Tears, well we must balance those with something happier. I know, it must be love, I will put a red rose in your left hand, a few petals at your feet". He continued his work in silence whilst Amy considered love.

Wasn't it love she had felt for Douglas? She had been so happy in the spring. His touch had excited her, his kisses stirred greater feelings in her. There had been talk of a weekend away together, sometime when Douglas could extricate himself from the constant hospital visiting. Close to him in some secluded hiding place, her heart thumping, Amy had agreed. Once back in her own room, away from his magic Amy knew she could not succumb, not until they were married. She so wanted to be the up to date 'flapper' of the 'Twenties but a small voice inside her reminded Amy of her upbringing. Whatever would Sarah and Dinah think of her. What would Mother and Father say if they were to discover her secret. No she must wait for the proposal of marriage that would surely soon be forthcoming. Now all that was over, the dreams and the hopes - the tears too she trusted.

Amy's neck ached, she moved slightly. "Keep still" barked Charles.

Why couldn't she be like Ivy, wondered Amy. Ivy fell in and out of love so easily, so often, without tears it seemed. Poor, kind George had gone the way of several other young men and Ivy was out dancing and flirting with someone new whenever she had the chance.

"Finished for today, wake up Amy, you can relax now". Charles wiped his brushes, there was a smudge of yellow ochre on one side of his nose, a smear of burnt umber where he had passed his hand over his forehead.

His hair needs cutting, thought Amy. He looks like a grubby little boy with that paint on his face and untidy hair. She felt a surge of warmth toward him.

"Doing anything this afternoon?", asked Charles cleaning his fingers on a rag soaked in turps.

On an impulse Amy came forward, took the rag from him and wiped the offending paint from his face. For a moment or two the couple stood motionless, then Charles moved away, surprised by the excitement Amy's touch had aroused in him. Amy, shocked that she had been so intimate, blushed as she replied to Charles' question. "I was going back to Ilford", she said quietly.

"I'm going to visit the Art Gallery where I intend to hold my exhibition. Care to come with me?".

"Oh yes, I would love to come", said Amy, her face still burning with embarrassment.

It was the first of several visits to the gallery just off Bond Street. At first Amy was rather shocked at the paintings and drawings of the nudes that lined the walls of the ground floor. Upstairs, small watercolours were displayed and down in the basement artful lighting showed some oils to advantage. There were landscapes, flowers and various still life. Amy found it fascinating with Charles beside her to explain the artists' work.

That evening, sitting in the garden after supper Amy related her day to Imogen.

"I met Sasha who owns the gallery. She is very unusual isn't she? She was wearing a wonderful, embroidered coat, so colourful and I have never seen anyone with hair the colour of hers. Not really red, more like a copper kettle my mother has. I felt too drab beside her".

Imogen gave a kind of grunt and examined the leaves of a geranium in a tub beside her.

Amy continued, "Sasha was so friendly with Charles, she hardly took any notice of me".

"She was a little too friendly with Charles at one time but I soon put a stop to that" , said Imogen as she plucked off a dead head from the geranium. "I'm surprised that Charles has chosen to exhibit at her gallery, he could have chosen another I'm sure".

Then sitting back in her cane chair, adjusting the cushion, Imogen gave Amy her full attention. She at last uttered the words Amy so longed to hear.

"I have given thought to your proposition and if you still wish to find other employment I have no objection to letting you remain here. As you say, the work could easily be managed by a daily woman. If you cope with the chores you suggested I shall consider that enough payment for your room".

Amy, for a moment or two was too stunned to reply. She would be free, no more blackleading, no polishing brass. Her thanks and appreciation were given with shining eyes.

"Thank you so much Miss Imogen, thank you. I didn't dare hope you would agree. Shall I ask Ivy if she knows of a woman for the work?".

"Not so fast Amy, I can deal with that. You must start looking for a vacancy in one of the stores. I have an idea myself of something you may be interested in but....well, does it have to be a large store?".

"Not really", said Amy just so pleased with life that at that moment she would have accepted anything in a shop.

It only took a day or two for Dolly Wise and Imogen to come to an agreement to offer Amy a position with them. They decided between them that with her height, slim figure and dark, striking looks Amy could be of great use modelling the clothes for them. It would also mean there would be another pair of hands to assist Mrs. Berg in the workroom.

Imogen longed to get home to tell Amy. "You know Dolly, Amy does so love dressing up. I have, on several occasions, surprised her parading in front of a mirror wearing one of my coats or a hat, turning this way and that. She does it so well you know, moves gracefully. She is shy though and we will have to instil some confidence into the girl".

William and Lousie read and reread the letter their younger daughter had written. Louise was secretly pleased for Amy but to keep the peace grumbled a little with her husband about the way young people were behaving nowadays.

"I was right", shouted William, "She should have looked for a situation around here, not gone gallivanting off with Miss Imogen Lambert with her modern ideas. Fancy her giving permission to Amy to call her just 'Imogen' from now on, just as though our daughter was her equal. No good will come of all this, you mark my words" .

Sarah was given the letter to read. "I'm so pleased for Amy, Father. She will be happy away from cleaning the brass and blackleading the cooking range. She'll love shop life, meeting all those people, look how happy I am".

"A village shop is one thing, selling fine clothes to London ladies quite another", mumbled William.

However, his thoughts were with Amy the Monday morning she started work at the salon. William thought affectionately of his little girl, hoped she was not feeling too nervous. He was glad he had sent a postal order, something toward the season ticket Amy would have purchased for her daily journey.

Amy was quick to learn. Once in the salon she was called Miss Clayden, a novel experience. Surnames were used for them all when clients were within earshot. A welcoming smile and a quiet 'Good Morning' or Good Afternoon' for the clients, her whole attention given to the prospective buyer and no gossiping with Ruth Jacobs. Not difficult instructions for the well mannered Amy.

After a day or two of making tea and helping Rose Berg in the workroom, Amy was instructed by Dolly in the art of 'showing' the exclusive clothes to advantage. "Walk slowly dear, touch the lapel lightly to draw attention to the stitching on the collar" or "with this skirt make a sharp quick turn that the pleats swirl, bringing the garment to life".

Amy found it all quite easy except perhaps when she had to unbutton a jacket, remove it gracefully and then let it hang nonchalantly in her hand as she continued the slow walk to show off the blouse and skirt.

"Do you wear a Flattener, Amy?", enquired Dolly one day.

"A Flattener, what's that?".

Dolly studied her new assistant. " Yes. I can see you will have to get one. You must not have even a suggestion of a curve. This new style of brassiere flattens the bust and allows the clothes to hang perfectly straight. I do not need one myself but I know Imogen wears one. She'll tell you where to buy them".

Ruth began to unbend a little but was not above the odd unpleasant remark. The two girls lunched together in the minute kitchen and every day Amy had to listen to details of Ruth's social life. Shocked by some of Ruth's escapades Amy was, in spite of herself, a little envious of the blonde girl's sophistication. Was she ever going to be anything other than a 'country mouse' Amy wondered.

The salon was becoming well known. The quality of the clothes was excellent and they were expensive. The clientele were happy to purchase the expensive garments knowing they were unlikely to meet another woman at a function wearing the same model. Dolly bought wisely, often with a particular client in mind. She attended the Paris Fashion shows and Imogen was happy to leave the buying of their stock to her partner.

Mrs. Berg was a talented needlewoman and a client, not stock size, requiring a special dress could be catered for by Rose Berg. She could design, cut and make, beautifully.

Dolly told how a cousin of hers who lived in America and was a clothing manufacturer, had forecast that soon, the sizing of English made clothes would be greatly improved. American factories were already employing new methods and American women could now buy garments in various sizes, no waiting for alterations to be made. Meanwhile, Rose worked in her untidy room, Amy and Ruth helping with hems, sewing on buttons and generally making themselves useful. Sometimes as Amy sat there making tiny stitches on a hem Imogen or Dolly could call. "Miss Clayden, are you available?".

Amy knew then that an important client had arrived, ensconced in one of the little armchairs she would be waiting for Amy to walk backwards and forwards, face almost expressionless so as not to detract attention from the cut and design of some exquisite evening dress. Tall, elegant Amy, moving gracefully maybe in front of a short middle-aged matron who was convinced that once the dress was hers she would look as stunning as the dark mannequin.

Ruth was envious of course and never once gave Amy any praise, only remarks like 'No wonder you have not got a young man, men like girls to be small and blonde, you're too tall, too dark'.

Five-foot eight-inch Amy looked down on five-foot-two Ruth, noted the navy blue parting in that blonde hair and just smiled.

* * * * *

The portrait was finished, varnished and a gilt frame chosen. The exhibition date drew near. About fifty pictures, all painted by Charles were to be displayed on the first floor of Sasha's gallery. A number of guests would be invited to the opening evening and Imogen made herself responsible for the refreshments.

Amy received an invitation, the white, gold edged card was propped up on the shelf next to Tessie and after the 14th September would be placed in the gold chocolate box along with other mementoes, to be kept forever. Amy was a hoarder, she knew it and was teased about it by Imogen and her mother.

The question of what she was to wear on the important night was answered immediately Amy asked.

"Why Amy, you will of course wear the dress and sash we lent you for the sittings. Charles and I have decided to make you a present of the dress, sash and shoes".

Amy had been paid quite generously by Charles for her time and had considered that enough, to now possess that lovely silk dress was wonderful.

It was planned that Imogen would go straight to the gallery from Theodora's to supervise the caterers and Amy to Chelsea where she would change for the evening in Charles' spare bedroom.

Amy had her hair trimmed, she used a silk handkerchief to polish the smooth bob. Imogen had instructed her in the use of vanishing cream and a Dark Rachel face powder. A tiny blue and white round box contained Bourjois Rouge and Amy felt rather wicked giving her pale cheeks a soft becoming glow. A rosy red lipstick completed the transformation. Amy was no longer the sallow, old fashioned girl of Shearfield.

She came slowly down the lovely curving staircase and into the drawing room where Charles was waiting, nervously fiddling with his gold cufflinks, whistling softly to himself.

He looked up and a delighted smile lit up his face. "You look wonderful, just topping. That dress is so right for you, move the sash a little lower Amy, that's right, perfect".

"It doesn't look quite the same without the pearls", remarked Amy. "May I wear them tonight please Charles?".

Charles frowned, rubbed his nose as he always did when embarrassed and said, "I don't think so Amy, I'm sorry, but well, you see .." Then putting his shoulders back, standing up straight he said, "Why not, of course you can wear them. I'll run upstairs and get them".

He came down with the velvet box, lifted out the long rope of pearls and put them around Amy's throat. He fixed the Turquoise clasp and as he did so it would have been the most natural thing in the world to kiss the fragrant nape of her neck. Instead Charles drew away and said, "Lovely scent Amy, what is it?".

"Mrs. Wise gave me a small bottle of Guerlain's Mitsouko because I helped to sell three dresses last week to a very difficult customer".

"It suits you Amy, if you like it, wear only that one, make it your signature". Then feeling he had gone too far, "I'm sorry Amy, I have no right to tell you what to do, but it does suit you so well".

The evening went extremely well. Amy did not see Imogen for the first two hours, there were so many people, a continual buzz of conversation. Soft music played, a background to 'Look at this one darling isn't it spiffing?' or 'Love the colours in this Charles, must find Johnny and ask him to buy it for me'.

Glasses were continually refilled, trays of canapés appeared and were quickly demolished. Ash trays were filled and emptied and all the time the high pitched voices went on and on. The pink satin shoes that Amy wore, hurt her feet and they were trampled on time after time. Those pretty, dainty, pink satin shoes ruined in just one night!

Charles endeavoured to stay by Amy's side and introduced his model to as many viewers as possible. Impossible to remember all their names but Amy retained some snatches of conversation. 'Just come from the Cooper-May's, went for cocktails, super flat' and 'Hugo and Thelma want us to join them on their yacht next spring, isn't it super?'

On her own for a while Amy tried to get up the stairs to view the pictures. What a crush it was, men and women sitting on the narrow staircase and Amy could not avoid jolting against them as the pushed her way through.

Amy's portrait had pride of place, the largest picture on show. She listened to some of the comments around her. 'How clever he is, just look at those eyes'. 'The model isn't English, is she?'. 'I have always said Charles is at his best with portraiture and he has excelled himself with this one'.

The catalogue listed about a dozen pictures as 'Not for Sale', Amy's portrait among them. The remainder, more portraits, still life and landscapes were priced and several people were producing cheque books at Sasha's desk. She sat there resplendent in a purple velvet dress, the crimson and gold silk shawl that Amy had been shown on her visit to the studio was thrown across one shoulder. Sasha was smoking a Turkish cigarette in a long slim holder, the blue scented smoke rose above her copper coloured hair as she noted buyers names and addresses.

Amy had a feeling of being apart from all that was going on. She did not belong, an outsider amongst Imogen and Charles' friends. She felt incredibly lonely and looked round for Charles. Not Charles but Dolly caught her eye, standing at the top of the stairs with a short round man who was smoking a cigar. Dolly introduced her husband, Samuel Wise. He had a warm smile, dark friendly eyes and Amy felt at ease with him. Dolly looked ravishing, unusual. With her rather large nose she would not be expected to wear one of those close fitting evening caps that were so fashionable. On Dolly the beaded, white silk helmet fitted so close not a vestige of her black hair could be glimpsed. Her vivid colouring, dramatic bone structure and black and white dress gave her the look of an exotic bird. Samuel was obviously immensely proud of his wife and not a bit embarrassed by the attention her unusual millinery attracted.

The crowd had thinned, Amy could hear Charles' voice coming from the ground floor. In spite of the feeling of 'not belonging' Amy had enjoyed this, her first taste of London social life. She made her apologies to Samuel and Dolly and went to join Charles. He came towards her, placing a hand under Amy's elbow he asked, "Had a good time Amy? Let's find Imogen to thank her, she did us proud, at one time I thought we might run out of the bits and pieces, so many people weren't there?".

Imogen saw them coming toward her, laughing, close. As they drew nearer, Imogen's smile froze.

Her voice was hard, icy, as she asked, "Charles, why is Amy wearing the pearls, tell me, at once".

Amy looked first at Imogen's livid face and then at Charles. He coloured, the blush spreading from his neck to cover his face. "Just for tonight Imogen, just for tonight. It seemed the right thing to do, for Amy to look exactly as she does in the portrait".

Imogen ignored her brother and turned her angry face on Amy. "Be sure that you hand those pearls back to Charles before we go home, do you understand?".

She then continued with the stacking of wine glasses her lips in a straight line.

Amy immediately removed the pearls, how beautiful they were with their soft gleam, how intricate the silver filigree around the turquoise. She handed them reverently to Charles who slipped them into a pocket as though they were nothing but loose change.

The evening was over, a success for Charles. The elation Amy had felt was evaporating, why had Imogen spoken so sharply to her? What was wrong, it was so unlike Imogen to be anything but kind, had she wanted to wear the pearls herself?

The pearls were not mentioned again but Amy was conscious of a restraint in Imogen's manner on the journey to Kensington for the next day or two. Dolly, aware of a slight atmosphere, made a suggestion to Amy that she may like to dress the window to her own taste. She hoped this would bring back the happy look on Amy's face that had been missing since the opening night of the exhibition.

Amy, of course was delighted with this opportunity to use her imagination. Ruth was enlisted to help move the pleated, black silk screen from the rear of the salon to the window. A gilt chair and small round table were also manhandled into the small display area. Dolly was requested to bring from home some sundry items and out of these Amy placed on the table a lace cloth on which she laid a wine glass, a pair of white kid gloves, tiny enamelled opera glasses and a silver cigarette case. Draped across the back of the chair was one of their evening capes. White velvet, trimmed with white Fox. The dress Amy chose to display was also white, long, draped and beautifully beaded by Rose Berg. The white garments with the backdrop of the black silk was dramatic. Dolly was pleased with the effect and Imogen admitted that the display had a greater impact than a small window overcrowded with their wares.

"For that Amy, I shall take you out to lunch", said Dolly. How pleasant it was not to have to sit in the tiny kitchen with Ruth and listen to her empty chatter for an hour.

"I am going to have cheese omelette and salad", announced Dolly. "You order whatever you fancy, I never eat much".

Amy stole a sly glance at the man sitting at the next table. He was obviously enjoying the steak pie in front of him. It reminded Amy of the pie her mother would sometimes serve and her mouth watered.

"Yes, I know what I would like", she said, then added rather lamely, "I'll have the same as you".

"Has something happened between you and Imogen?" Amy told Dolly about the incident and the pearls. "Then I know exactly what it is", said Dolly. "You must have noticed that at the gallery almost every woman there was accompanied by a man. Imogen does feel it so, being on her own. You may not be aware, she does not talk about it, but Imogen lost her fiance in the war. She was heartbroken at the time. Now she feels it is too late for her to meet someone else. There is a shortage of men you know".

Amy ate the last mouthful of the omelette and wiping her lips on the overstarched napkin said, "But Imogen is so pretty, there must be many men who would love to marry her. She is always out to tea-dances and she has Charles to take her around".

"I hadn't finished Amy. Charles, now there is the problem. As you know Imogen and Charles lost their mother when they were both very young. Imogen has become far too possessive of Charles, he is such an attractive young man, always some girl in tow. As soon as Imogen thinks he may be serious about them she intervenes. The pearls you were wearing have been in the Lambert family for some years. It is the custom for them to be passed down to each successive bride. Seeing you with them around your neck maybe Imogen thought...."

"No, no", interrupted Amy. "It was all my fault, I asked Charles if I could wear them, persuaded him against his will to let me. Oh I do wish I hadn't asked".

She studied the menu, feeling her face getting hotter, knowing she was blushing.

"I am so fond of them both Dolly, I would never come between Imogen and Charles, I just couldn't do it".

As they walked back to Theodora's in the autumn sunshine, Amy was thoughtful. She noticed how the leaves were changing colour, felt some of the fallen leaves crackle under her feet but her thoughts were really on Charles.

He had asked her to spend the coming Sunday with him. Had suggested they may go to Richmond, enjoy a walk by the river. Amy knew that from now on she would only accept invitations from him if Imogen were invited too. There was no way she would jeopardize the friendship she had with the brother and sister. They had both been so good to her.

CHAPTER EIGHT

Several commissions resulted from Charles' exhibition. He was busy in his studio but found time for the partying and dancing that was all the rage in the 'Twenties. Amy was asked quite often. At first she made excuses for not partnering him but later accepted if Imogen was also invited. It was not Amy's favourite way of spending an evening, she was not enamoured of the dancing and felt clumsy and inadequate when forced to join in conversation which she considered flippant.

Theodora's was thriving, Rose Berg was finding it difficult to keep up with the work and a second dressmaker was taken on.

Gabrielle Chanel had a dramatic, powerful influence on fashion, her shops in Paris and Deauville selling clothes of an elegant simplicity, easy to wear cardigan suits and straight dresses. The shops in London soon followed her ideas and Theodora's window reflected her genius. Amy loved the jersey suits and the long ropes of glass beads. The style suited her and she modelled the clothes for Dolly and Imogen to perfection.

For her birthday in 1923 Amy received from her employers a bottle of Chanel 5 perfume, a new venture for Coco Chanel as Gabrielle now liked to be known. Amy was delighted, even put a spot on Tessie's wedding dress that the doll might share in her pleasure.

One winter evening Charles gave a small dinner party. Sasha and Stefan were at the table, also Dolly and Samuel. Mrs. Gurney, with the help of a young girl hired for the evening served a memorable meal. Amy thought of the times at Shearfield Hall when she had helped Sarah at dinner, now here she was, a guest herself, being waited on, sitting at a table beautifully laid with silver and crystal. She looked around at the ladies, so fashionably attired, at the men in their dinner jackets a perfect foil to their colourful partners. She accidently caught Stefan's eye, he winked at her and grinned wickedly. What a good looking man, how sure of himself. Amy was fascinated by the very slight accent in the voices of Sasha and Stefan, listened to their lively, interesting conversation but was too shy to contribute very much herself...

* * * * *

What a long time ago it was since she had lived at Welbeck Gardens and worked in Kensington. Amy smiled at her recollections; she still had the nightdress and negligee given her that first Christmas in Ilford. They hung together on a padded satin hanger, part of her collection of clothes from the past. The gold chocolate boxes in a wardrobe.

Eighty year-old Amy, still upright, her face only slightly lined, put a spot or two of Mitsouko behind her ears and lifted the front of her new hairstyle with a tail-comb. That new girl had done a good job with the silver hair. Sally was her name, Amy hoped she would remain in the salon; so many girls did not stay anywhere for very long these days.

The ringing of the telephone broke the silence of the morning. "Hello, who's calling?".

"It's Margot, Aunt Amy. How are you? Becky gone back to London?".

"Yes dear, yesterday afternoon. I did so enjoy the couple of days she was here. I do wish she came more often".

"Well, you know Becky better than anyone. She will go her own way to the end of her life, you can't make her do anything she doesn't want to".

"The meal was good wasn't it Margot, so nice to be with you all. By the way did you notice the little man, the dapper fellow who paused at our table during the evening?".

"I know the man you mean, I noticed him in the bar, with a hard-faced woman wasn't he. Why do you ask?"

"I felt Becky knew him, she was embarrassed, unusual for my daughter but I saw her discomfort. Wondered if you had any idea who he was".

"Can't help I'm afraid. O.K., to pick you up next week, 10 o'clock on Wednesday? Thought we'd spend the day in Exeter".

"Sounds fine to me dear, we're sure to chat again before then I'm certain. 'Bye for now, love to Tom".

Amy went downstairs, already the day was warm and soon she was in the garden; it was colourful and fragrant on the patio. A box of notelets in front of her, she sat writing her 'thank you's' for the gifts, flowers and cards received for her 80th birthday. Her writing, she noticed had deteriorated after the first few cards had been penned. What a nuisance it was, getting old, the stiff fingers, the failing sight and hearing. She flexed her fingers and continued .... 'so thoughtful of you, how kind to remember I have always loved that particular soap'.

A blackbird, his head on one side was surveying her, some raisins had been scattered for him on the patio. Most had been taken but the bird had spied one or two near to Amy's sandled feet. Dare he advance so close? Amy stopped writing, made no movement and the blackbird hopped toward her, took his bounty and flew away. She continued, warm and content in the June sunshine. The correspondence completed, Amy sat back in the whicker chair, closed her eyes and slipped her feet out of the leather sandals. The patio stones were hot from the afternoon sun and the warmth was pleasant on her bare feet.

Birds were twittering in the hedge at the end of the garden, maybe a cat was lurking there. Closer to hand, bees were investigating the sweet smelling honeysuckle, their humming incessant but pleasant. Amy listened to these summer sounds, breathed in the summer scents and thought of such an afternoon at Berrycombe years ago, it must have been some time in the 'thirties; then she remembered exactly when it was, her 26th birthday, so it would be 1930 and her first meeting with her baby neice, the year following her return from Paris.

* * * * *

Early in 1928 Dolly invited Amy to accompany her to the Paris Spring Fashion Shows. "We can stay in a small hotel I often use Amy and you will have the opportunity to see the exciting creations of some of the most important designers in Paris. You'll love every minute, I promise you".

They arrived at the Gare du Nord one wet Sunday evening. Dolly led the way through the busy station to the line of taxis and directed a driver to take them to the Hotel Colombier. Amy, tired as she was with the long journey, sat bolt upright and turned her head from side to side, wishing to miss nothing as the taxi sped along the boulevards. So many cars, horns sounding all the time, brakes screeching on the wet roads. It was an exciting ride to their hotel just off the Rue du Maubeuge.

Dolly's face was radiant, her eyes glowed as she spoke of Lanvin, Worth and Vionnet. "We shall travel on the Metro each day to the St. Honore district where many of the designers have their salons", she explained.

It was a wonderful week, Dolly had prophesied that Amy would love every minute and Amy did. She walked past Maxim's, stared at 'The Ritz' in awe. London had seemed so sophisticated, so alive after Shearfield to the young country girl but Paris, well, Amy was enraptured by the extravagance of it all. The traffic was louder, faster, the people excitable, fascinating, smart; 'chic' Dolly called them. The wide boulevards with their glamorous shops filled with expensive luxuries, this was the Paris Amy saw during that week.

The mannequins, the clothes, the opulent salons of the famous designers, their heady perfumed air, Amy drank it all in and was intoxicated.

The women sitting on the tiny gilt chairs in those showrooms in the Rue du Faubourg wore extravagant 'avant garde' clothes, fantastic hats and were invariably escorted by handsome men. Husbands, lovers or whatever they were, all studied by an avid Amy.

At one of the salons Dolly had arranged to meet an old friend, Mireille, directrice of Maison Ravel. The two women embraced and kissed each other on both cheeks. Mireille, after a few sentences in French continued her conversation in an attractive mixture of English and French which Amy did not find difficult to follow. It transpired the two women had started their training together at the House of Worth. They had been midinettes, running errands before graduating to improvers and later seamstresses and embroiderers.

"We have both done very well 'cherie'", said Mireille to Amy. "I have been Directrice for Monsieur Ravel for three years now and my dear friend Dolly has the exclusive shop she always dreamed of".

The journey back to England on Saturday went by in a flash. There was so much for Dolly and Amy to discuss. They had met Mireille and one of her mannequins on Saturday for lunch. A tiny cafe with tables on the pavement not far from Notre Dame. A suggestion was made. The Fench mannequin had a sister living in London and wished to work in the English capital for a year. "I thought maybe Amy and Madeleine could change places for a year. Amy could take over Madeleine's share of the apartment she has with Nicole and I should love to have a tall, elegant, English mannequin in the Ravel salon". Mireille's voice was persuasive, her large eyes pleading, looking first at Dolly then at Amy.

Dolly looked rather worried. "I'm sure it would be a splendid opportunity for Amy; Imogen and I will not stand in her way if she wishes to work for Ravel's. We are not able to offer Madeleine a similar position at Theordora's though. Maybe, Mireille I have misled you. The salon is modest, we sell exclusive clothes, have a good clientele but nothing on the scale of Maison Ravel".

Madeleine said something to Mireille and there followed quite a lengthy exchange of French spoken at high speed. Dolly tried to follow but had to wait with Amy for a translation. "Madeleine is quite happy to accept a position at Theodora's Dolly. She wishes to learn English and the business of running a small salon, so you see the exchange will be ideal". Mireille smiled at them all and considered the matter closed.

Now on the train from Paris to Calais, Dolly and Amy could talk of nothing else. "I do hope Imogen will agree and that she will be willing to let me return to Ilford when the year is over", remarked Amy.

And so began the next phase of Amy's ambition to make something of her life. Maison Ravel was situated off the Champs Elysees, a tall narrow house, wide steps leading up to an imposing front door which displayed a large brass plate inscribed with the words 'Alain Ravel, Haute Couture. Paris.'

The workrooms were on the top floor, light and spacious. How Rose Berg would have loved the space to work that Ravel's cutters and embroiderers enjoyed on the second floor. The first floor was given over to the mannequins and dressers. Amy thought the girls resembled a flock of pretty, colourful birds. They chattered away in their fast fashion that convinced Amy she would never be able to master the French language.

She studied the exotic females with whom she would be working. In the main they were shorter than she, small boned, dark haired French girls and one or two exquisite young women with almond eyes and complexions of a shade that Amy guessed were the result of mixed parentage. And then there was Nicole. Nicole was petite, not beautiful but she had a gamin look, an arresting, unusual face and hair that was cut like a boy's. What appealed to Amy was her command of English, how wonderful to have someone to speak to who could understand. It would be a pleasure to share the appartment that Madeleine had vacated with this vivacious girl who was half French, half English.

The salon on the ground floor was large, high ceilinged with ornate, crystal chandeliers lighting up the cream painted walls. Tall, narrow windows ran down one side of the room, they were draped with a fine, filmy cream material and large oval gilt framed mirrors were placed between each window. A wide staircase with gilded balustrade swept down in a curve from the floor above. A staircase of wide shallow steps, down which Alain Ravel's mannequins glided to show his creations to his wealthy clientele.

How different it was to show clothes at Maison Ravel. No tiny kitchen or workroom to act as dressing room, here each girl had her space. A rack held the clothes in order of appearance and there was a dresser to assist in the hurried changes, to ensure that the correct shoes were worn, that the jewellery was pinned securely and put away safely. Amy found her dresser invaluable in the chaos that always seemed to abound.

With a dress half on and half off Amy would hear two other girls fighting over the clothes they were to wear. Marie had taken the hat that Chloe was supposed to be wearing. Someone was screaming that Amy was wearing her silk stockings and so it would go on. At the door stood a calm vendeuse, dressed in black, holding a sheaf of papers, checking each girl as she passed through the door to start her unhurried gliding walk down the curving staircase to be announced by Mireille who sat at a Louis VXI table with her carefully written programme, not seeming to even look at the mannequins but in fact her eyes missed nothing.

Amy at the begining had felt 'gauche', a word she had learned from Nicole. It was not long however before she felt at home walking, turning, posing in front of the well dressed women who were devouring the gowns with their greedy eyes. Gowns they did not need but wanted so badly, gowns they must have in order to see the envy on the faces of other women at one of the many functions these wealthy Parisians would attend.

Nicole was a friend to be treasured, she was an even tempered girl and there was no conflict between her and Amy in the small apartment they shared. The mornings started with cafe-au-lait and croissants and later the friends would shop at the outdoor markets for their evening meal. Some evenings it would be supper at a small restaurant on the Left Bank. Omelette and salad and the coffee that Amy now preferred to tea. She visited night clubs where 'le Jazz' was the rage and met young friends of Nicole's. Amy even had little flirtations with two Frenchmen, nothing serious, short lived pieces of nonsense really. Amy was still waiting for the thunder and lightning of a big romance. Perhaps it was not to happen in Paris.

The sight of so many artists in Paris often brought Charles to mind. Nicole and Amy sometimes visited Montmartre which had the air of a village somehow. Artists mingled with shady looking characters around the Pigalle where also poverty stricken immigrants were to be seen. Amy had never seen such a wealth of contrast. The sights, the smells, the sounds of Monmartre stayed in her mind for a long time.

The Metro too, was something Amy would never forget. She quickly learned where to change trains and to read the Metro maps. It was the smell of the carriages she would instantly recall, if in later years anyone mentioned Paris Metro. The odour of garlic and the smoke and the sweet sickly smell of the cigarettes or Gitanes as they were called, pervaded every carriage; empty blue packets littered the floor, but this was Paris and Amy loved it.

Ravel's Autumn Show was over, a success for the designer who recognised the need for garments for 'le sport' and had designed his collection to include items for Golf, Tennis and Swimming.

"You have been a great asset to us Amy", said Mireille. "In sports clothes you looked especially well, your long legs. Ah, I wish we French girls had the English legs".

Mireille tapped her teeth with a gold pencil. "I need you to show winter dresses and coats to our regular clients Amy. Also there will be furs to be modelled. It may cause a little jealousy amongst the girls but I do feel that you are the one to wear the Mink coats, the Sables and other models the furrier will supply. Our girls are swamped by these furs, you will look well in them".

So Amy worked until the middle of December in that overheated salon, the cloying scents of the women sitting on the little chairs forever in her nostrils. As she walked and turned and opened coats to display the expensive linings Amy dreamed of her Christmas in England, at Shearfield with Mother and Father, Sarah and Jack too. Walks over the fields in the cold frosty mornings.

Amy received a great welcome on her return to England. Imogen could see a new confidence in her friend, a polish there had not been evidence of before Amy had worked in Paris. Everyone at Shearfield, family and friends alike remarked on Amy's well groomed appearance. There was a barrage of questions from all, only father showed little sign of curiosity. His concern was for her health, her accommodation and her diet. "I hope you are eating sensibly Amy. I know all you young women are starving to keep your figures but you need some good puddings inside you. Don't suppose those Frenchies know how to make a decent suet pudding eh Mother?".

Christmas was all Amy had dreamed of. Sarah and Jack were happy to walk off the huge dinner and in spite of the cold wind, the three of them strode past the cowsheds and over the fields. Amy breathed in long, deep breaths of the fresh air and returned to the cottage unbelievably ready to eat Christmas cake and drink the tea that only her mother seemed able to make. Was it the brown china pot that made it special?

On Amy's return to Maison Ravel in January there was already talk of the Spring collection. Amy, showing dresses and coats, displaying jewellery, wearing exquisite hats, was not enthusiastic. Another show, the noise and hysteria that acompanied the run up to the event. She looked at the women staring at her as she paraded Ravel's winter clothes for their inspection. Was this what Amy Clayden wanted, really wanted, could she stay for the Spring Show?

For a few days Amy continued, hating the stuffiness of the salon. The air was never fresh, the windows never opened, the heavy, cloying, expensive scents of the visitors to Ravel's was always present. Amy recalled her walk at Shearfield, over the fields, the wind blowing her hair in her eyes, her shoes covered in mud. 'I'm a country girl and nothing will ever change that' thought Amy as she stood before a chic Frenchwoman who was examining the trimming on the coat Amy was showing.

Mireille was annoyed, Nicole sad and the other mannequins heard the news of Amy's decision to cut short her year with Ravel's with mixed feelings. They liked this English girl, she was kind, had fitted in very well but she often got to wear what they considered the 'creme de la creme' of the clothes. Certainly when Amy returned to England she was the self confident, perfectly groomed young lady she had always wanted to be. Amy would never be 'pretty' but she had a style of her own and had learned from the chic Frenchwomen exactly what suited her and also just what she must never wear.

Dolly and Imogen had opened, in 1929, a small salon in Ilford, which Imogen managed and on her return from Paris Amy divided her time between the two 'Theodoras'.

Several men, French and English, had wined and dined Amy and there had been two mild love affairs but nothing to really stir any great emotion in Amy's heart. She had learned how to deal with unwanted attention in a pleasant manner. She was no longer shy in sophisticated company and her husky low voice could be heard adding her comments to the conversation.

Yes it had been her 26th birthday when she had visited Berrycombe for a few days holiday.

CHAPTER NINE

Dinah stood by the open window in her comfortable kitchen. It was warm, too hot for cooking really but this was a special day, Amy's birthday. Jim had been so pleased when his sister had accepted their invitation to stay for a few days and tonight Dinah was having a small gathering for supper. It had been such a hectic day, the baby fractious, the telephone ringing at inconvenient moments and the hands on the old Dutch clock had just whizzed round.

Jim had driven to Newton Abbot to meet Amy from the three o'clock train and soon he would be returning with his glamorous sister. Dinah pictured Amy, twenty-six today, tall, attractive, self confident. That shy, awkward gipsy-looking child had disappeared. Dinah sighed, she too had changed, plumper than ever, never enough time to spend on herself. How happy she was though with Jim and now there was Margot, such a lovely baby. Life just couldn't be better. She must run upstairs and change into a clean cotton dress, run a comb through her hair before the car returned.

In the hall Dinah stopped in dismay, Jim's usual trademark was there. A trail of sawdust on the red carpet, woodshavings clinging to the curtains where they touched the floor. He had left by the front door instead of using the kitchen as she had instructed. Dinah turned back to the broom cupboard and picked up a dust-pan and brush. She was emptying the shavings into a bin when the car drew up on the gravel.

Jim jumped out to open the passenger door and Amy's long legs appeared, shapely in pure silk, her narrow feet encased in strappy, kid sandals. She stood up and smoothed her dress that was barely crumpled from the long train journey. Dinah hardly had time to recall in horror that she had not after all had time to change before Amy was hugging and kissing her.

"Lovely to see you, you look so well Dinah and you smell wonderful too, talc and apples and ..... well don't know what else but so good, yes just so good".

Dinah, for a brief moment, felt shy of her old friend. That husky voice, the expensive perfume, the clothes so obviously of the best quality. The moment passed. Dinah remembered to say 'Happy Birthday' and led the way into the kitchen.

"Where's the baby?" asked Amy looking round eagerly.

"Sleeping, I am very glad to say", said Dinah, filling a kettle at the sink. Jim was busy with Amy's luggage and just smiled when his wife reprimanded him on his appearance.

"The same old Jim, fancy coming to meet you in his working clothes", laughed Dinah, not truly cross. Shabby trousers, his shirt hanging untidily out at the back.

"As usual I forgot the time", replied Jim as he hoisted at the offending trousers. "What about this cup of tea then?".

"May we have it in the garden? that train was so hot and stuffy".

Dinah carried out the tray she had prepared. They sat on the lawn by the summer-house that Jim had built. Amy removed her sandals, lay back in the whicker chair and listened to the birds and the humming of the bees busy about their work on the honeysuckle that grew up the side of the summer-house.

Through half closed eyes she looked at the stone house; she did not visit often enough, it must be two years since she was here. How peaceful this was after London. The upstairs windows were open, white lace curtains stirred slightly in the breeze. There was ivy on the walls, a tub by the kitchen door with an abundance of herbs. A path led to a gap in the hedge and Amy could just glimpse the workshop where, according to Dinah, her brother spent too much time.

Eight years had passed since Charles had painted Amy's portrait. He was now living in Eze in the South of France, capturing on canvas the old buildings of that hilltop town, the colours, the flowers and the faces that surrounded him.

Imogen and Amy had holidayed with him, unforgetable weeks in the hot sun, visiting Nice and Cannes, meeting the many artists who made up the circle of Charles' friends.

The house in Chelsea rarely saw Charles now. Mrs. Gurney kept things in good order, Sasha and Stefan still occupied the first floor. When staying in town Imogen occasionally entertained friends in the lovely dining room where now Amy's portrait hung over the fireplace.

Amy at twenty six was quite a different young woman to the girl portrayed in that picture. Two quite well know artists had requested that she sit for them. One of the portraits Amy had liked, it had shown her as she was, an eighteen year old in a 'Twenties style coat and cloche hat. The second picture she really could not understand; the artist, a Frenchman, had painted her entirely in shades of green, portrayed as a woman with an eye on her chin, half her face emerald green and the other side in a pale lime shade. It had sold immediately and the artist commissioned to paint four more in a similar vein. But that was six years ago, before Amy lived and worked in Paris.

The tea was delicious and Dinah was chattering nineteen to the dozen.

"Amy your dress is longer than I have seen you wear for ages, is that the fashion now?"

"Yes, and waists are back where they belong, thank goodness".

Dinah laughed ruefully. "It always happens, whenever I pluck up courage to wear what I think is up to the minute I find I have missed the boat and fashion has moved on. Oh well, we are bound to be out of date down here in 'dear ole Devon, m'dear".

"You look fine to me Dinah, so young and happy. Now what about the baby, she must be awake by now".

Margot was presented to her Aunt Amy. Just over five weeks old she was rosy and crumpled from sleep. Amy held the tiny bundle that smelled so sweetly of baby powder, she buried her nose in the soft white shawl. Was she like Dinah or Jim? How stupid to think that any resemblance could be detected so early. Amy scrutinised the tiny face; her own parents, her grandparents, great grandparents had all had a hand in producing this baby. How wonderful and mysterious life was. She handed the baby back to Dinah.

Jim had some work to finish and hitching up his trousers he ambled along the path, through the gap in the hedge to his beloved workshop.

"Uncle Walter, Aunt Anne and a colleague of Jim's will be here to supper tonight, your birthday supper".

"That's lovely Dinah, will be nice to see Uncle Walter again. How is Aunt Anne, is the arthritis any worse?".

"Afraid so, she is in a wheelchair most of the time. It is hard on Uncle Walter, he sold out to Jim last year but his heart is still in that workshop and he is often giving a hand with a piece of furniture. Aunt Anne sits with me in the kitchen enjoying a gossip as usual. Neither of them ever complain but I know it is hard for them to cope and we are all getting older".

"I know, mother and father have slowed up a bit. Father is sixty six now, Mother sixty four. Can you imagine Dinah, before we know it ten years will have flown by and we shall both be forty". The friends laughed at the ridiculous idea that they could ever be forty!

By seven thirty the family were having drinks in the garden awaiting Jim's colleague, an antique dealer from Torquay. Amy had bathed and dressed leisurely. Her black hair was worn longer now, Greta Garbo had set the fashion of a longer bob, still sleek but softer and shoulder length. She thought of Charles as she touched her wrists and ears with Mitsouko. He had commented on her perfume when she had first worn it. Would things have been diffeent between them, she wondered, if Imogen had not shown her jealousy that night? Amy sighed, he hadn't married but according to Dolly, living in France away from his possessive sister, Charles enjoyed the company of a variety of attractive ladies.

Amy joined Dinah and Jim, she kissed Uncle Walter and Aunt Anne and gave them news of William and Louise. There was the sound of a car pulling into the drive, the quiet engine was turned off, a door slammed and Amy heard footsteps on the gravel.

Jim jumped up and went to greet his guest. Amy was listening to a description of Uncle Walter's new bungalow when Jim said, "Amy, I would like to introduce Mr. Serovsky. Stefan, my sister Amy Clayden".

They looked at each other and laughed. Stefan took her slim hand in his own. "Well, well, I did not realize that you were the sister of whom Jim speaks".

Amy explained the connection to her family and looked past Stefan for Sasha.

"Where is your wife?".

"I have no idea Amy, I have yet to meet her".

"But Sasha....?", said the mystified Amy, thinking how handsome Stefan looked. He was cleanshaven now and his grin even more wicked now that the creases in his cheeks could be seen when he smiled.

"Sasha is my sister, surely you knew that Amy". Stefan looked down into those questioning, large dark eyes.

"No one told me, I expect they thought I knew. Took it for granted that as you lived together in Charles' flat she was your wife. I feel such a fool, do forgive me Stefan".

Over supper Amy learned that Stefan had a house in Torquay which he used to display the antiques he collected. He dealt in furniture and porcelain mainly and it was to Jim be brought furniture for repair or restoration.

"I just get used to the scoundrel lumbering up my workshop, drinking all the tea Dinah can supply then off he goes, back to Chelsea and his sister to ferret around for more junk", teased Jim.

Amy found the man fascinating, it was almost impossible to turn away once he looked into her eyes. He seemed to have a mesmeric effect on her. Amy thought of the dinner party that Charles had given, how Stefan had caught her studying the other guests and the unexpected wink he had made. She blushed at the memory and looked up to see him watching her intently.

Dinah had produced a feast. The poached salmon was excellent and Uncle Walter had supplied the new peas and potatoes. Amy reminded him of the meals she had eaten on her first visit to Devon and of the junket she so disliked.

"No junket tonight Amy", whispered Dinah and hurried out to the kitchen to bring back raspberries and clotted cream and, to please the men, a large apple tart.

Dinah pushed Aunt Anne in her wheelchair into the kitchen, put a tea towel in her hand, one for Amy too and the women set about the washing up.

"Fancy you knowing Stefan Amy, he is a very charming man but I never feel quite at ease with him, I feel overwhelmed by him, he is larger than life isn't he?".

"I know what you mean. It was some time ago when I last saw him, I've never exchanged many words with him until tonight. I used to be so shy in those days".

It was impossible to sleep that night. Amy lay in the tiny bedroom wide awake. Stefan filled her thoughts. His eyes, his tanned high cheekboned face, his strong hands with fine blonde hairs on their backs. His voice was memorable. Stefan had the slightest accent French or Russian she did not know which. Imogen had spoken of how Sasha and Stefan had left Russia in 1917 and had been living in Paris before settling in England. His voice held a caressing note when he had spoken to Amy, his voice lowered, his whole attention given to her.

Amy turned on her side, she must get to sleep. She thumped her pillow turned over again but still sleep eluded her. She re-lived her entire conversation with him that evening, then went back to her first sight of this man who was proving so intrusive. They had met on that gracious staircase in Charles' house, she had been about to enter a bedroom to change out of that pale silk dress and Stefan had come bounding down the stairs from his flat, a small bow, a 'good morning' and she had said to herself 'a handsome blonde giant'.

Dawn was breaking, the birds were singing their chorus and still Amy had not slept. She was so grateful to hear at last the rattle of china in the kitchen below her bedroom. Dinah would soon appear with an early morning cup of tea, I must look a wreck, thought Amy, no sleep at all!

Dinah came in bearing a small tray, a tiny china tea pot with matching jug, cup and saucer. "How pretty", exclaimed Amy, sitting up at once.

"You look wonderful, no need to ask if you slept well", said Dinah.

"No, don't ask", smiled Amy.

Breakfast was hardly over before the telephone rang and Stefan stated he would call for Amy at eleven o'clock. He wanted her to see his shop and take her to luncheon.

"I hope Jim and I are going to see something of you before you go back to Ilford", said Dinah, giving her friend a hug to soften her words.

Margot was in her pram under the apple tree and Amy peeped in at the sleeping baby. Who knows, before long I could be looking at a baby of my own? The thought appeared from nowhere and Amy shook her dark bob briskly as though to shake the thought away. Whatever was wrong with her?

The car was a large, open tourer, long and sleek. Amy settled back in the comfortable leather seat and waved goodbye to Dinah as Stefan drove out of the gate and then much too fast down the narrow country lane toward Torquay.

Stefan slowed the car as they drove along the front. "Do you know, this reminds me very much of Cannes or Nice", said Amy. The sea that morning certainly had a blueness to rival that of the Riviera and the white houses and hotels perched on the terraces above the town had a continental air. Palm trees lined the coast road, Princess Gardens were brilliant with geraniums, lobelia and alyssum. Women smartly dressed strolled in the morning sun.

The Strand was busy with shoppers and holiday makers and they turned into a small road on the left. Stefan parked the car outside a house sandwiched between two shops. A pretty girl was arranging flowers in the florist's windows and waved to Stefan. Amy saw that the other shop was a milliner's, the window displaying some attractive straws, beautifully trimmed. The front door of the house was imposing, white paint, heavy brass knocker and letter box. To the left was a bow window in which was displayed a fine Georgian chair, a large blue and white vase and a small card informing those who may be interested that Stefan Serovsky opened the shop by appointment and gave his telephone number.

"Very casual", remarked Amy.

"Very convenient when taking young ladies out to lunch", was the reply.

The house was a treasure trove. The hall floor was covered with an oriental carpet in rich, dark colours. An elegant table held mother-of-pearl boxes. The walls were hung with pictures depicting Dutch interiors. They moved into the large room which looked onto the road. Amy saw that it contained so many beautiful and interesting pieces of furniture and porcelain that she did not know where to look first.

A long-case clock standing in one corner caught her eye and she went over to admire the workmanship. "That is a William and Mary walnut long-case Amy, made in London around 1700. It needed a small repair and your clever brother used his skill on a moulding that was damaged".

Stefan opened a door in a Sheraton bookcase to disclose glasses and decanters and poured some sherry for them both. A warmth and an energy emanated from him standing so close as he handed Amy her glass.

She wanted to ask so many questions, to touch the objects, to feel the damask curtains, to pick up the tiny porcelain figurines. More important, Amy wanted to know about Stefan. So many thoughts were buzzing around inside her head. She knew he was of Russian descent, that he had lived in London for several years, but there was so much more to discover. Were his parents still living, was he happy here, did he and Sasha plan to return to their country in the future?

"I have a comfortable flat upstairs", Stefan was saying, "but I think we should lunch first, get to know each other a little more and then I shall bring you back so that you may enjoy the treasures I see you eyeing so greedily. If by that time you still trust me I shall take you upstairs to partake of tea in my dining room".

The midday sun shone down on the hotel terrace, small tables under colourful parasols looked inviting. Not many were occupied and Stefan was able to choose a position where his companion could be seen to advantage. Amy deserved to be seen; she wore, with her simple, cream linen dress, a caramel coloured straw hat, shallow crowned, wide brimmed. It shaded her eyes and she did not need to wear the very latest accessory from France, large spectacles with lenses so dark they were almost black. Amy had purchased them in Nice the year before and as yet, very few women were wearing these 'sunglasses'. She placed them neatly on the table next to her cream gloves and handbag.

Heads were turning to observe the handsome couple, Amy composed, aloof, Stefan attentive, discussing the menu with the waiter ensuring that Amy's preference regarding the salad ingredients were adhered to.

"Tell me about your time in Paris", instructed Stefan.

"It was everything I had always imagined. The clothes I modelled were fabulous, the French girls were friendly and I was never lonely. Nicole was kind enough to let me share her apartment and from her I learned to speak reasonable French and to make the perfect omelette".

Amy smiled across the table at her attractive escort and continued. "It is certainly true that April in Paris is rather special. My fondest memories of the spring I was there, is of the heady scent of the chestnut trees along the Seine, just after a shower of rain. I can smell it now, mmm, heaven. I have only to close my eyes and I am there again, strolling toward the Pont Neuf".

"I know exactly what you mean Amy. I'm familiar with Paris, especially the Left Bank. Some of my family still live there and whenever I am in the city on business I spend some time with my aunt and uncle, my cousins too if they are available. We have happy, noisy meetings in a cafe in the Latin quarter, the old ones talking of their young days in Russia and we younger element try to convince them that life is not so bad in France and England and that they must not pine for a Russia that does not exist anymore".

"Your parents?" enquired Amy, not looking into his eyes but crumbling an unwanted roll on her side plate.

"Both dead, only Sasha and me left now". Stefan's voice was sombre and although Amy hoped he would enlarge on the fate of his family he concentrated on his 'Chicken veronique' and the conversation petered out.

Amy decided to remove her hat and she put on the fashionable dark glasses and waited for her coffee.

"Imogen and I went to Eze last year. We stayed with Charles, have you been to the villa he is renting?".

"Haven't had that pleasure yet Amy. Charles has invited me, I hear the villa is perched high over the sea and that the little town is ancient and beautiful".

Amy smiled at the memory she had of Charles waving goodbye at the end of their holiday. "He is as dark as a Spaniard, Stefan, out painting in the sun from morning until it is too dark. He really is turning out some good work. You would hardly recognise him, he wears brightly coloured shirts and neckerchiefs and looks extremely happy".

"Glad about that, good for him to get away from possessive Imogen. She spoiled things between Charles and Sasha you know".

Amy did not comment, she was loyal to Imogen, they lived happily together and there was never a cross word between them. To steer the conversation away from Imogen, Amy described the holiday on the Riviera that she had enjoyed so much.

"Charles gave us a holiday I shall never forget. We motored each evening to dine with different friends, he has so many on the Cote d'Azur. I met Daisy Fellowes at Cap Martin, elegant in her plain linen dress, wearing her famous emerald bracelets. Josephine Baker dazzled and slightly shocked us when we saw her at the Casino in Monte Carlo. Everyone, but everyone was living life to the full. How incredibly rich some of those people are. One afternoon we visited a French couple in their white villa not far out of Nice. I shall remember their garden for the rest of my life. It was terraced, masses of flowers dropped down to sea level, but what impressed me were the steps leading down from the highest terrace. The steps looked as though they were a staircase carpeted in green with narrow stripes either side of purple and pink. Of course, it was grass and the stripes, borders of pansies and dianthus. One gardener was employed wholly to maintain the staircase, clipping and snipping, weeding and dead-heading. Fantastic".

Stefan had listened to this long description but at the same time he studied Amy's expressive face, eyes and hands as she relived her holiday.

Aware of Stefan's scrutiny Amy continued but now rather self consciously. "I never used to like dancing and small talk but out there in those warm scented evenings it all seemed so right. We never saw our beds until the small hours but were never tired. Imogen and I spent the mornings on the beach while Charles worked. We were daring and wore those new Beach Pyjamas, bought some of the first sunglasses and felt very chic. I sunbathed, the latest craze, but Imogen had to protect her fair skin". She broke off and touching

Stefan's arm said excitedly, "Oh look Stefan, over there, by the Gardens. There's a girl wearing shorts, can you see her?".

Stefan gave the girl a cursory glance and said "Stupid fashion, ugly, it won't catch on and her skin is as dark as a peasant's".

"The fashion will take on" argued Amy. "Last year shorts were worn a lot in America, Dolly told me and as for sunbathing, well you wait and see, everyone will want to be tanned".

"You love fashion don't you Amy", stated Stefan. Amy sipped her coffee and confessed: "I love the whole aspect of fashion. Do you know I have kept one garment or bag or shoes from each season since the time I left school. I have quite a collection and it is fascinating to see just how fashion evolves".

"Now, that is a good thing to do", said Stefan. "Collecting I can understand. Providing you have enough room for storage to keep on with it. Who knows, one day you might even open a Museum of Fashion".

They both laughed at the idea, Amy old, the clothes dusty and housed in a dark room. People shuffling through, having paid their twopence for the honour of looking at Amy's treasures.

Later that afternoon Amy had a second look at Gentian House where Stefan displayed and sold the antiques.

"If this were mine I would arrange this room to look like a home that is lived in. I wouldn't put furniture and ornaments all higgledy piggledy as you have done. I can just imagine it looking so opulent, your customers would love it". Amy paused for breath then said: "If I had my way you wouldn't recognise this house, it's beautifully proportioned Stefan and you have such wonderful furniture and pictures to display. As said before, I can imagine it all so clearly".

"I've heard of your imagination Amy", was all Stefan said. He lived on the first floor amongst dusty tables, books and bric-a-brac. A space was cleared for a tray of tea and Amy admired the Crown Derby cups and saucers and gave the brown china tea pot a withering look.

"It's sacrilege to put those cups on the same tray as that awful tea pot", she remarked. "Look at the lovely strong tea that comes out of the spout though".

Amy studied the pot and saw the kitchen at Shearfield. The white cloth on the end of the long table, two cups and mother warming the brown pot for the tea for the little girl home from school, warm memories.

Stefan drove her back to Berrycombe in time for supper and as he left said, "Be ready at 10 o'clock in the morning. I am going to take you over the moors".

"Sorry Stefan, I must spend a day with Dinah, we have both so looked forward to these few days together".

"As I said, be ready at 10. Wear something comfortable and tonight be sure to pray for fine weather".

"But Stefan.........."

The blond giant opened the door of his car and helped her out. He raised her hand to his lips and gave a slight bow as he lightly kissed her smooth brown skin. "Until tomorrow".

Dinah was rather put out when over supper Amy announced she would again be out most of the day. Jim looked rather worried. "Be careful Amy. Stefan is a very attractive man I know, but he can turn on the charm when he wants his own way and just as quickly turn it off again".

As Amy described her day, Dinah soon recovered her good humour, she so wanted her friend to enjoy her few days here and she certainly was looking radiant. They would make the most of the rest of the week together.

Whether she prayed or not the weather the next morning looked very promising. Amy tried to subdue the excitement she felt at the thought of spending another day with Stefan. She dressed casually in sweater and skirt of light navy and carried a blue and white striped pullover with her as she descended the stairs.

Dinah appeared in the hall. "Oh there you are, a delivery has just arrived for you".

Flowers, a large fragrant bouquet of roses, carnations and lilies. A white card nestled amongst the blooms. A single word in a large definite hand.... Stefan.

Soon he would be here and she could thank him. There was a feeling of apprehension in Amy each time she took a deep breath, she was aware of a small ache begining in her stomach and extending to fill her chest and throat. What was there to be frightened of? During the last few years Amy had learned to stand on her own two feet, make decisions, deal with difficult people. With Stefan somehow she felt she was not in control. He was masterful, imperious and Amy knew she must be assertive otherwise he would take over her precious holiday.

Amy stretched her legs, the car was comfortable and it purred its way along the country lanes. There was only a slight breeze and her black hair hardly moved. She was very much aware of Stefan's presence, she looked at his hands on the steering wheel, they were large capable hands, a large gold signet ring gave importance to his left hand's smallest finger, he had well manicured nails. Fine blonde hairs on the backs of his hands grew thicker where they disappeared under the white cuffs of his expensive shirt. Amy found she was picturing what his arms would be like without the covering of his shirt sleeves. Sitting close to him she occasionally had the pleasure of a waft of scent from his soap or cologne, an aroma of sandalwood, lavender and something reminiscent of leather. Quite delicious, Amy thought.

He was a pleasant companion so Amy, no longer nervous, relaxed as they chatted about the picturesque countryside. They drove through Bovey Tracey with its narrow steets above its river, the Bovey. Amy remembered the bridge from her holiday fifteen years before and related to Stefan how Bovey Bridge had been built during the civil War and Royalist troops quartered there were surprised by Cromwell as they were playing cards. The troops only escaped because they threw their stake money through the window where the Parliament men scrambled for what they could get, thus enabling the Royalists to escape unchecked.

“I don’t know a great deal of English history”, admitted Stefan. “I was brought up mainly in St. Petersburg and love the history of my own country. However, I am knowledgeable of your Royal Family I am pleased to let you know”.

“Our King is very much like your late Czar isn’t he, Nicholas and George were cousins I believe?”.

“Yes Amy”, smiled Stefan. “That makes us almost related wouldn’t you say?”.

They laughed at this idiotic remark and Amy tied her silk square over her head as Stefan increased his speed and the summer breeze lifted her dark hair.

A hamper was produced from the boot when they parked the car near Postbridge. Stefan took out a bottle of wine and stood it in the river to cool. Chicken and salad tasted so much better out of doors decided Amy. Afterwards they lay back on the tartan blanket, lazy and content. We could be the only people in the world, thought Amy, there was only the sound of the water to disturb the silence. No other cars, just peace, perfect peace. She closed her eyes revelling in the warmth of the midday sun.

A cloud must have passed over the sun, she no longer felt the heat on her eyelids. She opened her eyes and blotting out the sun’s rays was Stefan’s face. Close, so close to hers, his eyes crinkled at the corners with his smile. Amy smiled back and he leaned right over her. There was now only an inch or two between them and Stefan, his expression serious now made the move to kiss her open lips. Amy felt the weight of his body on hers, his lips seemed to set her on fire. She returned his passionate kisses, her body melting under the warmth of his. Stefan kissed her again and again. “Let me make love to you Amy, here, now, please”.

Amy struggled to sit up but Stefan held her down, she turned her face away that he could no longer take possession of her lips. “No Stefan, no. Please let me sit up”.

"But you are going to marry me Amy. I want you, you will marry me. I made up my mind yesterday, you have to be my wife".

The shock of this proposal, if it could be called that, calmed Amy, her pounding heart quietened. She had so nearly lost control, it would have been so easy to succumb to his caresses. Marriage, to suggest marriage when they hardly knew each other, he must be mad. She must talk to him, seriously.

Stefan sat up, got to his feet and pulled Amy up to stand beside him. "I meant that Amy, you will marry me, you have to, it will make me so happy".

Amy picked up the rug, made a fuss about shaking off the grass, folded it carefully before she said, "Let us drive on to Widecombe, there should be somewhere there for a cup of tea and when we have both recovered from this ....well, when we feel calmer I'll discuss it with you". That was better, she was in control again.

Neither spoke very much as they drove toward the tall church tower which could be seen miles before they arrived in Widecombe-in-the-Moor. That morning, in her happy state Amy had planned to sing to Stefan the old legend of 'Uncle Tom Cobleigh and his Grey Mare' as they approached the moorland village but now she remained silent, endeavouring to sort out her disturbed thoughts.

Tea was found and with it their tongues, they talked to each other over the tea and Lardy cake.

"You are rushing me Stefan, I hardly know anything about you, about your family. What do you know about me, only what you may have heard from Charles and Imogen. How can you be so sure I am the girl you wish to marry?"

"I know you very well Amy. I know you are the most attractive girl I have had the pleasure to lunch with. I know you are a good friend of my friends Charles and Imogen. I know you have lived in Paris which I love and where I have also lived. I know you are most exciting to kiss and I know you find me just as exciting".

In spite of herself Amy laughed.- "Rubbish", she said. "I have to go home on Saturday, when you are next in London contact me and we will get to know each other better".

"I'm thirty six Amy, time I was married".

"And I'm twenty six with plenty of time. You must meet my parents, be familiar with my background. See me in my various moods before you contemplate spending the rest of your life with me".

Stefan brushed the cake crumbs from his jacket and said in a decisive voice, "I intend to marry you Amy, not your parents. Your moods I shall deal with in my own way. We shall not mention the subject again until we are in London".

The sun was behind the clouds when they emerged from the shop and Amy put on her pullover. She was silent as Stefan drove, rather too fast for the narrow lanes through Ilsington and Highweek. Newton Abbot was still busy Wednesday being market day. Farmers' wives were packing up their stalls, men cleaning up the cattle market. They were at Berrycombe before the first drops of rain fell.

Dinah offered Stefan tea but he declined and made his way to Jim's workshop to collect a chair he had left for repair. "Had a nice day?", enquired a flustered Dinah. The baby was crying for her feed, a saucepan was boiling over and there was a smell of burnt pastry from the oven.

Amy moved the saucepan from the heat and avoiding Dinah's eye said, "This evening I have to talk to you. You and I, we must have a chat".

Stefan put his head round the kitchen door, "I'm off now. Might see you before you leave on Saturday Amy. Thanks for your company today, bye Dinah".

Amy was furious at his sudden exit and had to remind herself that she didn't care at all if she never saw him again. No sooner had the thought materialized, she knew she was lying to herself. Why hadn't he asked to see her tomorrow or Friday? She would have refused of course, she must spend some time with Dinah and Jim, but all the same ....

Sitting in the garden after supper, knowing that Jim was in the dining room engrossed in his detested paperwork, Amy gave Dinah a detailed account of her day.

"At last Amy, you have fallen in love and Stefan appears to be besotted with you".

"You haven't been listening Dinah. I have said nothing of love, Stefan has said nothing of love. He is rushing me, he assumes I will marry him. I am so very annoyed with his imperious manner".

"As I said, you have fallen in love. I recognise the symptoms. Look how you have described him to me in detail. How his eyes remind you of Hugh and his blonde hair too. You love his very faint accent, you find his hands fascinating. Even his soap and cologne have been analysed. You just won't admit it, even to yourself".

Amy frowned and looked at her friend. "Dinah he never mentioned love, only that I must marry him, then it would make him happy. Now he has gone back to Torquay without saying a proper 'goodbye' and I don't know when I shall see him again".

"Tomorrow", said Dinah with a smile. "Tomorrow Stefan will be here, stealing you away from me. If not, then there will be more flowers, telephone calls".

Thursday and Friday came and went but no Stefan, no flowers and no telephone calls for Amy. Dinah and Amy pushed Margot to the village and back each day and Jim had instructions to listen out for the ringing of the telephone.

Amy's thoughts were in turmoil; she was angry at Stefan's behaviour. Fancy thinking she would let him make love to her on such short acquaintance; what audacity - and then to walk off so casually. Then moments later, remembering his smile, her response to his passionate kisses, her anger faded.

She wanted to see him again, soon. wanted him to kiss her again and tell her in his low, attractive voice that he loved her. To tell her about his life, his family and well, just everything she did not know about him.

Dinah was concerned that there had been no word from Stefan and compared his offhand manner with Jim's thoughtfulness during their courtship.

Amy listening to her friend said, "There Dinah, as I said we do not know each other at all. I admit I find him exciting but I am cautious enough to realize there is a lot to find out about him before I give up my independence and become Mrs. Serovsky".

"Oh Amy" , exclaimed Dinah, "Whatever would ...."

" ....my father say", finished Amy and they collapsed with laughter.

Packing her case on Saturday morning Amy was sad that her short holiday was over. There had not been enough time with Dinah. An hour or two had been spent with Jim in his workshop and whilst holding a piece of moulding steady for him Amy had discussed the possibility of between them, negotiating to buy the cottage their parents had lived in all their married life. William, sixty six now would be thinking of retirement and to leave their home to live in one of the new council houses near the bridge at Shearfield did not appeal at all.

"When we are up for the Christening in October we'll speak to Jack Yeldham, Amy. Father has been a good employee and it may be possible to get Yeldham to sell to us".

Amy gave her brother a hug. "It would be wonderful to do something for them both Jim. I took so much for granted when I was a child, looking back I can see times must have been hard with four children to bring up. Mother never complained did she?".

"Jim will drive you to the station in plenty of time to catch the 2 o'clock train. I've told him it leaves at 1.45", said Dinah with a smile. "You know what he is for leaving everything until the last minute".

Jim was putting her case in the car, Amy saying 'goodbye' to Dinah and Margot, when Stefan's car drew up at the gate.

"Don't worry Jim, give me the case. I'm driving Amy back to Ilford".

Dinah and Amy looked at each other, Dinah raised her eyebrows, shook her chestnut curls at Stefan and Amy tried to look annoyed. How could she be cross, he smiled his charming, disarming smile, opened the door of his immaculate car and hardly gave her time to kiss Jim before Amy was in the passenger seat and he had started up the engine.

They stood at the gate, Jim and Dinah, Margot held in Dinah's arms while Jim waved until the car had turned the corner.

"Stefan, why on earth did you not let me know you were going to do this?".

"Didn't know myself until half an hour ago. Suddenly thought, good idea to take Amy home and stay in Chelsea for a while to buy some stock. You're glad to see me I hope?".

Amy's heart seemed to be beating in her throat, there was a lot of motoring to do before she was home. Was Stefan going to use the time to charm her into saying 'Yes' to marriage?

Today, as the weather was cooler the hood of the tourer had been raised. Confined like this, Amy was even more aware of the vitality that Stefan exuded. He seemed almost to crackle with electricity. To Amy's relief the conversation of Post Bridge was completely ignored. Stefan asked again about her year in Paris and listened with interest to her replies.

"Have you ever flown Amy?"

"Oh no, I always went to Paris on the Boat Train".

"Then I must arrange a flight when I take you to Paris".

"I'm not sure I should be happy in a plane Stefan".

"You silly goose, of course you would. What about your namesake, Amy Johnson, she flew all the way to Australia alone in her little Gypsy Moth in April. Surely you could manage to hop over the Channel with me beside you".

They stopped at Shaftesbury for afternoon tea in an old inn. As Amy poured the tea, Stefan looked at her hands, at those long artistic fingers with their well shaped nails, buffed to a pearly sheen. "Has anyone ever told you Amy that you have beautiful hands?".

"Yes, once, a very long time ago", said Amy, thinking of Hugh and how this man somehow reminded her of the fair haired young man she had idolized.

Stefan took her left hand in his and slowly, without taking his eyes from hers began to kiss each finger. "Did he do this?" he asked.

Amy lowered her eyes and shook her head.

"Your eyes are magnificent Amy, I remember my grandmother had eyes such as yours. As a child I was almost frightened to look into them, so large and dark. When she looked at me I felt that she knew every one of my secrets, could read my very thoughts".

"Your tea will be cold Stefan", was all Amy could think to say. Her heart was beating quickly and she knew a blush had given away her secret. She was not quite as composed and sophisticated as she would have people believe. Not quite a woman of the world.

"I must telephone Imogen to let her know you are taking me home, how awful if she went to Paddington to meet the train". Amy rose from the table and made her way to the reception desk to make her call. She had to pass an old man who had witnessed the hand kissing but he now appeared to be engrossed in his Madiera cake and Amy was grateful he did not look at her.

The remainder of the journey was pleasant. Stefan remarked on how lucky they were to have the quiet A30 to take them to London. "In twenty years or less there will be so much more traffic Amy. Everyone will learn to drive and want to own a car".

"Even me", said Amy who enjoyed the convenience and comfort of motoring. She lay back in the leather seat and recalled her first drive in a car. Hugh at the wheel of the Major's car, herself looking quaint in a straw hat and flowered dress from Ashdowns store in Ongar. Mother and Father excited to be going on holiday to Berrycombe.

"Are you fond of the ballet?", Stefan's question brought her back to the present.

"I've never been".

"You've never been in a 'plane, never visited the ballet. I can see I am going to be busy finishing your education". Then Stefan had to give his attention to driving, the traffic was increasing as they drew nearer to London.

At home in Ilford, Imogen was looking out for the car and opened the front door before Stefan turned into the drive. She kissed and hugged Amy. "Missed you so much", she said. Then turning to Stefan she looked up at him towering above her. His blond good looks never failed to impress her, she admired his wonderful smile, his perfect teeth but Imogen was one of the few women immune to his charm.

"Hello Stefan, it is nice to see you again, do come in for a drink. How convenient that you were travelling back to Chelsea today that Amy was able to beg a lift".

I don't think Imogen likes him, thought Amy and felt a sense of disappointment.

Later as she saw Stefan off at the door he bent down and kissed her lightly on the cheek. "Make arrangements for a November wedding", he instructed, revved up the engine and was gone.

Tessie, sitting lonely in the back bedroom was the recipient of Amy's thoughts on Stefan, private thoughts she would not yet share with

Imogen. The doll stared back, her dark brown glass eyes expressionless. No encouragement, no remonstrances came from her pretty, pink china lips.

CHAPTER TEN

The serious wooing began. Stefan stayed in his flat with Sasha in Charles' house. During the day he was searching for antiques, attending sales and auctions. His evenings were given over to Amy. They went to concerts at the Albert Hall, enjoyed Revues and new plays at the many theatres in London. Stefan introduced Amy to the ballet which she loved, the fairy tale quality of the dancers, the beautiful, haunting music and the georgeous costumes left Amy in a trance-like state as she left the theatre on Stefan's arm.

That summer Stefan was proud to 'show off' the tall, slim, dark girl he intended to marry. Amy always attracted attention from both men and women when she entered a room. Her carriage and dramatic colouring teamed with immaculate grooming made her an outstanding companion and Stefan basked in the reflected glory.

The London *Theodora's* was expanding. Dolly had been able to buy the premises either side of her small salon and after consultations with Amy and Imogen the merchandise now included jewellery, belts, gloves and bags. Amy did most of the buying for both the Kensington and Ilford shops and was extremely happy with her career. She no longer wore the 'Flattener' of the 'twenties and her figure was rounder, her arms and legs nicely covered. Mitsouko was still Amy's perfume although she also used Guerlain's 'Jicky' and more rarely, Chanel No. 5. Amy Clayden looked the typical sophisticated 'thirties well groomed business woman but the old Amy, the shy country girl was not buried too far under that shiny veneer.

Amy was waiting for an invitation to visit Stefan and Sasha's flat. She wondered if Stefan had confided in his sister that he intended to marry. Apart from kisses in taxis and Stefan's car their relationship was friendly and he did not repeat his impassioned pleas of that afternoon on the moors. Amy was becoming used to his imperious manner. She had ignored his request to arrange a November wedding and was awaiting what she considered a proper proposal and a declaration of his love.

July and August passed. Stefan returned to Torquay at the end of August and escaped the heatwave that made life almost unbearable in London. It was over 90 degrees on 28th August and Amy was envious when Stefan telephoned and described to her how blue the sea was in the bay, how a gentle breeze stirred the leaves on the trees in Abbey Gardens.

"Keep Wednesday 24th September free Amy, I'll be back in London again and we are doing something special", and then the receiver was replaced.

Letters from Dinah arrived regularly and always contained reference to Stefan. Was he serious about a November wedding? Had Amy introduced him to her mother and father? If she married him it would mean living in Devon, was she happy at the thought of saying goodbye to *Theodora's*?

Amy wrote back but did not answer any of those questions, evaded them by saying she and Stefan would have discussions on the subject when he returned to London.

The gold chocolate box which housed many of Amy's treasures was bursting with cards and letters, menus and invitations. A red ribbon was tied over the bulging lid, the box no longer had the slim elegant shape Amy had discovered when she had unwrapped Charles' present to her that Christmas which now seemed so far away. Tessie sat on the shelf, next to the mis-shapen box, aloof, confident that her shape would not change over the years. The family photograph in the oval frame showed Amy's loved ones with unlined, smiling faces. Amy sighed as she studied a younger Louise and William. There were no sign of the grey hairs that she had noticed the last time she had visited. There was nothing one could do to slow down the passing of time.

The passing of time had changed Ilford too. The population when Imogen and Amy had moved there in 1920 was in the region of 85,000 now in 1930 it had risen to almost 131,000. New shops were opening to cope with the estates of houses being built. The Penny Bazaar in the High Road which had opened in 1922 had become, in 1930, Marks and Spencer. The A.B.C. and J. Lyons had tea shops in the High Road and there were several drapers and furniture stores in the High Road and Cranbrook Road. Imogen in her small gown shop was happy with her growing clientele. Each week Amy spent two days at the small *Theodora's* to enable Imogen to have some free time. There was a young assistant, Sadie, a bright girl eager to learn the trade. Amy knew that if she married Stefan it would be as Dinah had said, she must say goodbye to the career for which she had worked so hard.

On the 11th September flowers arrived at *Theodora's* in Kensington. They were for Amy and a small white envelope contained a note in Stefan's distinctive writing, 'To remind you that it is now three months since I decided you must be my wife. Have your 'glad rags' ready for the 24th Sept we are attending the premier of Private Lives. Arrange for rest of week off, we fly to Paris to meet my family. will see you 23rd.... Stefan' .

Delight, apprehension and excitement swept over Amy as she read and re-read the note. What would Stefan's relatives be like, would they be able to understand each other, would they like her? She must be brave and endure the flight across the Channel, pretend she was enjoying it, for Stefan's sake.

The day before the theatre visit, Stefan appeared at *Theodora's* to take Amy to lunch. His tall, muscular body seemed to fill the salon. He raised Amy's hand and lightly brushed it with his lips, Dolly was also treated to this old fashioned courtesy.

In his imperious manner Stefan said, "I am sure you will not need Amy for the next three hours Dolly, we have so much to discuss and I do so hate being rushed over luncheon".

Dolly, unlike Imogen, was not immune to his charm and though it meant she would have to miss her own lunch and attend to a very important client who always requested that Amy modelled the clothes she was interested in, Dolly smiled her agreement, still savouring the sensation of Stefan's lips on her hand.

To walk with Stefan on that September morning was a pleasant experience. The pavements were dappled with the sun shining through the leaves of the trees lining the busy road. Amy was so aware of his closeness, the caressing note in his voice when he spoke to her, (was it this that reminded her of Hugh?) the thrill she felt when his hand cupped her elbow as he steered her across the road. Yes, the magic was still there, it was not something she had imagined had happened between them in Devon. Amy was sure, yes this was love, there was no doubt in her mind.

He chose a small imtimate restaurant for their lunch, a secluded table. "We fly to France on Thursday morning Amy. We shall stay a night with my Aunt and Uncle, unless of course you will agree to me booking us a room at a hotel? No? I thought not, no matter. Aunt Margot and Uncle Sergei are impatient to meet the woman I love and give their approval".

"The woman you love, you love me Stefan?".

"Love you, of course I love you Amy, I adore you".

Her happiness was complete, he loved her, he had said it. Amy put down her knife and fork, she could eat no more. There was nothing to worry about. What did *Theodora's* matter or her home with Imogen. Not long to plan and arrange the November wedding Stefan wanted.

Amy looked around her, how beautiful the restaurant was, how handsome the waiters. The women lunching in their pretty hats were georgeous, to Amy that day everything was beautiful. She gave Stefan a dazzling smile, her large dark eyes were glowing with love.

The first night of Noel Coward's 'Private Lives' was a success. Amy and Stefan had good seats and thoroughly enjoyed the clever playwright's performance. Gertie Lawrence opposite him was magnificent, the audience forgot they were watching a play so realistic were the performances of the two stars in their quarrelling and fighting. Amy almost felt embarrassed by the shouting, the ferocity of the quarrel in one scene, the kicking and rolling on the floor, almost as though she were eavesdropping.

In the interval, with drinks in their hands they mingled with the theatregoers and the Press. Well known society figures were being photographed, dressed by Worth, Lanvin, Chanel and Amy saw a dress of such clashing, bright colours she guessed it may be a Schiaparelli; she was not sure that she liked the marrying of the outrageous colours for which that designer was becoming known.

A bright flash startled Amy, a young man, no doubt mistaking the tall svelte young woman for someone well known had taken a photograph for his newspaper. Stefan was amused, "I can see the heading tomorrow, Count and Countess Serovsky at the premier of Mr. Coward's new play", he said.

Later, over supper they discussed the play and Noel Coward. "Do you think his talent is all they say Stefan, or do you expect in just a year or two he will be forgotten?".

"Hard to say Amy. I certainly think he has another success in 'Private Lives'. Coward is a clever young man but we must wait and see. He may well last".

The dreaded flight was in fact quite enjoyable. Amy was rather pale as she boarded but once over the sea and sighting the French coast so soon after 'take off', the experience was a happy one and Amy was sorry when the plane began it's descent. She wanted to see more of the colourful patchwork of the fields below her.

Paris was as busy as ever, bathed in the hazy golden autumn sun. The air scented with flowers, leaves and newly baked bread brought back to Amy memories of her year living and working in the capital.

The rendezvous with Stefan's aunt and uncle was a small, dark cafe not far from Notre Dame. The greetings and the first few minutes of conversation with Maria and Sergei was in Russian and then, in deference to Amy, the three switched to French interspersed with broken English which she found easy to follow.

Sergei and Maria were happy to enlighten Amy on Stefan's background, his family and childhood. Amy learned that his father had been a jeweller employed by Faberge in his St. Petersburg workshops. On his marriage to Dagmar, a golden haired beauty from Riga the brothers Sergei and Micha had opened a jewellers in the city. The business thrived, the brothers becoming well known for the excellence of the design and quality of their rings and brooches. Perfect stones and gems in restrained settings was their hallmark. Sasha and Stefan had an English nanny followed by a good education at well chosen schools.

In 1914 when Russia was at war with Germany, Stefan was in the army and Sasha an art student. As she ate her omelette and salad Amy listened to an account of the fashionable life in St. Petersburg before the revolution. Maria excitedly described balls at the Winter Palace, the magnificence of the gowns and jewels worn by the women, their escorts handsome, resplendent in their uniforms. Then came the rumblings of the trouble to come. Word came of minor skirmishes because of the discontent of the hungry and cold peasants.

More vodka was poured and drunk as Stefan and his uncle resorted once again to the Russian tongue to describe the violence and butchery that St. Petersburg had witnessed following these early warnings.

Maria looked at Amy who was no longer able to follow the conversation. She told in her broken English of the horrific day when Stefan's parents had been killed. The brothers had decided to leave Russia and make a new life in Paris. Many of their compatriots were escaping from the fighting and looting in the city. Plans were made, the stock carefully packed and at the last moment Dagmar refused to leave. What would Stefan do when he returned from the war to find his home deserted? His mother made the excuse that she had lost the bracelet Micha had given her at Easter. Like most Russians she was superstitious and refused to leave the house without it. She told Maria and Sergei to take Sasha and she and Micha would follow when the bracelet was found. Stefan's parents stayed in the home of which they were so proud, thinking to persuade Stefan to desert the army and join them in Paris.

It was impossible to contact Stefan and when he did return it was to find his parents had been murdered and his home ransacked. Stefan eventually found his way to Paris and made his home with Maria and Sergei. Sasha was continuing her art studies in Paris and he had settled in with her aunt and uncle.

"Enough of this sad talk Amy", said Maria, wiping away a tear. "We must take you to our apartment, Sergei, if you are able to raise yourself from that chair we will make our way home".

She led the way across an open market. The stalls depleted somewhat by now but still colourful with the reds and greens of vegetables and salads, fragrant too where huge bunches of flowers were waiting to be sold.

Stefan bought several bunches to the delight of the flower-seller and presented them, with a flourish, to his aunt.

A square just opposite the market place was their destination. Sergei opened a door, one of several in a brick wall, a door long overdue for a coat of paint. They were in a narrow, covered passageway, a few steps and the four of them were one again in the sunlight. A small courtyard furnished with a curved stone bench then wide steps leading up to a door which Sergei opened with a large key.

"We live on the ground floor", explained Maria. "other Russians live above us and on either side. Some are related to us and others have become our friends. We are quite a colony in this part of the Left Bank you know".

Amy had not seen rooms furnished as those in this cool apartment. Tall windows curtained in heavy cream lace, many small tables overloaded with photographs in silver frames jostling with tiny silver trinkets and pretty little enamelled boxes. The walls were hung with icons and on a larger table, draped as were the others with lace cloths, stood a Samovar of intricate design.

Stefan and his uncle disappeared into a small room off the salon and Amy was left alone with Maria. She hoped she was mistaken but she felt Stefan's relatives did not wholly approve of her. Amy was glad to find her French had not entirely deserted her and was able to hold a conversation of sorts with this Russian woman.

The door opened and Amy caught the tail end of a sentence in French, ' .....not happy but she does look a strong woman and will give you healthy sons'.

She blushed as Stefan caught her eye and gave a suggestive wink. "Come in Amy and sit down, Uncle Sergei and I have something to show you".

Sergei was closing the door of a small black safe in the corner of the room, on the table was a square of black velvet and Stefan pulled her down into the chair next to his. "Time to choose your engagement ring. Uncle Sergei has quite a quantity of jewels he brought from St. Petersburg and I have been looking through them, picking out several that you may have a choice".

Sergei lifted the black velvet and there displayed on the table was an assortment of such beauty that Amy caught her breath in amazement.

Diamonds, sapphires, rubies and emeralds. The Jewels were set in gold, mainly of a simple design that the stones could be seen to advantage. Amy tried on each and every ring, marvelling at the brilliance of the jewels. It took a considerable time to select just one. Maria was called in at the end to help decide between an emerald and a diamond.

"The emerald is lovely but if you wear blue often then I think the diamond would be the best choice. Amy slipped it on her finger once again, yes the diamond was beautiful.

"You have made a wise choice", said Sergei. "That diamond is flawless and of a good colour, not a hint of yellow. The setting and shank are 72 zolotniks gold".

"In English that is 18 carats", explained Stefan as he shooed Amy out of the 'room that he may complete the financial transaction with his uncle.

That evening a noisy party was given for Amy and Stefan. The many relatives living nearby came to wish the engaged couple good luck by drinking quantities of vodka. Someone brought his Balalaika and his music led to wild dancing and the singing of Russian folk songs.

"You will be married, of course, at the Russian Orthodox Church here in Paris?", someone was saying.

"No, at home, my village church", said Amy.

Stefan, his fair brows drawn together took Amy's arm and his voice was loud as he corrected her and announced that the wedding would take place at the Russian Orthodox in London.

Amy thought it best not to argue, she had noticed that Stefan's glass had been refilled many times, she would tell him tomorrow that the wedding, without doubt, must take place at Shearfield.

Wearing her ring proudly, watching the diamond flash whenever the light caught the facets of the stone Amy travelled back to England. Looking down at the coast of France, seeing the white cliffs of the English coast, Amy knew she must take Stefan to meet her family. Sarah would be pleased for her, she was so happy in her marriage and wanted her sister to be as happy. Father and Mother? Well that was another matter. How different her own relatives were from Stefan's family she had met the night before. Amy looked at the handsome man beside her, she squeezed his arm, smiled as she pictured Mother and Sarah captivated by his charm. Father ... she would just have to wait and see.

An invitation came from Sasha, lunch on Sunday week at Chelsea. Amy was apprehensive of meeting Stefan's sister again. She was a flamboyant character, the younger Amy had been in awe of her and the memory had lingered.

Imogen had not received the news of the engagement with much enthusiasm. "Are you certain Stefan is the right choice dear?", she had said. Later she had added, "It is not just because you will be leaving Dolly and me that I am unhappy about this marriage. Charles and I know Stefan quite well, he is a very charming man but...well, it is not for me to interfere. Just be sure Amy, very sure, If you have any doubts at all, break the engagement now".

Poor Imogen, thought Amy, destined to remain single. It was only natural she should make such remarks.

The Sunday lunch was a success. Sasha met Amy at the door of the flat carrying a silver tray on which sat a piece of bread, some salt and a few grapes. Stefan explained that this was an old Russian welcome but then followed a typical English Sunday lunch of roast beef.

Sasha, looking resplendent in her bright clothes, her hair redder than ever, was a good hostess and she had the Russian gift of storytelling. She kept her guests amused with tales of her student days in St. Petersburg and Paris.

Amy listend, enthralled. How different from her childhood in Shearfield. The tiny, nagging thought came back again. How wide the gap between the Serovsky's and the Clayden's.

Before Amy returned to Ilford, she left Stefan to chat to his sister while she went downstairs to see Mrs. Gurney. To her surprise she found that Charles had just returned from France. The hall was littered with luggage and he came out of the drawing room to greet her with a kiss like the old friend she now was.

"I hear you are soon to become Mrs. Serovksy", he said, his eyes grave. "I had hoped ..but that was a long time ago".

Charles looked so well Amy thought. Tanned, his brown hair streaked with gold by the sun he still looked very young. She did a quick calculation and realized that Charles was now thirty two.

"Come into the dining room and have another look at your portrait Amy, I do, each time I return home. I stand in front of it and remember the enjoyment I had in capturing your shyness and youth on the canvas".

Amy moved with him into that lovely room and looked up at her younger self. Her dark eyes looked out of the painting, the first thing of which the viewer was conscious and then she saw the silken texture of the pale dress, the bluish, black sheen of the hair.

"I was only an innocent child then", she said.

"Yes and you are still young, beautiful and I believe, innocent" said the artist with a smile lighting up his tanned face.

Mrs. Gurney brought them coffee and Stefan came running down the stairs. Charles said, "Now, you two, don't forget your old friends when you move down to Torquay permanently. Amy, you will keep in touch won't you?".

It was October, the weekend of the christening before Stefan met William, Louise and Sarah. The women fell under his spell but William was cautious.

Sarah was captivated by Stefan's looks and his charming manner. Amy saw them talking and laughing together and noticed that Jack was uncomfortable in Stefan's company. She went out of her way to be nice to her shy brother-in-law.

Margot was a lovely baby and she behaved with dignity at morning service followed by the christening. 'Margot Louise' the vicar named her, making the sign of the cross on her forehead. Afterward walking through the churchyard toward "the kissing gate", Amy looked at the spot where on such another sunny October morning she had sat with a young soldier so soon to die.

"Well Hugh", she thought, "I've kept my promise, I'm making something of my life".

The family were not happy with the wedding arrangements. The Russian Orthodox Church indeed! The subject had to be dropped for Amy could see that Stefan and her father were getting extremely heated over the matter. Dinah, also aware of the atmosphere, managed to change the subject and Amy and Jim took their father into the garden to discuss with him their plan to help him buy the cottage. Jim had already spoken to Farmer Yeldham and persuaded him to sell.

"I want no help from you Amy", snapped William. "You have separated yourself from us and our ways. I cannot understand why you couldn't have stayed here in Shearfield. You could have had a good domestic post by now, at the Rectory or the doctor's. You could have marrried a nice steady local boy, not some fancy foreigner. No Amy, I shall never understand you".

Jim tried to placate his father. "We just want to help you. Soon you will retire. Where will you live?".

"I've saved something out of my wages each week of my working life, boy. My savings will buy this cottage, no need for charity from my children".

Louise busied herself producing an enormous tea, her remedy for frayed tempers. Sarah helped her mother, she knew how unhappy Louise must be, she always was if there was any discord within the family.

Upstairs in her old bedroom, Amy sat nursing a fretful Margot. The baby no doubt crying because the surroundings were unfamiliar. Amy was crying because she had been rebuffed by her father. Dinah comforting both her baby and her friend tried to give good advice.

"If your father buys the cottage Amy, I'm sure you could help in another way. There will be solicitors fees and surveyors. There could be repairs and alterations to be carried out. Knowing your father, it won't be long before he regrets his outburst today and then you and Jim can step in".

"It's not just the cottage Dinah. What about the wedding? I always imagined I would be married in our church, dressed in silk and lace, you know, just like Tessie. Now I am thinking in order not to offend either family it would be better to have a quiet Registry Office ceremony".

"You may be right", said a sad Dinah, glad that her romance and wedding had been uncomplicated.

A Registry Office it was, on the 22nd November, with Sasha, Dolly and Charles as witnesses. William and Louise, Imogen also, had declined to attend. Amy was photographed wearing a plain wool dress and coat. The photographs did not show the dusky rose of the woollen material or the deeper rose of the felt hat worn to one side of her head. The glow of the warm pink brightened up the greyness of that cold damp November morning in London.

At the reception Sasha and Stefan described to Amy what she had missed by not being married in their church. There would have been no bridesmaids but there would have been a bearded High Priest in a cloth of gold raiment. Candles and icons, rowan berries would have decorated the church a symbol of eternal life. Crowns would have been held above the heads of the bridal pair. Amy thought of the 15th century church at Shearfield with its lovely woodwork on the 16th century screen, of the traceried font, carved with the shields of ancient families of the district. The old organ would have wheezed through the hymns she had sung since childhood.

Amy Clayden was now Amy Serovsky, she was married to the man she loved, did it really matter where the vows had been made?

CHAPTER ELEVEN

Amy was dusting the photographs and ornaments on the mantlepiece in her bedroom. It was a long process these days, she was very careful. Age had caused her fingers to become stiff and she often dropped things. These treasures were too precious to be dropped and broken.

She studied the black and white snap Dolly had taken with her Brownie box camera that morning in November 1930, on her way to the Registry Office. Had she ever had hair as black as that? Amy remembered the day clearly, the start of her marriage to Stefan.

Amy, duster in hand, sat on the little chair and pictured their bedroom in Gentian House. How happy she had been, what a wonderful lover Stefan had proved to be. There had been no honeymoon, just a night spent in a luxurious room at the hotel where they had given a small reception. What was it called, that famous hotel? No, her memory had let her down again; it was silly, she knew the name so well, it was always appearing in the newspapers, no, never mind.

* * * * *

The young bride had been so deliriously happy. It had not mattered that Mother and Father had not attended the wedding. After all it was quite a journey from Shearfield to London and they had sent a wedding present. A bread-board and knife and a carving set. To this day they were in the kitchen drawer and often used.

Just Stefan and Amy together, they needed no one. To be held in Stefan's arms, to learn from him the art of loving, to listen to the extravagant phrases he whispered in her ear. Amy was content, satisfied. Life was perfect now.

Yes, in spite of what was to come Amy was happy in those early years of marriage. Gentian House with Amy to tidy it up, to clean and polish, to rearrange and display the treasures, was a beautiful place.

Stefan was pleased to have Amy as his assistant. Customers now entered the front door into what appeared to be a delightful home instead of a room full of furniture with price tickets hanging from legs and handles.

Amy had taken off the offending labels and a book was kept to which she or Stefan referred should a client wish to purchase. Clients on arriving were invited to remove their coats and leave them in the small vestibule that Amy had recently decorated. Coffee or tea would be served in translucent china, there was no need to hurry over viewing the treasures, no pressure to buy.

Business increased as satisfied customers told of the charming hostess at Gentian House Antiques. Upstairs, Stefan's untidiness was brought under control. Amy created a comfortable sitting room and a dining area out of the large room over the shop. The kitchen was adequate, bright and functional with a view of Torbay from the small window.

Stefan left the decor and furnishing of their bedroom to Amy and was pleased with the result. She had applied a pale wash of apricot to the walls, the curtains and bedcover were of a deep turquoise and apricot chintz and a carpet the colour of clotted cream covered the floor.

Tessie sat on a chair, her wedding dress carefully arranged to disguise the fact the doll only possessed one leg. Tessie was the only thing in the newly decorated room to which Stefan objected. "I'm not keen on having that doll watching me make love to my wife", he said, only half joking.

It was only a matter of a few days before, in spite of Amy's protests, Tessie was in the showroom, not, definitely not, 'for sale', but placed high on top of a Queen Anne tallboy. She looked charming in her old fashioned dress and veil, but Amy looking at her one evening thought she had a reproachful look in her eye, a trick of the light no doubt.

Amy was now able to see Dinah and Jim most weeks and it was fascinating to see Margot developing; she was a happy, pretty baby and Amy loved her. Louise wrote regularly and Amy was delighted when her letters began to contain loving messages from Father. The rift that had occurred over the wedding was begining to heal. The purchase of the cottage was completed and Jim and Amy were satisfied that eventually they had both been able to contribute something towards fees and repairs.

* * * * *

'It was all so long ago' thought Amy as she continued with the dusting and picked up the studio portrait of Becky, a photograph, hand coloured, taken in Torquay's best studio on Becky's first birthday. A smiling, plump, blonde little girl. How proud Stefan had been of his daughter who had inherited his fair colouring, his imperious manner.

Amy smiled as she remembered the conversation when she had told Stefan she was pregnant.

* * * * *

"But you can't be Amy, it isn't convenient. I need you in the business".

Then later, "Be sure it is a boy Amy. Thinking it over I would quite like a son. Just be sure you give me a son and I will forgive you for getting pregnant".

Amy had worried throughout the remaining months. There was nothing she could do, maybe she was carrying a boy but supposing it was a girl. She had learned by now that charming as he was, as generous as he was, Stefan did have to have his way about everything.

Their daughter was born on the 25th November, 1931 and was named Rebecca after Stefan's grandmother and Stefan idolized her. There was not another baby in the world so beautiful, so intelligent, so good. He had quite forgotten about the son he had wanted.

William and Louise came to stay with Jim and Dinah that Christmas and the rift was completely healed. They were a happy family again. William the perfect grandfather with a baby on each knee.

* * * * *

Back in 1984 Amy finished the dusting and went downstairs and into the garden at the front of the house. She would walk to the gate, look along the road for Mrs. Monk. They would have a cup of coffee before that lady started on the real housework. Then it would be time for Margot to arrive and they would be off to Exeter for the day.

A red car stood in the road, partly hidden by a large rhododendron bush. Amy was surprised to see a man studying her house from the opposite side of the road.

"Can I help you?", she asked.

"No thank you, I was admiring your house, the mature garden, it is all very attractive".

He gave Amy a smile which she did not return and it was not until he got into the car and drove off in the direction of Buckfastleigh that Amy recognised the well-groomed man she had seen at the hotel on her birthday.

Yes, it was the man who had hesitated at their table, the man she was sure Becky knew and yet had not acknowledged. Just then Mrs. Monk arrived on her bicycle and the incident was pushed to the back of Amy's mind.

Mrs. Monk did not sit long over coffee and was soon about her domestic duties. "I've done my bedroom, no need to come upstairs today", called Amy as she checked on her hair and make up at her dressing table. Her jewel case lay amongst the silver topped bottles and she selected a gold brooch that had belonged to her mother to secure the Hermes silk scarf at her neck.

Leaving the bedroom Amy noticed her pearls lying on the bedside table; Margot had arrived and was sounding the car horn so Amy quickly hid the necklace under the skirt of Tessie's ageing wedding dress. Just in case I have a visit from the burglar everyone prophesies will come one day, she thought as she hurried to greet her neice.

"Do you mind stopping at Kent's stores Margot? Mrs. Kent requsted me to call this morning, something she wants to tell me it seems".

"Village gossip I suppose", said Margot with a laugh. "Whatever would you all do for news without the village shop?"

She waited for her aunt outside the tiny, shabby looking shop. How fortunate Aunt Amy was to have the convenience of a village shop; she could walk down most mornings and sit on the rickety bentwood chair for a chat. Far friendlier than the supermarket where Margot and Amy did their bulk shopping once a month.

Amy came out, carefully shutting the door behind her. Margot heard the 'ding' of the bell on its leather strap. She noticed how serious her aunt looked as she got into the car. "Everything O.K. Aunt Amy?".

"No, I'm afraid not", said Amy. "Mrs. Kent wanted me to be one of the first to know that at the end of next month the shop will close. She has for some time been trying to find a buyer but no one wants to take on a small shop with the new supermarket a mile or two away".

"I am sorry Aunt Amy", said Margot putting a hand on the old lady's knee. "You will miss your daily stroll, not to mention the friendly chat. You're not to worry about the shopping, we'll just visit the supermarket more often".

"I just have to accept that times are changing all the familiar things, complaining about them is a waste of time. Forget about it and let's enjoy our day out".

They did enjoy their day, Margot was good company and a considerate companion. There were several breaks for coffee and tea and their lunch was taken at a favourite hotel near the Cathedral, comfortable and quiet, giving Amy a chance to rest her feet. It was quite late in the afternoon that Margot remembered she had to collect a watch left for repair at a jewellers.

Amy sat on a chair and studied the bracelets and rings in a display case. She secretly thought that her own jewellery, collected over the years, was far superior to this modern stuff and how expensive it all was!

Margot was waiting for the assistant to finish serving a couple who were looking at second hand brooches. The man spoke, "My wife and I collect 'twenties and 'thirties items, we'll look at these whilst you attend to the ladies".

Margot and Amy exchanged surprised glances, it was the couple who had been at the hotel and only this morning their car had been parked at the front of Hope Lodge. They did not look at Amy and continued their perusal of the brooches as the jeweller went to find Tom's watch.

"Here we are madam, see it is exactly right, 5.03p.m."

Margot paid for the repair and she and Amy left the shop, glancing again at the dapper little man who was now relating how they had had no idea it was so late and that they must start on the long drive back to London.

The A384 was very busy and Margot concentrated on her driving. Amy was pleased when they reached the roundabout where the signs showed Newton Abbot to the left and to the right the A382 leading over the moors to Moreton Hampstead; they would soon be home now, Buckfastleigh could be seen in the distance. Oh to take off the smart shoes and to sink into an armchair. Amy hoped Margot would decline the offer to stay for a while, it had been a long day.

Margot drew up in front of Hope Lodge, got out to help her aunt and Amy said, "Coming in dear, or are you anxious to get home?".

"I'd better get going, Tom will wonder where I am, we've been out ages haven't we, but I've so enjoyed the day".

Amy got out her key and once in the hall she kicked off her shoes. A cup of tea, her feet up on a stool and after ten minutes she would prepare her evening meal. As she walked down the hall past the drawing room Amy noticed the curtains moving slightly in a breeze. Mrs. Monk must have left the window open, unlike her to be careless, she was usually so fussy about security. She hadn't left the kitchen very tidy either, drawers and doors open, lids off a couple of pots.

It was not until Amy had drunk her tea and went upstairs did she realise the awful truth. She had been burgled! Her bedroom floor was covered with the contents of drawers and her wardrobe. Handbags were open, upside down on the bed. The dressing table swept clear of the silver and crystal trinkets collected over the years. The jewel case had gone of course and Amy turned quickly to look for Tessie. Thank goodness, the doll sat there on her velvet covered chair, eyes open wide, the skirt of her yellowed wedding dress spread around her. Amy lifted the skirt and there were the pearls, safe in the hiding place Amy had decided on that morning. They lay in a heap, softly gleaming. Under the dressing table stool something caught Amy's eye, she bent down and thankfully retrieved the pearl and turquoise earrings.

The Police pointed out that the french windows in the drawing room did not have a secure lock and it would have taken no time at all to force an entry. The burglary followed the pattern of several that had recently taken place in the area. Small items and cash, nothing too difficult for disposal.

After the police had taken finger prints, Amy telephoned Mrs. Monk and she and her husband came to help tidy up. John Monk said that he had been returning, on his bicycle from Dartington about five o'clock when, passing Hope Lodge, he had almost been forced off the road by a small red car leaving Amy's drive at great speed. No, he had not recognised the driver or the car. Margot at once suggested that the couple in the jewellers owned a red car and hadn't Amy seen it parked outside earlier that day?

They began to connect the couple with the incident until Margot pointed out that it had been 5.03 p.m., when she had been handed the repair watch and the couple were at that time still in the shop. The policeman dealing with the break-in asked John Monk if he could be certain of the time he saw the car and his confirmation of 5 p.m., was accepted. It was just another case of a householder losing some valuables because the property was not properly secure. Some young man without a job making enough to live on by selling his ill gotten gains, that was the verdict of the constable.

Becky had to be told of course, and she was adamant that the time had now come for her mother to vacate Hope Lodge. "Supposing you had been at home Ma, anything could have happened. How will you now be able to sleep there alone at night. Listening to every noise and creak?".

Amy's heart was heavy, she felt sick, hated the thought that a stranger's hands had been amongst her scarves and gloves, her underclothes tossed carelessly on the floor. Within the next few days, locks had been fitted to the doors and windows, a burglar alarm installed and Amy was begining to give serious thought to Becky's advice.

Maybe it was time to move into a Residential Home. Mr. & Mrs. Monk were getting older just as she was; they seemed fit it was true but the years had made a difference to them all. The village shop was closing, Amy would miss it she knew. There was more traffic on the once quiet Devon lanes, life just wasn't the same any more. Nothing one could do, the best years had long gone. Those were Amy's thoughts as she began to search the advertisements in the local paper for likely Residential Homes.

Margot was a treasure, she drove Amy to view about a dozen Homes. Always there was something not to Amy's liking. Margot was patient, she admired the way the old lady had dealt with the unpleasantness of the break in, the loss of most of her jewellery. She was sad of course at the loss of some of the more sentimental pieces but she explained to Margot: "They were only material things, remember. Like you I have lost people cared for greatly, those were the big sadnesses in my life. A few baubles, well I can live without them I'm sure. Glad the thief left my old chocolate box alone though, I should have hated to lose my souvenirs, all those letters and theatre programmes. The postcards and invitations. I still like to take them out and look at them you know".

One afternoon Amy and Margot visited 'St. Annes', a large Victorian house on the edge of a park near Newton Abbot. Mrs. Tillson took ten residents, each having a spacious bedroom and eating with the family in a well furnished dining room. The airy lounge contained comfortable chintz covered chairs and useful tables. Interesting pictures and two glass fronted display cabinets full of pretty porcelain. Amy was fascinated by the house and also by the young proprietress and her children, Gemma and Thomas. They were all so attractive and so well mannered. The garden was large and well tended, there was a conservatory which housed exotic plants. Fees were discussed and Margot could see Amy's dark eyes sparkling. Was their quest at an end?

Driving home, Margot said, "Well, Aunt Amy?".

"If I must leave Hope Lodge, then St. Annes it will be. How nice to have young children around the house and what a lovely house it is. I can just see my walnut low-boy standing under the small window in the lounge. The nursing chair could stand on the first landing and..."

"But Aunt Amy ..."

"The outer hall", continued Amy. "Those black and white tiles are perfect. Can you imagine how attractive it would look with one or two of my white jardinieres filled with scarlet geraniums?".

Margot's voice was firm. "Aunt Amy, you must stop, listen to me. If you move into that Home you will have one room of your own. You will be able to take one or two small pieces with you, that is all. The house belongs to Mrs. Tillson, she has good taste, you can see how well it is furnished. You will not be able to interfere, you have to understand that".

The two women finished the drive back to Hope Lodge almost in silence. Margot, after seeing her aunt safely indoors, kissed her goodbye. "Think carefully about what it means to leave your home and live in someone elses, Aunt Amy. I know you want to please Becky, you have always given in to her. This is something you must decide for yourself. Sleep on it, there is no need to hurry".

It was a long evening of deliberation. Amy turned it all over in her mind, the unpleasantness there would no doubt be with Becky if she did not move. Becky had always been so difficult. Her teenage years were best forgotten. She had taken a flat in London, sharing with Margot but it was not long before Becky had moved in with a man somewhat older than herself. An affair that had ended in disaster with Amy trying to soothe her distraught daughter. That episode was repeated several times with Becky never heeding any advice. She was determined to have her own business, did not mind on whom she trod to raise herself to manager of the large estate agents who employed her.

Becky had at last reached her goal, with more than a little financial help from Amy. She bought premises in South London and worked extremely hard to build up the business of which she now was so proud. She was where she was today because of her determination and hardness of character. Amy would not let Becky's determination get the better of her now. She would remain at Hope Lodge, she had enough money to pay for any extra help she may need in the house, a nurse if necessary, a live-in housekeeper. Why worry about spending some of her capital, why worry about Becky.

Amy went to bed, her mind made up. She knew how unhappy she would be if she had no hand in choosing new curtains or chair covers in a house which did not belong to her. In her own home she could rearrange the furniture, change the colour of the paint, anything she chose. No, Amy could not and would not live anywhere but Hope Lodge.

As she lay in her bed Amy's mind went back to Gentian House in Torquay, when she was young and Becky a baby, a baby whose character had yet to develop.

* * * * *

Torquay in 1933 was a popular holiday resort, advertised as the English Riviera. The hotels smart and sophisticated, sun terraces and Cocktail Bars. In the evenings, guests would dance to tunes like 'Smoke Gets In Your Eyes' and 'Stormy Weather'. During the day the promenade was a fashion parade. Women strolled past Abbey Gardens to the Pavilion and back again dressed in pale linen suits or lowbacked sundresses with flared skirts mid calf in length. Hair was longer now and the permanent wave was no longer a novelty.

Amy treasured the time she could take off from the antique shop that she may push Becky, as the baby was now called, along the promenade. She missed Imogen, Dolly and *Theodora's* more than she had thought possible. Amy revelled in the sight of the fashionably dressed holidaymakers.

A young girl had been employed to look after Becky when Amy was busy in the showroom. Stefan left Amy to run the business more than ever, he spent a lot of time in London and Paris looking for and buying unusual pieces. Amy did not worry about this too much as to rearrange the showroom and entertain clients was a fulfilling occupation. The excitement of Stefan's homecoming from his buying trips almost made his frequent absences worthwhile.

Amy missed the salary *Theodora's* had paid, Stefan was generous and would usually buy Amy anything she asked for but it was not the same as having her own monthly income. One morning a customer, a local hotelier, was having coffee in the showroom with Amy. He had been telling Amy how he admired her taste, the showroom was now so much more attractive, when he suddenly put down his cup and saucer and looking rather serious said, "Mrs. Serovsky, I have no idea if you would be interested but I have just built a new wing on the hotel, could you... would you consider advising me on the decoration of the rooms? As I have told you I admire your taste, what do you think?".

"I've had no formal training in interior design but I do so love planning colour schemes. If you think that is enough, if you are not worried about qualifications yes, I should love to advise you".

"Good", said Mr. Browne, "Come over as soon as you can to look at the rooms then give me an estimate. Now let's look at the Davenport I came in to see".

Amy sold him the piece of furniture and promised to call at the hotel that evening. So began Amy's own business, a small begining but the start of

'Gentian Interiors'. Stefan was not pleased; having Amy to run his business had left him free to do what he enjoyed. Staying in Chelsea, being fussed over by Sasha. Lazily chatting to other dealers, searching for bargains in unlikely places. Going to Paris, amusing himself with the city's nightlife. Bartering with his fellow Russians for the few treasures they had left. He would then return home to a warm responsive wife who would spoil him until he took off again.

Stefan had to remain in Torquay while Amy organised painters, carpenters and found a woman to sew curtains. She looked at carpets, chose bed linen and visited furniture stores. Amy Serovsky was in her element.

Jim's business was doing well, he bought Dinah a car and taught her to drive.

"You must learn Amy, it's easy", said the excited Dinah after taking Amy and Becky to Babbacombe for a picnic one Saturday. Margot and Becky were good friends and sat happily on the back seat clutching their teddy bears as their mothers chatted.

"Easy?", said Amy. "Then I will ask Stefan to teach me". When she was proficient Amy was able to buy herself a little car with the proceeds of her first assignment. What a difference it made to her life. Dinah and Jim could be visited so quickly. She could take Becky to play on the beaches at Paignton or Teignmouth. Shopping was easier and Amy was independent.

Stefan was away again before Amy became involved in another commission. "I'll be at Sasha's", he said. "Don't bother to telephone me there, I'll be in touch, let you know when I'm returning".

Ten days went by, Amy was confined to the showroom. Lily, the nursemaid was a boon and Amy was grateful for the way she was firm with Becky who could be troublesome. Stefan spoilt the little girl and would not listen when Amy remonstrated.

A client was very interested in a Laquer commode but disputed the price put on it by Stefan. Amy, not wishing to lose a customer asked him to leave his telephone number and when she had spoken to Stefan she would contact him.

She dialled Sasha's number at the Gallery, "Sasha, Amy here. I know Stefan will not be with you at the Gallery but when you see him tonight, I should be grateful if you would tell him to get in touch, a business matter" .

Sasha's throaty voice with the slight accent accentuated by the telephone replied, "Amy, my brother is not with me, not staying at the flat".

"You mean he has left Chelsea and gone over to Paris?".

"He hardly ever stays in London these days. You must be aware of this Amy, most of his buying is in Paris. Have you not a telephone number that you may contact him? Must go, customer here. Love to Becky".

Amy was puzzled but not unduly worried. Stefan was a law unto himself but it would have been sensible to have let her know of his whereabouts. Supposing Becky or even herself had been taken ill. He would be staying with Sergei and Maria. Amy found their number in Stefan's desk and called.

Over a crackly line it was difficult to understand Maria's broken English but Amy had it made quite clear that Stefan never stayed with his aunt and uncle on his business trips. The conversation was short and terse, no message for Becky, no enquiries as to their wellbeing. As she replaced the receiver Amy felt regret that Stefan's family had never really accepted the fact that he had married an English woman.

As promised Amy telephoned the client, dropped the price and sold the commode.

The next evening Stefan contacted Amy. He had finished his business. London was awful after Torquay and he was longing to get home.

"Have you had a successful few days?", enquired a subdued Amy.

"Fine, I've found a mahogany Toilet Mirror in very good condition, about 1820 I should think. A Hepplewhite style armchair of carved mahogany and several pieces of Meissen which you will love and beg me not to sell. Sasha has looked after me very well but it will be wonderful to get home to your cooking. Sasha sends her love and says it seems ages since she heard from you".

"Did she indeed", said Amy and replaced the receiver without saying 'goodbye'.

On his return the confrontation was painful but Stefan was so plausible that Amy accepted his explanations. He sulked for the whole evening because his wife had questioned his honesty and when they went to bed turned his back on her. Amy couldn't bear it. She ran her index finger down the length of his spine, kissed his shoulder blades lingeringly and Stefan turned over, put his arms around her and their reunion was as joyful, loving and perfect as ever.

Word of Amy's flair for interior design, her sense of colour and choice of furnishings was begining to spread; several commissions came her way. Two large houses on the road to Babbacombe benefitted from her ideas. Stefan was able to supply some furniture and sold an old dinner service that was in good condition and complete. Unemployment was spreading, the North of England fared worst but some hoteliers in Torquay were complaining that their bookings were down considerably. Stefan noticed his stock remained in the showroom much longer these days and was relieved that his clever wife was making a success of her business.

Because of the slowing down of his sales, Amy was surprised when Stefan announced he was off once more to Paris to see what he could buy. He returned a week later with nothing other than a small French carriage clock.

"Not worth the fare", remarked Amy as she served dinner on his return.

"Oh, I don't know", said Stefan giving her his most charming smile.

He looked after the showroom whilst Amy was off seeing her clients. Discussing furnishing fabrics, paint finishes and carpets, Amy was content.

She came home one afternoon from supervising the hanging of curtains for one of her clients and on entering the showroom felt there was something missing. Amy looked around, something was different, ah yes, the Hepplewhite card table which had stood open by the fireplace had gone. Stefan must be delighted to have sold such an expensive piece, his first for some weeks. It wasn't just the table though, something was amiss, Amy's eye travelled upwards and it was then that she noticed that Tessie was not perched in her usual place. Amy looked around but the doll in her wedding finery was nowhere to be seen.

"Stefan", she called, "I see the card table has gone, well done, but where have you put Tessie?".

"Tessie?", he said, coming through the door, smiling, running his fingers through his blonde hair. "Oh, you mean the doll. I've sold her to the chap who bought the table".

Amy couldn't believe it. "Sold her? Sold Tessie? How could you. I'll have to buy her back, immediately. Who was it who bought the table, where does he live? I'll go straight away".

"Sorry Amy, don't know the chap. He wanted the table, didn't like the price, so after haggling a bit he agreed to buy if I threw in the doll for five pounds".

She was speechless, it took several moments before Amy found the words to describe her horror at his action.

"You know how much Tessie means to me. She has been my friend since I was ten, I've always told her all my secrets. Oh Stefan, how could you sell her?".

"Grow up Amy, it's only a doll and a broken one at that. I'm glad it has gone, staring down at us from that tallboy. You speak as though the thing was human. Be your age for goodness sake ... ".

Amy by this time was in tears. "Imogen gave her to me; Hugh brought her to the cottage for me to look after. She is real to me Stefan, can't you understand? You are selfish and unkind Stefan, you must get her back, we can trace the customer from his cheque".

"He paid by cash, had a van parked outside and drove off with his purchases, a happy man. Afraid you've seen the last of your 'friend' Amy".

* * * * *

Early in September 1934 Imogen and Charles spent a holiday in Buckfastleigh. Charles wished to paint in the area, especially views of the Abbey at Buckfast. He admired the work of the monks, an incredible feat, the building of Buckfast Abbey. Never more than six monks at any one time working on the project since 1906. The magnificent building housed many treasures and Charles spent hours studying the series of windows in the style of a famous window at Chartres. His skecth book was always at hand and he longed to reproduce his sketches in colour.

There was of course time for Imogen and Charles to visit Stefan and Amy at Gentian House. Amy was proud that Becky was such a sociable little girl, a friendly, attractive three year-old. 'Princess Rebecca' as Stefan called his daughter, was fascinated by Charles' sketches of her and of her toys.

Amy and Imogen talked incessantly about Dolly, *Theodora's* and the present fashions. Princess Marina of Greece had made a great impact on the London scene. Her marriage to George of Kent was to take place in November and shops and magazines were showing 'Marina' hats, little felt pillboxes that the princess often wore and there were copies of the simple dark coloured dresses she favoured, unadorned except for small lace collars. The elegant princess even had a colour named after her - Marina Blue, a lovely bluish-green shade, like the sea around sunny Greece.

Amy could not bring herself to tell Imogen about the loss of Tessie and dreaded that her former mistress might ask to see the doll but the subject did not come up.

One evening at the end of their holiday, Charles drove over to collect Amy that she may dine with them at their hotel. Stefan stayed in to look after Becky and he sat with a bottle of Vodka beside him as he perused his accounts.

"I could have driven myself over you know Charles, there was no need for you to make this journey".

"I know Amy", replied Charles, "but I thought this way I would have a chance to be alone with you. It must be years since you and I could chat together. Are you comfortable, I'm not driving too fast for you?".

"No, just right", Amy remembered, Charles was always courteous, thoughtful; he was a dear.

They chatted for some time Amy answering his questions about her parents' health, about Dinah and Jim; he was interested in her family's welfare. If only Stefan were not so self centred, she thought.

"Amy, are you happy? Forgive me, I do not mean to pry but Imogen and I, well we can see a difference in you. Are you maybe working too hard? I know it must be wonderful for you, this venture into business on your own but with Becky and Stefan to look after, well, just don't overdo things. Is Stefan still away a lot of the time?".

Before she answered, Amy fiddled with the diamante clasp on her evening bag, pulled down the skirt of her crepe dress. "I am happy Charles, I have no regrets that I am involved nearly all day, every day in my business. Becky is well looked after but as Stefan probably told you the other evening, the antique trade seems to have tapered off. He is still away quite a bit and... well Stefan is Stefan isn't he and providing I go along with his whims and fancies he is affectionate and generous".

"Does he still go to Paris to buy? I know he rarely stays at my house these days?".

Amy turned that she may look directly at Charles. "Stefan goes away for three or four days each month to Paris. He says that he visits relatives of his and looks for unusual 'objets d'art' for us to sell. Charles, he seldom brings back anything of value and yet he is spending money, a lot of money. Not very loyal of me to discuss my husband like this but Charles I am worried, very much so".

Charles continued his steady drive through the narrow lanes, his face serious. He said nothing and Amy concentrated on the lovely views of Dartmoor, soft in the evening light. Soon they would pass the white house that Amy loved, she always slowed up in order to stare at the house and garden, her dream house.

"I'm going to stop shortly Amy", said Charles. "Something I want to show you and then we are almost at Buckfastleigh". The car slowed down and then they stopped outside the very house of which Amy had been thinking.

"There", said Charles, "Isn't that perfect, a Georgian house, not too big, not too small. Set in a beautiful garden that will be even better in a few years when those rhododendrons and trees have matured. What lovely views all around. It is my dream house".

"You won't believe it Charles but it has been my dream house too for some time. If ever I am driving this way I slow down to admire 'Hope Lodge' as it is called".

"Hope Lodge", laughed Charles. "How appropriate, I 'Hope' one day it will come on the market and perhaps one of us can buy it".

He started the engine and they drove on. "Look Amy, if ever you need any help or advice you must remember Imogen and I will be only too glad to be of assistance. We both care very much for you".

"Thanks but why should I need help?" It sounded curt, that reply, and on the spur of the moment Amy decided to tell Charles about Tessie. She asked Charles to stop the car as she had something to say.

Charles listened, his expression grave, his eyes sad. He put his arms around Amy. "How could he have done that. I know what that doll meant to you Amy and he must have known too. Oh my dear Amy. I am really so sorry", and he hugged her tightly.

The familiar smell of his cologne was there; Amy recalled a moment so long ago when she was serving dinner at the Hall and had first been aware of that lemony, pleasant, fresh scent. She felt safe and at home in Charles' arms and did not want to pull away but Amy sat up, straightened her skirt, re-arranged the cowl neck of her dress.

"Come", she said in her husky voice, "Imogen will be waiting".

CHAPTER TWELVE

"Mummy, Mummy, can I sit next to Margot?" Becky ran over the grass to where Dinah and Amy were helping to lay the long trestle table set on the grass outside Berrycombe Village Hall. A white tablecloth was threatening to blow away and the women were hurrying to put down plates and cutlery.

"I expect that will be alright", said Amy. The vicar's wife who was in charge of this tea to celebrate the Silver Jubilee of King George V and Queen Mary, nodded her grey head. Becky should have been at the celebrations in Torquay but Dinah had arranged for her to join the Berrycombe tea party that she may be with her cousin Margot.

Dinah and Amy looked at each other and smiled as Margot, so grown up now at five years old, re-tied the sash on Becky's dress; it was forever becoming loose and Becky was never still a minute. The sash, the Peter Pan collar and the puffed sleeves of the white cotton dress had a narrow edging of red, white and blue. Most of the children had something to wear that was of the patriotic colours. White canvas T-strapped shoes trimmed with red and blue had been on sale in Torquay and Becky was proud of hers. So proud of them that she was always looking down at her feet instead of where she was going and fell over often.

Union Jacks were flying over the door of the Hall. Mugs bearing pictures of the Royal couple were handed to the school children and Becky cried because there was not one for her. Kind little Margot let her cousin hold hers; this was a mistake on Margot's part as Becky held on tight and it would have to be prized from her little fist before she went home.

Sandwiches, jelly and cake were hardly on the table before they were devoured. Some of the children sat sedately, Margot and Becky amongst them; others, mainly boys, preferred to eat running round and round the long table.

"Can you remember if we had a tea at Shearfield for the Coronation?", enquired Amy of her school friend.

"I can't remember", said Dinah. "I don't suppose there would have been anything as impressive as this. I would expect you to know, you seem to be able to remember everything that has ever happened to either of us".

The sun shone down and melted the icing on the buns that Amy was distributing as she stood still and tried to recall such an event; no it was not amongst her many memories of childhood. The Coronation was a blank to her.

After tea, Becky being too young to stay and attend the concert in the Hall, Amy said her 'goodbyes' and drove back to Gentian House.

The lanes were quiet, the hedges and trees were a wonderful, fresh new green. Another few weeks and everything would be quite different, the colour and the perfume of the flowers in the hedgerows. It would still be beautiful to see but this, this was a perfect May evening. Becky fell asleep beside her and Amy, free from entertaining her young daughter, thought of Stefan. She hoped he would be in a good mood when they arrived home.

Recently he had been critical of Amy, her hair style was not becoming, why didn't she pluck her eyebrows like all the other women were doing these days? Did she have to wear mannish trousers and jackets just because Marlene Dietrich had set the fashion?

At other times, usually on returning from Paris, Amy would be showered with gifts, jewellery or chocolates. His behaviour was erratic, even little Becky suffered, spoiled one day and shouted at the next for bad behaviour.

Stefan was using the telephone when they came into the sitting room. He was speaking in Russian, waved his fingers at Amy and brought the conversation to an end quickly.

After bathing Becky and reading her a short story before she lay down to sleep, Amy set the table for herself and Stefan. A bottle of wine was opened to drink the health of the King and Queen.

"Think you can manage the showroom for a month Amy, on your own, completely?".

"I don't know Stefan, I believe Mr. Hext out at Berrycombe will accept my estimate, he more or less confirmed this afternoon when I saw him. If so I shall be very busy, all the summer".

"Then we'll close Gentian Antiques during June or a better idea, close for good. You probably make enough to live on now with your venture. My business, as you know has dropped off a lot".

Amy couldn't believe her ears. Close down! Stefan close down his showroom? "What are you doing in June, why won't you be here?".

"I shall be away for the whole month, maybe more Amy. Family matters in Paris, nothing for you to worry about".

In the next three weeks Amy saw Stefan in all his moods. The two of them shared some happy days and there were some nights when Stefan was especially loving, as he had been at the begining of their marriage. On nights such as those Amy wondered why she always carried around with her a sense of foreboding. There was nothing wrong, nothing for her to worry about. Then followed days when nothing was right. Becky was not being brought up correctly, the food was not to his liking and Amy's attempts to express her love for him were rejected.

Amy saw him one afternoon, his arms around Becky, with tears spilling down his cheeks. Stefan looked up and saw Amy, pulled her down beside him and held her tightly. "Oh Amy, Amy", was all he said as he buried his damp face in her warm neck.

No amount of cajoling could get Stefan to explain his behaviour. Amy had disturbing dreams, she couldn't eat. On two occasions on waking in the night and finding Stefan was not beside her Amy found him, head in hands, at the dining table, a bottle of Vodka beside him.

At the begining of June, as he had said he would, Stefan had departed for France.

* * * * *

Now in 1984, brushing her silver hair in front of the dressing table mirror, Amy smiled wryly as she remembered her first few silver hairs.

It had been a wet evening during the second week of June 1935. Amy, answering the telephone, hoping to hear Stefan's voice, was surprised when it was Charles who spoke.

"Amy my dear, are you alright?".

"Yes Charles, fine. How nice to hear from you. Are you well?".

"Listen Amy. Has Stefan spoken to you today?".

"No".

"Now look Amy, I know it is late but Imogen and I are on our way down. We are in Exeter, buying petrol and will be with you as soon as possible. 'Bye for now".

The present day Amy put down her hairbrush, looked at her abundant silver hair, studied the face she had looked at all her life. Anything to take her mind off that terrible June evening. She never wanted to think of it again, even after all these years. The memory refused to be shut away and she could see once more Charles and Imogen arriving just as she had picked up the telephone. It was Stefan and he shouted in his excitement, shouted from Paris. "Amy, I have a son, a son Amy. Do you hear?"

Imogen put her arms around her, held her close. Charles took the receiver from her rigid fingers. No, she would not think about it, ever again it was too painful.

It appeared that Stefan had telephoned his sister to shock her with the news that he had a mistress and that Anna, as the girl was called, had given birth that day to a fine boy. He knew he must break the news to Amy. He would do so later, he needed a few Vodka's first.

Sasha had run downstairs to tell Charles and he and Imogen had immediately left to drive down to Devon to be with their friend. It was soon after that traumatic evening that Amy had noticed her black shiny hair was sprinkled with silver at the temples.

A divorce was inevitable. Stefan gave Amy the whole story, she listened quite calmly, her senses numbed as he related how he had fallen captive to the charms of Anna. She was a dancer in the Ballet Russe, with a promising career. On one of his trips to Paris in 1934 Stefan had taken her to supper after a performance. She was so fragile, he said, not strong like Amy. So beautiful and it was wonderful to show her off to his family. Stefan could converse in Russian, speak Russian words of love, look into those huge dark eyes set in the tiny pale face and forget he was a husband and a father.

The strong Amy heard how stressful it had been for Stefan in May and June when he had worried about what to do when the baby was born. Now he and Anna had a son his mind was made up, Stefan would live in Paris, marry his mistress. He knew Amy would survive. She had her business and Becky, they would all remain good friends.

Amy, nearly fifty years later could remember the conversation clearly. He had made his excuses, his apologies and thirty one year old Amy had seen her whole world collapse. Her first thoughts were, 'What have I done? How have I failed him? If he had so wanted a son why hadn't he suggested that Amy had another baby?

There was no answer except that Stefan Serovsky, imperious, spoiled Stefan always had to have just what he wanted.

Charles and Imogen had stayed until Sarah had come to be with Amy. Sarah was such a comfort, a wonderful sister. She looked after Becky and encouraged Amy to get on with her commissions. Dinah and Jim were so very upset by the whole business and gave all the help and time they possibly could. William and Louise wrote often. Loving, understanding letters. No one said, 'I told you so' and Amy then realized how very fortunate she was in her family. It was true, she had gone her own way, had grown away from the good country folk they were, but now she was in trouble she was surrounded by their love and compassion.

Gentian House Antiques became Gentian House Interiors. Amy displayed velvets, brocades and chintzes together with wallpapers, lamps and bedroom accessories. Business was good and Amy threw herself into her work to try and forget the hurt that was inside her. She dare not think too often of Stefan for she knew the tears would fall and once they started the flow was difficult to stem.

Becky, used to her father's absences, did not appear to be badly affected but Amy guessed there would be problems later when Stefan came to visit and wanted his daughter to stay in France for holidays.

"Are you going to do something about those silver hairs?", asked Dinah, her head on one side surveying her friend's temples.

"No, I'm not", replied Amy. "I've earned these pieces of silver. Anyway, I think they add a kind of distinction to my looks".

"But we are only thirty-one Amy, I don't want you to look old, you will if you go grey".

"I'm quite happy as I am thank you".

The year was nearly at an end, a sad year. Stefan leaving Amy, then Aunt Anne had died in September and only a few weeks later Uncle Walter had succumbed to a heart attack. Louise had been staying with her only brother and was with him when he died.

Amy was writing her Christmas cards and she crossed out Uncle Walter's name from her list. A card was chosen for Stefan and Amy signed it, just plain 'Amy', no kisses or love this year. She passed the card to Becky for her to scrawl her name and some xxxxxx's. Amy sucked on her pen, strange that she felt no animosity toward Stefan, only a deep sadness that what had once been between them no longer existed. Why did she not hate him? Maybe she was not a passionate woman; had Stefan turned to another woman because passion was missing from their love-making. Amy did not know the answer. Part of her still loved the man who had caused her so much pain. How could she be indifferent, they had shared so much. She would never entirely forget his lovemaking, his adoration of her in the early days. Amy sighed and continued to sign the colourful cards, just the names 'Amy' and 'Rebecca' this year.

CHAPTER THIRTEEN

Coronation year, London in early May 1937 had an air of expectancy about it. Would the weather be fine and dry, would the sun shine on Wednesday the 12th? The London parks were green and tidy, forever being swept and weeded. Colourful with geraniums, trees heavy with blossom, they would give a good impression to the many overseas visitors here to enjoy the pageantry that would accompany the crowning of George VI and his wife Elizabeth.

Amy and Becky had come to London for a few days, staying at Charles' house in Chelsea. Mrs. Gurney, an old lady now, made a great fuss of Becky, glad to have some company. These days there was only Charles living there. Sasha, to the surprise of everyone, had married quite suddenly, a Dutch art dealer, given up her little gallery and now lived in Amsterdam. Imogen would sometimes stay a night to avoid a journey back to Ilford after a theatre visit. There were times when Charles and Imogen would give a dinner party for friends and use the lovely dining room. Mrs. Gurney then did her best for them, watched by the young Amy looking down from the gilt frame over the mantlepiece.

On the Monday before Coronation Day, Amy took Becky on the train to Ilford. "I'll show you the house I first lived in when I left Shearfield. I was very young then Becky".

"As young as Princess Elizabeth?", asked Becky whose mind was full of the two little princesses these days.

"No dear, older, I was sixteen and not at all like a princess".

"Daddy called me 'Princess Becky' didn't he? I never had a crown though. Will the little princesses wear crowns to the Abbey on Wednesday?", asked an excited Becky.

"Wait and see, wait and see", replied a harrassed Amy. She hoped that Dolly would be successful in her quest for seats for their party. She had been half promised seats in a window on a first floor office on the Coronation route to the Abbey.

She and Becky were now walking down Welbeck Gardens. Amy noticed it had not changed very much in the six years she had been away. Steps still showed signs of careful cleaning, the brass knockers too. Where was Ivy now, she wondered, and George, that kind milkman, married no doubt. Amy hoped he was happy.

Imogen opened the door, a smile lighting up her lovely face. She will be forty three in June, thought Amy and she is still a very attractive woman. The hair not quite as bright maybe but still a red-gold frame for her face.

After tea, sitting in the summerhouse at the bottom of the garden, a recent acquisition, Imogen surprised Amy by the remark, "I am going to try and persuade Charles to sell the Chelsea house. It is far too large for him".

"Sell the house? Charles will never do that will he Imogen?".

"Well, I think he should. These days though my brother does as he thinks best. There was a time when Charles listened to my advice, took notice of me. I had to look after him, protect him after Mother died. It took me a long time to accept that he was no longer a little boy and I sometimes think I may have spoiled his life being so possessive. I hope not".

"I'm sure you haven't", said Amy gently. "I do agree with you that he does not need such a large house now Sasha no longer has a flat there. I've noticed too that Mrs. Gurney is finding it all a little too much. I believe she would welcome retirement" .

The two friends had to listen then to Becky's chatter about Princess Margaret-Rose and how Becky was almost as old as her idol. The little girl was even able to describe the clothes that the Royal sisters wore.

"Just like you Amy", said Imogen. "Interested in clothes already. Are you still adding to your collection?".

"All the time, about fifteen years of fashion stored in a room at Gentian House. I really ought to dispose of it, no sense in collecting all those dresses, shoes, hats and bags. They are not old or valuable enough for a museum to be in any way interested".

Imogen considered for a moment then said, "Don't stop now Amy. One day you may do something with them. If not, just think how Becky and Margot too will enjoy dressing up in them".

Dolly had managed to pull a few strings and on Coronation Day, Charles escorted Amy and Becky to an office in Trafalgar Square. They were in their places, together with Imogen and Dolly by 9.30 a.m., an hour before the golden coach was due to leave Buckingham Palace for the Abbey.

Becky loved the spectacle, the horses especially. Charles and Amy couldn't believe the size of the crowds, hundreds of people, waiting, hoping for even just a tiny glimpse of the shy man and his wife who had suddenly had their lives changed because of the love Edward had for Wallis Simpson.

Dolly and Imogen, a pair of binoculars between them, were taking it in turns to pick out elegant women, like themselves, sitting in chairs by the windows for which they had paid handsomely. Their hats and dresses came under discussion, where had they been purchased, did they suit the individual? Dolly and her friend never left their work behind.

Charles was watching the crowd, concerned that the rain which had been threatening since early morning would now fall and drench those people down in the roads below them, people not as fortunate as themselves in their comfortable seats. He turned to find Amy looking at him. She smiled at him, a smile that reached her eyes. Charles took her hand in his and said quietly, "Haven't had much time to talk to you, alone, since you came up from Torquay. How are things? Does Becky see her father often and are you over the nasty business at last?".

"I'm fine thanks, we're both fine. Stefan is very good and visits Becky quite often. Glad to say I now feel comfortable with him again. It was hard at first, I thought it the end of my life but I had to think of Becky and my business. Two years have gone by you know, incredible isn't it?".

"Becky tells me she is going over to Paris to stay with Stefan and his... Stefan and Anna. Are you happy about that? Isn't Becky a little young to leave you?", Charles rubbed the side of his nose, embarrassed that perhaps he had said too much.

Amy squeezed his hand. "You are a dear to be so concerned over us Charles. Becky will be alright, she is a very confident six year-old, you must have noticed how grown up she is?"

Imogen and Dolly had been investigating and returned to tell of an elaborate buffet set out on the floor below and suggested their party make a move in that direction. Charles released Amy's hand and as they made their way to lunch said, "Do you have an evening free before you return to Torquay? I should like to take you out to dinner, Thursday, Friday?".

"Friday would be fine for me Charles. Mrs. Gurney can look after Becky. I shall look forward to being with you and to bring you up to date with my family's news".

They watched Becky selecting her salads, taking fresh salmon, choosing a dressing. Amy was always amazed at her daughter's self confidence but then she was Stefan's daughter too.

Friday evening Becky was put to bed early, protesting a little until Charles appeared and sat down to read 'Winnie the Pooh'.

Amy prepared for the evening. Her hair was now worn parted in the middle, a style made popular by the now unpopular Wallis Simpson. Amy swept back the sides, displaying, not disguising, the silver streaks at her temples, and she curled the hair into the nape of her neck. She wore a prized possession, a Chanel evening jacket, deep blue cire satin over a dress of a paler shade, a matte crepe, halter necked. The removal of the jacket during dinner would reveal Amy's perfect back, a back of which she was justly proud.

A discreet make up. Mitsouko sprayed lightly and Amy was ready. This was exciting, she had found no time during the past two years, or more truthfully, had not had the inclination to accept invitations to dine. Work had been a good excuse and it was true, Amy had to spend a considerable amount of time to satisfy her growing clientele.

Charles smiled his approval when Amy appeared in the drawing room. So many women these days were aping their favourite stars. Hollowed eye sockets, the plucked eyebrows of Dietrich. Hair dyed platinum blonde like Jean Harlow. Red lipstick drawn in a bow á la Crawford.

Amy was Amy, no attempt to colour the stray silver hairs, no obvious plucking of her blue-black brows. Yes, Charles approved.

As they dined, at a secluded table in a fashionable restaurant, Charles leaned towards Amy and said, "I'm going to surprise you. I haven't told Imogen yet but I'm seriously thinking of selling my house. Goodness knows what Imogen will say, our grandparents lived there all their married life. We both have such happy memories but I just don't think it is sensible now to keep it going. Mrs. Gurney has told me she wishes to retire. Do you think I am right to sell?".

"I do think you are right Charles", and thinking of her conversation with Imogen, Amy added, "I'm sure Imogen will agree with you. Where will you live, with Imogen?"

"Heaven forbid", replied Charles, his green eyes open wide. "Now, here comes the real surprise. Remember Hope Lodge on the way to Buckfastleigh?".

"Of course I do", said Amy. "My dream house, that lovely white house with the well tended garden. You have not beaten me to it have you Charles?".

"Not yet, it is on the market though, that is why I am trying to make up my mind. If the price is right, well why not".

Amy's heart leapt. To have Charles living only a few miles away would be wonderful. He was so kind, so considerate and Becky loved him. Amy would not allow her thoughts to go further than that.

"Do you think your house will sell quickly?".

Charles put down his knife and fork and sat back in his chair. "Property in Cheyne Walk and Cheyne Row, in fact anywhere in Chelsea is well sought after. I don't visualize any difficulty in selling".

Amy smiled at him, a soft look in her dark eyes. "I should be very happy to have you as a neighbour".

They fell to discussing Charles' ideas on building a studio on to the back of the house, or maybe a separate building in the garden. His name was now well known and the distance from London should not be a problem in selling Charles' work.

Amy's mind, as always, rushing ahead impulsively, imagined a part of Gentian House as an Art Gallery. She did manage however not to divulge to Charles her ideas. He had to buy the house first.

As they travelled home on the train from Paddington, Amy thought of Tessie. If only her doll were sitting in the showroom to welcome her, to listen to the things Amy could have whispered, things Becky sitting opposite was too young to understand. Poor Tessie, where was she now? Amy wondered.

* * * * *

It was almost Christmas when Charles finally moved into Hope Lodge. Things had not gone smoothly but at last the white Georgian house belonged to Charles Lambert. A perfect house, thought Amy, as she stood, tape measure in hand, at one of the large windows on the ground floor. Charles had commissioned Amy to decorate and supply soft furnishings. Together they had disucssed colour schemes. Charles had some definite ideas of his own and Amy found it interesting to work with him.

Jim and Dinah planned a gathering on Christmas Eve. Jim promised faithfully that he would walk away from his workshop at midday and not re-enter until 1938 was a few days old. Dinah planned, shopped and cooked in addition to wrapping endless presents for all the family. Amy and Becky of course would be guests and Charles too had received an invitation.

"Becky, for goodness sake hurry up. Uncle Charles will be here any minute and you know he doesn't like to be kept waiting".

Becky, a stubborn look on her face said, "I don't like to hurry. If Uncle Charles doesn't want to wait, you can drive us over to Auntie Dinah's".

Amy sighed, she always seemed to be battling with Becky these days. There was so much of Stefan in their daughter. She was self-willed, determined, not an easy child to live with. Becky was an affectionate little girl though and naturally, Amy loved her.

The telephone rang and Amy raced Becky to answer. "Charles here, look I'm awfully sorry but I've been held up in Exeter. I'll go straight to Berrycombe. Do you mind driving yourself over there?".

"Of course not Charles. Becky and I are ready so we'll be off. See you later, 'bye".

Jim, looking unusually tidy, his shirt well tucked into his trousers and wearing a tie, opened the door and that special Christmassy aroma greeted them. Amy sniffed appreciatively, sausage rolls, sage and onion stuffing, pork roasting and the fruity smell of mince pies. Margot was not far behind her father; at eight years old she was remarkably like Dinah had been as a child. Amy almost expected to see herself, thin and sallow, black hair hanging straight and shiny also appear. The two girls went to look at the Christmas tree and Amy made her way to the kitchen where she knew she would find Dinah. Over a sherry Dinah and Jim learned that Charles would arrive later, they were also expecting a local builder and his mother and the married couple from the cottage opposite.

"You've been terribly busy Dinah, we've made a lot of work for you I'm afraid".

"I love it, you know that, this doesn't seem like work to me. Margot has helped me too, she cut out the pastry for the mince pies and filled them for me".

Jim, in the act of refilling the glasses, stopped and said, "Listen, I think that is Charles' car".

"You finish that Jim, I'll open the door", said Dinah as she walked out of the kitchen. Amy followed her, glass in hand and saw Charles apologizing to the hostess, presenting her with a bouquet. Charles left his coat on a chair together with a brown paper parcel he had been carrying and came to greet Amy and Jim.

"Doesn't your house look festive", he said to Dinah, then with a smile, "Nothing like this in my house, my interior decorator would never allow it".

Becky and Margot pointed out the holly, the paper chains they had made and the mistletoe hanging over the dining room door.

Charles bent down to whisper to Becky, a whisper meant to be heard by Amy. "I once kissed your mother under some mistletoe, a long, long time ago. Expect she has forgotten that".

Amy wished she could stop the blush that crept over her face as Charles looked at her. "I've not forgotten, Charles", she said.

The other guests arrived, Jim was a good host and kept the conversation going and the glasses filled. A flushed Dinah went backwards and forwards to the kitchen, forever surprising her guests with her luscious seasonal fare.

Much later, the married couple, the builder and his mother having departed, the sitting room was quiet. Dinah and Jim sat on the rug by the fire, Becky and Margot engrossed in a jig-saw puzzle, Charles reading a newspaper, Amy was almost dozing in a large comfortable armchair when she heard Charles say, "There's a present for you, in the hall on the chair with my coat. Go and get it and bring it in here to open".

As Amy jumped up, awake now, she had a feeling of *deja vu*. Yes, she was certain, this had happened before.

She came back with the parcel, oblong, wrapped in brown paper. There was a Pembroke table behind the settee and Charles came and stood beside her as she placed the parcel on the table and began to take off the paper. A cardboard box was exposed, Amy removed the lid and there, unbelievably, reposed Tessie. No orange blossom wreath, no yellowing tulle veil but the doll in her wedding dress of silk and lace. Eyes closed, her cheeks still had a pale pink blush. Her china lips still pretty, pink and slightly parted over the pearly teeth.

Amy gave a cry of delight, she threw her arms about Charles to kiss him, full on the lips. "Oh where did you find her? Thank you, thank you, I don't know whether to laugh or cry. I just don't know what to do".

"Then just kiss me, as you did before".

This time Charles put his arms around her and their kiss was long and warm. Amy did not pull away, she responded fully, not aware of anything or anybody except the closeness of Charles and the beating of her heart.

Dinah and Jim gathered up the girls and quietly closed the door on the couple.

When, at last, Charles released her from his embrace, Amy sat down on the settee and pulled him down beside her. "Tell me, where did you find Tessie, who had her, when did you find her?".

Charles smiled down into those shining dark eyes and told her, whilst shopping in Exeter that afternoon, he had glanced in what only could be described as a bric-a-brac shop and caught sight of the doll, upside down. There was only one leg, the clothes had fallen over the head, the shabby toy was almost hidden in a pile of second hand clothes. Charles could not be certain but decided to go into the shop. It was closed, no sign of an assistant, no lights, no sign of life at all.

"I had to make enquiries of neighbouring shopkeepers, Amy. It took me quite a time to trace the proprietor. Eventually he arrived, none too pleased to have to open when he had started his Christmas holiday. As I turned her the right way up I knew this dirty, shabby doll was your little friend. Her eyes stared at me, her face was streaked with dirt, her hair dishevelled but I think I have made a fairly good job of cleaning her up, don't you?"

"I can't thank you enough. The best present I shall get this Christmas I'm sure", said Amy, then blushed as she recalled the passion in their embrace only moments ago.

Charles looked around. "We're alone, one more kiss and then we had better find our hosts. It must be time to go home and I shall look forward to Christmas Day with you".

The kitchen looked a mess, empty glasses, plates, cups and saucers. Jim and Charles set about the washing up. Dinah looked at her friend, squeezed her arm and asked, "Everything alright? Happy now?".

"Very, very happy", was the descisive reply.

* * * * *

Charles arrived before Jim and his family at Gentian House the next day. He had to see the presents Becky had found in her pillowcase early that morning. Showed surprise at the Dolls' House he had helped Jim make for her and admired the book of Shirley Temple cut out dolls and clothes. Then he was able to talk to Amy. "I hardly slept Amy, we have wasted so much time. Please say you will marry me, I love you, that you must know by now. I've loved you I think since you were sixteen, shy and with all that lovely hair escaping from its pins, remember?".

"Could I ever forget it? It was the bane of my life".

"Seriously Amy, how do you feel about me, are you ready to love again, do you feel you are able to marry again after the way you were treated by Stefan?".

Amy put her arms around his neck, kissed him slowly. "Charles, my darling, I love you, I love you very much. Let's wait for a while before we discuss marriage, do you mind?"

* * * * *

The Christmas dinner, served at three o'clock was a great success. Amy always worried a tiny bit when entertaining Dinah and Jim, her friend was such a perfect cook. Today nothing went wrong, Amy's kitchen was small but she was a good organiser and artistic in the presentation of her food. Charles complimented her on a wonderful meal and suggested that after he and Jim had washed the dishes, they all went for a walk along the front, get a breath of sea air.

Margot and Becky dragged the men over to the Pavilion to look at the posters for the Pantomime and Amy and Dinah walked on ahead. Dinah made a suggestion to her friend. "Shall we take Becky home with us tonight? She could sleep with Margot for the next night or two. It would be company for Margot and Becky could bring some of her new toys over. What do you think?".

"But why? What has made you suddenly suggest this?"

Dinah looked at the mystified Amy. "You goose, anyone can see how things are now between you and Charles. You are in love with each other, no don't deny it Amy. Have you not thought that tonight he may not wish to go home, not want to leave your warmth for an empty house?"

"Dinah!", said a shocked Amy. "The thought never crossed my mind. Do you think I should let him stay, isn't this rushing things a bit?"

"You do just whatever you feel is right", said a wise Dinah. "If it worries you then don't suggest it. If it seems natural for him to stay the night, then let him".

The delighted Amy took Dinah's hand and said, "I'm not going to say it and you mustn't either".

"Say what?".

"Whatever would my ..." giggled Amy.

Amy didn't worry about Father a bit, never gave him a thought as later that night she carefully lifted from the tissue paper in her bottom drawer an ivory Crepe-de-Chine nightdress and negligee, as yet unworn.

CHAPTER FOURTEEN

"Happy Boxing Day", said Charles as he leaned over to kiss Amy. Her face was almost buried in her pillow and she turned to look into his eyes, eyes she now knew were not really green but hazel with flecks of green and a golden brown. Charles' chin had a dark shadow, it was several hours since he had shaved.

Amy looked at the clock. "Goodness, it is almost nine o'clock. I must get some breakfast, you must be starving".

"Before you rush away Amy, you are going to marry me aren't you?"

Amy slipped on the negligee before she replied. "Please let's not talk about it yet. There's so much to consider, Becky, my business, this is my home here at Gentian House. No Charles, it is too soon to think of all that marriage to you entails".

Amy bent to kiss her lover's stubbly face and left the bedroom.

Tessie sat on a Victorian chair by the window, her eyes open wide. Charles looked at her and smiled at his thoughts. Yes, he would paint the doll, as she was, on that chair with the velvet upholstery. She would make an attractive picture, he may even use pastels instead of his usual oils. Part of his wedding present to Amy for he was sure she would not keep him waiting too long, not after last night. Amy was not the type to just want an affair, she would be thinking of a wedding, planning it all by the time they had eaten breakfast, of that Charles was certain.

How wrong Charles was, Amy did not give her answer. He was patient, understanding of her fear to commit herself to marriage again. They worked together on Hope Lodge for although Charles had moved in, there remained many details to complete. It was not a large house, the usual Georgian design of well proportioned rooms either side of the front door. Three good sized bedrooms and a bathroom led off a landing that was large enough to show to advantage an early Victorian worktable which had belonged to Charles' grandmother. It was made of rosewood and the work-bag hanging below was of pink satin. Amy suggested that Charles put with it the low, Victorian nursing chair, also of rosewood, upholstered in a faded brocade of pinks, cream and red; the chair, rescued from the old nursery in Chelsea took on a new life.

The drawing room was finished and Amy and Charles were delighted that their combined ideas had resulted in such a tasteful, attractive room. "I was very much afraid you would make me use the current craze, of the colours orange, fawn and brown", joked Charles.

"You know me better than that I'm sure".

They had agreed the walls should be painted a soft Adam green. Amy's portrait hung above the white marble fireplace and now that the Chinese carpet of cream and green had been laid over the parquet floor and the curtains hung, heavy velvet in a dull gold colour, the room had an air of opulence, a richness and serenity. The garden, beautiful in its spring colours could be admired from the french windows and Amy felt that in spite of arguing over the curtains, with Charles having the final word, the drawing room gave her great satisfaction.

"I hope you are pleased with your room, I still think lighter curtains, patterned chintz, would have been more in keeping with the 'Country House' theme I had been working on. Tell me Charles, do you like your drawing room?"

Charles put his arm around Amy's slim waist. "It's our room darling, not just mine. You belong in this house. Say you'll marry me soon, please don't keep me waiting any longer".

Amy couldn't tell him everything that was in her mind. Charles knew she was worried about Becky's reaction. At present the little girl spent weekends at Dinah's, quite happy to be with her cousin Margot, not yet aware that Charles spent Saturdays and Sundays with her mother sleeping in the bedroom that her father had once shared with Amy. Charles was also aware that once she married him and moved into Hope Lodge, Amy would have almost an hour's journey to Torquay to carry on her business at Gentian House. A business of which Amy was proud, she had studied and worked hard in the two years since the Antique venture had evolved into Gentian House Interiors. Amy was always searching for a solution, she just could not think of closing down something she enjoyed so much.

What Amy had not discussed with Charles was the slight nagging worry, a worry of which she was half ashamed, that would not go away. There was nothing, not a thing about Charles that reminded Amy of Hugh Lodge. Douglas had looked so much like her childhood hero, Stefan, at the begining of their relationship had seemed to remind her of the young soldier. Other men with whom Amy had enjoyed mild flirtations had all possessed something she could relate to her sister's deceased fiance. Amy had decided many years ago that any man she married must have somthing of Hugh about him. She had always found Charles attractive, loved his youthful light-hearted manner but Amy could see nothing in Charles to remind her of her obsession.

When the thrill of their love affair quietened a little, when the passion, (for now Amy knew that she was capable of passion) subsided somewhat, what then? Would Amy, as she had with Stefan, pretend it was Hugh making love to her? Would she see Hugh's face above hers, his fair fine skin, his long eyelashes, not Charles' face, weathered by the sun and the wind, his day's growth of beard, dark and coarse?

Amy pulled away from her lover's arm. "Charles, I do love you but I'm frightened to commit myself. Perhaps I'm not ready to love fully again, give me a little more time, please".

Charles turned away, walked into the kitchen and Amy sensed that this time he was annoyed with her, rightly so. She mustn't keep him dangling much longer.

One of the bedrooms at Hope Lodge had been set aside as a makeshift studio. Arrangements had been made for a studio to be built at the end of the garden but meanwhile Charles was working in the bedroom on the picture of Tessie. He had made sketches of the doll, secretly at Gentian House. Dinah had presented Amy with a replacement veil and head-dress made from her own wedding veil and wreath. Yellowed with time the veil did not look out of place with the doll's dress. Amy had no idea that Charles, working in pastels, an unusual medium for him, was creating a delightful picture of the treasured doll.

Imogen was not fully aware of her brother's involvement with Amy but Charles had discussed that he hoped to marry Amy before too long. She maybe would not have been surprised or even shocked if she had known about those weekends at Torquay but the lovers had decided not to divulge this piece of information.

Amy, chatting on the telephone to Imogen one day, said, "You haven't mentioned Dolly and Sam recently, are they well?".

"Worried people, Amy, very worried".

"Why what is wrong, business, health?"

Imogen sounded serious as she explained to Amy, "They both have relatives in Austria and in Germany you know. They are having a terrible time, the Jews. Dolly hears of the harrassment the shopkeepers experience. Some of the tales I can hardly believe but I think they must be true. Sam says Hitler must be stopped at his 'Spring Cleaning' as he described his purge to dismiss Jews from their professions. As you have probably read, we are ready to go to war to defend France and Belgium if necessary after what happened with Hitler driving into Vienna like that".

Amy did not like to admit she hardly ever read a newspaper these days, she was far too busy. She was out of touch and did not really know what Imogen was talking about. Surely there couldn't be another war. There mustn't be, how could what was happening in Austria affect them down here in Devon?

Amy discussed her fears with Charles that evening and the elated feeling she had experienced since Christmas, the carefree, youthful exuberance of being in his company seemed to evaporate. War, memories of Harry, Hugh, Sarah and her parents in those days of the Great War came back vividly.

"Don't worry", said Charles, "you know how Imogen dramatizes everything. I know some of Dolly's relatives have been emigrating to America in the last three or four years, but that is probably because they have seen what a success her cousin has made of his manufacturing business. England cannot afford another war, the Government will sort it out with Hitler and his Nazis".

Amy looked at Charles, sitting there on the floor of her sitting room, mending a piece of furniture from Becky's dolls house. She knelt down beside him, looking directly into his eyes and said: "I'll marry you Charles, as soon as you like". He put his arms around her, hugged her to him and did not say a word.

* * * * *

Later as they drank a glass of sherry to celebrate, Charles took Amy's face in his hands. His eyes were grave, not dancing with merriment as they usually were when he was in her company. "Listen to me darling", he said. "If you marry me it must be because you love me for myself, not because the back of my head looks like Hugh's or some such nonsense. I'll tell you now, I will not play second fiddle to a man who has been dead for over twenty years".

Amy kissed his nose, "You're nothing like him Charles and I love you for being you". She crossed her fingers as she continued, "Don't worry, I hardly ever think of him these days, honestly".

Becky was difficult just as Amy had feared she would be. The seven year old announced she would go to Paris, live with her father and Anna, have a wonderful time with her baby brother. When Amy pointed out that Becky would be far away from Margot, only see her perhaps once a year, the little girl changed her mind. "I'll live with Auntie Dinah and Uncle Jim then. They wouldn't send me away at weekends like you have done", sobbed the frightened child. Another big change in her life imminent, a new school, a new home. She would have to share her mother with Uncle Charles, it was all too much for her to contemplate.

Becky accepted it in the end of course and looked forward to the wedding. An April wedding in Torquay. Amy had hoped to marry at the village church in Shearfield but the Rector had declined to marry a divorced woman in his church.

Amy had written to William and Louise with the news; William refused to have the telephone installed and Amy imagined the scene when the letter had arrived. William had retired and had settled down to a comfortable life. Lazy mornings until the garden required his attention. Louise read the letter to him over breakfast and they were both very happy for Amy. Her father had mellowed and Amy guessed correctly that he did not bring up the subject of marrying out of her class. Her parents had always liked Charles and were certain that this time Amy was making the right choice of husband.

"You would think it was Dinah getting married", said Jim one day when Amy was talking to him in his workshop. "She talks of nothing else and you can guess she is thrilled to be giving the reception here".

"No one could do it better", stated Amy fiddling with a white sheet which was covering what she guessed must be a small table.

"Take your hands off that", said Jim quickly. "It's a surprise, leave it alone"

"Don't be mean Jim, let me see, please", said a curious Amy. Jim would not give in and no cajoling by his sister would make him change his mind.

"Right, you mean thing, I'll leave you and go and gossip with your wife".

Amy settled down in Dinah's comfortable, warm kitchen, a cup of tea in her hand. She wouldn't tell Dinah what she planned to wear on the 30th April, it was all secrets these days. Exciting days, busy days so much to organize and only three weeks left. Dinah asked about Gentian House Interiors, was it to be closed?

"No, I shall keep it open at the moment, will have to travel in each day but I plan to let the flat as soon as possible. Charles and I are looking for a small shop in Totnes, something quite tiny and it will not be too great a distance from Hope Lodge".

"Such a pity you and Charles did not marry years ago", observed Dinah. "Before you, well you know, before Stefan. Why didn't you get together? You always were attracted to him, I can remember you telling me that when he was painting your portait. Why didn't it happen then?"

Amy sipped the hot tea, studied the willow patterned china and said at last, "Many reasons, Dinah. I'm sure I told you at the time how Imogen was so possessive of her brother. They had both been so kind to me, I decided to concentrate on a career instead of coming between them. Father did not approve of my friendship with Charles and Imogen, how the relationship between myself and my employers had progressed. Later, well you know of my romances and my mistakes, looking for someone like Hugh".

"Glad you've forgotten all that nonsense about Hugh. It was only a childhood crush, we all have them. Look at me and Fred Thurley, remember? I soon forgot him but you, you carried it in your mind all those years and made some silly mistakes. Charles is nothing like Hugh and I'm certain from now on you are going to be very, very happy".

Amy felt a tiny stab of pain, near her heart. No matter what anybody said, she would never, ever forget that 'nonsense' as her friend liked to call her first love.

She jumped up. "Must go now, I have to pick up Becky at lunchtime and take her over to her new school to meet the headmistress. Can you imagine the effect my daughter is going to have on the poor woman?".

As Amy drove out of the gate, Dinah watched her go and thought about Becky. Yes, she would have an effect. Becky was an unusual child, a strong character. Her self confidence was amazing until you remembered her father. Becky looked like Stefan, blonde, tall, the same eyes which could look very cold. She had his imperious manner, his determination and his confidence. Becky could be infuriating, always having to get her own way and then just when you had made up your mind that she was a deplorable child, she would do something thoughtful and kind. She was well mannered, charming and very affectionate. Amy and Charles, in a year or two were going to have trouble, of that Dinah and Jim were certain.

* * * * *

Presents began to arrive at Hope Lodge. Whenever Amy went over, as she did several times a week, there was a parcel or two to unwrap, with Charles looking on with interest. Stefan sent an antique timepiece. A brass, French carriage clock, small and perfect. It was beautifully packed, together with a card written by Stefan to them both, sending his good wishes. Becky and Margot had been taken shopping in Torquay by Dinah and spending money they had saved for weeks bought a joint present. It was a rather ugly vase of Devon pottery that Amy unwrapped and she and Charles thanked and kissed the excited little girls and placed it with the Minton vase just received from Dolly.

The evening before the wedding, Jim and Dinah were invited to Hope Lodge for a drink or two. Jim arrived and asked for Charles to give him a hand with a parcel. Between them they carried into the hall something wrapped in a sheet and tied with red ribbon. Amy and Charles were instructed to stand at the foot of the stairs and close their eyes. "Open", called Jim and the deep glow of the polished top of the small walnut table that he had unwrapped was almost matched by the glow of pride on his face.

"Jim, how lovely, thank you, oh thank you", said an excited Amy. Charles joined in the thanks and they moved over to inspect Jim's work. "Look Amy", he said, "See the crossbanding, the inlay,. What a lovely colour the walnut is".

Jim opened the centre drawer, took it out and showed them the plaque he had fixed in the back. 'This copy of a William and Mary side table was made by James Clayden of Berrycombe in 1938 for Charles and Amy Lambert of Buckfast'. "That is in case you try to sell it as a genuine 200 year old piece one of these days", he joked.

"Sell it", exclaimed a shocked Amy. "We'd never sell it would we Charles". They all laughed at her serious expression.

"Everything is 'right' about it", continued Jim. "The handles, the bun feet, the stretchers, the turning on the legs. Even Stefan would have difficulty in knowing whether it was a fake or not". He blushed when he realized he had mentioned Stefan's name, tonight of all nights, but it seemed to go over the heads of the happy couple as they opened the drawers, admired the handles and the wood.

"I know exactly where it should stand", said Amy. "In the drawing room, to the left of the fireplace don't you think Charles?".

But Charles had disappeared and Amy was talking to herself. He was back in the room in a minute or two holding a picture. "This can go above it", he said as he displayed the pastel of Tessie.

The soft shades of cream and the 'off' whites of the doll's ancient wedding finery were shown to advantage against the turquoise velvet upholstery of the Victorian chair. It was not a large picture but Charles had managed to convey the fine detail, the perfection of Tessie's lovely china face, the softness of the silk dress and the richness of the velvet.

Amy was overcome, it was such a surprise. She had no idea that Charles had been working on something for her. Something she would certainly treasure forever. She thanked her husband-to-be with a long kiss. Amy looked at Jim, smiled at Dinah and said, "What clever men they both are, don't you agree Dinah?".

"I do indeed, but I would have you know I am still waiting for an ironing board, promised in the first weeks of our marriage and a door for the cupboard Jim built in the bathroom two years ago". Dinah squeezed her husband's arm and the smile she gave him reminded Amy of the look her mother had given father when he had kissed her in front of ten year-old Amy.

"I hope this marriage to Charles will be as good as Dinah's and Jim's", thought Amy.

* * * * *

It was a quiet wedding, Sarah and her husband came on the early train Saturday morning and Imogen and Dolly travelled by car. Louise and William had planned to be at the ceremony but ill-health, that these days seemed to dog the couple, had decided Louise it was best to stay at home.

Charles had given his present to Amy, the rope of pearls, those pearls with the silver and turquoise clasp that had been passed down to successive Lambert brides. Amy wore them with the silk dress and matching coat she had bought from *Theodora's*, the dress patterned with flowers of many shades of blue, the coat a plain blue, lined with the patterned material. Becky had helped to choose the hat from the milliner next door to Gentian House, a shallow crowned natural straw, trimmed with blue ribbon.

The reception was informal and the guests chatted happily. Sarah and Jack had at first felt rather out of place in the company of the sophisticated Imogen and Dolly but after a glass or two of champagne all was well. Dolly had been admiring Becky's dress, it was very short and worn with white silk socks and black patent ankle-strap shoes. "I love your dress", she said to the little girl.

"It is a copy of a dress Shirley Temple wore in a film I saw", said Becky. "The lady who makes curtains and covers for Mummy made it and the one Margot is wearing. We love Shirley Temple and we are learning to tap dance like her".

"Good", smiled Dolly. "I hope that you are going to like your new school and living at Hope Lodge".

Becky studied her mother's friend and decided to confide. "You had better not say anything but I might run away. I want to live in Paris, it's much nicer there you know".

Dolly, unused to seven year olds, hurried to find Dinah and was soon reassured that all was well between Becky and Charles.

The honeymoon was spent in Lynmouth. Charles knew North Devon fairly well but Amy had never visited Exmoor, its lovely villages or the North Devon coast. She found Lynmouth unbelievably lovely, the deep valley, the trees and the birdsong and the little streams, East Lyn and the West Lyn. The streams joined forces in the village where fishermen's cottages stood, there was a beacon tower on the stone pier and very few people to spoil the serenity. Charles and Amy walked every day, so much to discover. Amy particularly loved the wooded walk up the valley to Watersmeet. She was ecstatically happy, Charles spoiled her, he was considerate in every way, tried to grant her every wish. Charles sketched for an hour each day and Amy made use of her camera. The resulting black and white prints did not do justice to the beauty she saw all around her and Amy envied her husband his skill in colouring his sketches.

On their last morning they walked around Hollerday Hill to the Valley of Rocks, back along North Walk and into Lynton for lunch. The cliff railway took them down into Lynmouth again and Amy savoured the view below her. "I'll never, ever forget this holiday", she said. "This must be my favourite place, it must never change".

"We'll come back, often", said Charles as all holiday makers say at the end of a perfect week.

In June of that year Amy would have her 34th birthday. She felt young and carefree, In fact younger than she had ever felt. Stefan had been a serious man, they had shared happy times of course but Charles had changed her life. He had quite a different outlook on life, laughed a lot, made a joke of mishaps and didn't take life too seriously. Married life was going to be fun with Charles Lambert.

CHAPTER FIFTEEN

Now, in 1984, Amy looked back on those early days of her marriage, the days when she thought she had reached the peak of happiness. Amy smiled, she had been wrong, as the years went by the love and contentment grew. All these years later Amy could recall the wonderful feeling of Charles' arms around her, the sense of security, the certainty of his love for her.

Dinah had noticed a change in her friend during the first year of the marriage. "You are evidently very happy, I'm so pleased for you both", she said as she sat with her friend, enjoying the last rays of the October sun in Amy's well tended garden.

"I feel happy, relaxed and content", said Amy. "With Stefan there was always a sense of conflict, I strived to live up to his image of me. Stefan fell in love with the well groomed, elegant, apparently self confident young woman I was at twenty six. He liked to show me off, as though I were one of his priceless porcelain pieces. To keep the peace I nearly always let him take the lead in our lives but I had begun to resent his dominance.

"And I thought you were so much in love with him", remarked Dinah.

"I did love him Dinah, in spite of his faults but I was not completely happy. I can see it quite clearly now. These days I am myself, I'm not acting a part any more".

It was 1938, Charles still did not agree with Amy that there might be a war with Germany. Amy told Dinah of her fears. Neville Chamberlain had returned from Munich in September with the promise of 'Peace in our Time'. Charles chose to believe this, Amy told her friend but Dolly passed on information she gleaned from her friends and gave Amy an uneasiness that slightly marred the happiness which Dinah and she had been discussing.

As the friends sat drinking tea in that peaceful English garden, warm in the October sun, Hitler's troops had marched into Czechoslovakia and in less than a year Amy would be proved correct.

The 'click' of the garden gate brought Amy back to the present and looking out of her bedroom window she saw the postman coming up the drive. She always wanted to run down the stairs to catch the mail before it dropped on the floor and had to remind herself once again that she was 80 years old, slightly lame with arthritus and that the post probably only consisted of a bill or two. No one seemed to write letters these days, a telephone call was so much less trouble.

Her hand firmly on the rail, Amy carefully descended. The letter, for there was only one, reposed on the door mat. She bent awkwardly to retrieve it and went into the kitchen to find her spectacles. Where had she put those 'specs? Amy screwed up her eyes, she did not recognise the writing, impossible to decipher the postmark without her spectacles. Of course they were beside her bed with the book she had been reading. Up she went to find them and as she hurried down the stairs began to put the spectacles on, not holding the rail, anxious to discover who had written the letter. Amy said later that she didn't know how it had happened, that fall to the bottom of the staircase. It was suggested that she may have had a momentary blackout, she did not recall tripping or losing her balance, only a blackness and the sensation of falling into a pit.

Amy lay on the floor for what seemed an interminal time. The pain in her ankle was bad, her right wrist had twisted under her. Thank goodness Mrs. Monk would soon arrive thought Amy only to remember at once that her daily help was on holiday. Margot was due to call at some time during the day. Amy decided to ignore the searing pain that came when she attempted to move and crawled to the 'phone. She must get in touch with Margot. She dialled the Berrycombe number but there was no answer. As she replaced the receiver Amy heard a car, a door slam and light footsteps, Margot's footsteps, coming to the front door. "Have you the key Margot? Can't get to the door to open it" called an exhausted Amy.

After that it was an ambulance of course. Hospital and a young doctor to examine her. The young man had used a lemon scented aftershave before he came on duty. Amy took deep breaths of the familiar smell. She delayed the moment when she would have to open her eyes and find it was not Charles' dear face so close to hers. "I'm pleased to say there are no bones broken, but you have a badly sprained ankle and wrist" , the doctor was saying. "You'll be uncomfortable from the bruising too for a while".

It was suggested that Amy should stay in the hospital for a few days for observation. Becky came down from London, annoyed at being called away from her estate agency business. She was a very busy woman she reminded her mother, this accident was most inconvenient, she had staff on holiday this week.

Margot, as she always did, smoothed things over. So different from her cousin. Margot never appeared to be ruffled, had a warm smile for everyone. She was gentle, very much like Dinah thought Amy.

"I hope it's O.K. with you Becky but I have arranged that when Aunt Amy goes home Mrs. Monk will work a few hours extra each day. I thought you would feel easier knowing your mother had company most of the day".

Becky gave Margot one of her cold stares. "No it is not really what I want Margot. I discussed with Ma the last time I saw her, the possibility of a Residential Home. She is too old now to live on her own. Too frail to be alone at nights".

"I am not too old", came Amy's firm voice, "I feel the same inside as I did at 40. I'm not frail, I can manage. You will never talk me into leaving Hope Lodge, never".

Margot held her aunt's hand. "You don't have to do anything you don't want to do, darling".

"Oh, doesn't she?", snapped Becky. "What about me? Don't I get any consideration. Miles away, worrying about what may be happening to Ma, imagining all sorts of things. My business will suffer, I cannot concentrate now for thinking about her and it will get worse, I can see that".

Amy looked at her daughter, Becky was not that worried about her she was sure. Money would be the reason Becky was worried. Was she short of money again? Amy had explained to her, only a few weeks ago that. she could not touch her capital. Becky had done very well in the past, Amy had been generous in financing Becky's business but that had to stop.

Her daughter stood at the foot of the bed, legs apart, chin held high, her blue eyes flashing. "I will get my way about this Ma, I will. I know you are going to be difficult but I'm determined. You must leave Hope Lodge, I know a client who would snap it up and then you can spend a comfortable time in a Home and save us all a lot of worry".

Margot sat quietly, her face pink with embarrassement. Amy remembered a similar scene many years ago. Becky's stance was the same, the words similar. Margot had been there then wearing the same embarrassed look.

* * * * *

It had been August 1940, Becky on learning that her father was working in London was anxious to see him. The nine year old had suggested she spent a week or two with Imogen; Stefan could then visit her in Ilford. Charles and Amy refused to let her go. She was far too young, they said, and anyway children had been evacuated from London, it was out of the question.

Becky stood there, legs apart, chin held high, her lovely eyes flashing with anger. "I will get my way about this Mummy, I will, I will. I'm determined to go".

Margot, pink and embarrassed said quietly, "I think it would be best if you agreed Aunt Amy".

Charles and Amy stood firm, London was out of bounds. Then Becky's attitude changed, her face softened, she put her arms around Amy, "Mummy,

I love Uncle Charles very much but I love Daddy too and I have been so worried about him. I know he escaped from Paris and the Germans and is safe but it is ages since I saw him. Please let me go to London, please". She put her pretty face, wet with tears against Amy's, cuddled up to her and pleaded again. It had no effect on her mother, the answer was still a definite 'no'.

Amy now wondered if this older Becky would do the same, put her arms around her old mother, kiss her and with tears of remorse say, 'Sorry Ma, of course you are still young and able. It's because I love you so much I want you to be looked after. Please say you'll do as I say'.

Becky did nothing of the kind. She went back to London, to her clients and her staff whom she could manage without any trouble.

Lying in the hospital bed gave plenty of time to reminisce and Amy recalled the follow up to nine year old Becky's request.

* * * * *

It was almost the end of August and Amy had decided to close Gentian House. No one was inclined to spend money on interior decorating now the war was 'hotting up' as they put it. The Torquay shop had been sold a year ago and a little shop in Totnes had displayed the sign 'Gentian House' for the past ten months. Business had never really taken off there and Amy had decided she could work from home. Charles' studio had been built and the bedroom that had been his temporary studio cleared of paints and canvases. Amy commandeered it and was in the process of transferring the stock from Totnes.

"Mummy", said Becky one Friday evening. "Margot has asked me over for the day tomorrow. When you go to Totnes in the morning, if you put me on the train, Margot and Uncle Jim will meet me at Newton Abbot. Is that alright?".

Amy, knowing she would have a busy weekend agreed willingly. It would certainly be easier to have Becky out of the way. "I'll have a word with Auntie Dinah", she said.

An excited Becky ran out of the room calling, "No, I'll ring her, I'll make the arrangements, leave it to me".

All went well that Saturday morning; at Totnes station Amy put Becky in the charge of a young woman she recognised. Becky was to alight at Newton Abbot where she would be met. Amy worked hard, driving back and forth between Hope Lodge and her tiny shop. There was no message from Becky, no doubt Jim would drive her back and stay for a drink.

"Perhaps I should go and collect Becky, what were the arrangements?", asked Charles.

Just then the telephone rang. "Amy?".

"Yes Dinah".

"We've been waiting to hear from you, shall Jim come over for Margot?".

Amy's mouth went dry, she felt the pulse in her neck beating strongly. "Margot's not here Dinah, we understood both girls were with you for the day". She gave her friend the details and Dinah told how Becky had 'phoned on Friday, spoken only to Margot who in turn had said she had been invited to meet Amy and Becky at Newton Abbot station to go to Teignmouth for the day. "Jim dropped her off at the station entrance when he saw Becky waving", said a frightened Dinah.

"Oh, why didn't Jim...", began Amy, then: "It's no good me saying anything now, we must find the girls. My goodness I think I know what they have done".

"What Amy, what have they done, where are they?".

"Becky has Stefan's address in London, she has been worrying me for ages to let her go to see him. Dinah I'm so sorry she has led Margot into this".

"Amy, the air-raids!".

"I'm going at once Dinah, don't worry, no I'll go on my own. I will 'phone as soon as I can". Amy replaced the receiver. Her mouth was dry, her hands shaking.

The journey seemed to go on for ever. Amy sat on the train in a daze. How could Becky have done this, to involve Margot and cause Jim and Dinah all this worry. They would be with Stefan at his flat, they must be. Why had Stefan not telephoned when the girls had arrived, he might know how worried she was. Perhaps she was wrong, maybe she had jumped to the wrong conclusion. No, Becky had planned this, Amy could see it now. Margot had said in her quiet voice that it would be best if Amy agreed to a holiday with Imogen, had she known that her cousin would stop at nothing to get her own way?

Twenty pounds was missing from the desk in the hall. Earlier that day Amy and Charles had, what was for them an unusual occurrence, a bitter arguement. Charles had discovered that twenty pounds was missing from his personal drawer in the desk. "If you were short of cash Amy, you only had to ask me, you know I would let you have some money. To take it without asking, well, I'm surprised at you. Don't ever do that again".

"You must be mistaken Charles, I haven't been to your drawer".

"Don't make it worse by denying it Amy, that is just stupid".

Amy began to get cross. "I've told you, I have not taken your precious money!".

The argument continued and was not resolved as both were certain they were in the right. Now Amy knew the money had been taken to purchase tickets to Paddington.

Amy looked at the scrap of paper in her hand. Fairfield Road, Bow, a taxi from the station and she would find the children safe and sound. The rhythm of the wheels seemd to say, 'They'll be with Stefan, they'll be with Stefan', and sometimes: 'Let them be safe, let them be safe, let them be safe'.

Paddington at last, it was dark now and the blackout regulations gave the station a grim, foreboding look. Amy had to queue for a taxi, waiting impatiently, a growing fear inside her. Supposing the girls were not at Stefan's flat, where to look then? Stefan would be there to help her, she felt a tiny jab at her heart at the thought of meeting him again.

The taxi pulled up outside a tall, grey looking house. As Amy paid the cabbie she saw to her relief, Stefan open the door and the figures of Becky and Margot behind him. Stefan shepherded them all upstairs whilst giving an explanation. "I had been to the cottage in Suffolk where Anna and Micha are living. Got back about an hour ago to see these two sitting on my doorstep. I 'phoned Hope Lodge and Charles intimated that you should be arriving any minute. We've been looking out of the window for you, haven't we girls?"

Amy knew she should be chastising Becky but she was so relieved that for the moment the chastisement was delayed. Margot was very contrite but Becky behaved as though it were perfectly normal for a nine year-old to travel nearly 200 miles to a city under attack each night by the Luftwaffe. She spoke to Charles and Dinah to put their minds at rest. 'Thank God for telephones' she thought.

Amy had seen Stefan only a few times and then briefly, since their divorce. She looked at him as they sat with the girls at a small table, eating beans on toast. Thinner now, he was still a big, powerful man. His hair not so bright, he looked older. Stefan had grown a beard again, a beard with a few grey hairs Amy noticed. His presence was still electrifying and Becky and Margot were enthralled as they listened to his anecdotes, embroidered no doubt, regarding his flight from France before the Germans entered Paris.

"I'm working for the Red Cross, helping trace missing persons. There are so many refugees looking for relatives. My office is in London but I couldn't let Anna stay here with Micha, they are happy in the country and I visit when I am able".

Amy enquired after the health of Stefan's young wife and his son. How strange it was, she had once been married to this handsome man, thought herself perfectly happy. Amy thought of Charles at home, dear Charles with his whistling, his dancing up and down the hall, the jokes he played on Becky and herself. Charles had carved C.L. loves A.L. on a tree in the garden, life was fun and she was sure of his love in a way she had never been sure of Stefan.

"The girls have been telling me of what they hope to do when they grow up", Stefan was saying. "Becky seems quite determined to run her own business, doesn't know what sort of business it will be yet, something where she can make a lot of money I understand".

"Has Margot surprised you with her ambition?".

"Yes Amy, she certainly has. Why an actress? Margot has always appeared so quiet, so shy" . Stefan looked at pretty, plump Margot, mystified. He was not to know then of course of Margot's success at drama school a few years later, of her career which began with small parts on television and the steady climb to the top. It was all in the future but the little girl eating her baked beans knew she was going to be an actress and a very good one.

"Remember one of our nights at the theatre Amy? Noel Coward and Gertrude Lawrence, he didn't fade away did he. I can see your face as though it were yesterday. Eyes shining, your hair black and glossy, discussing the young actor with me".

Amy blushed and jumped up to clear the table. Stefan followed her into the kitchen. Standing so very close in that tiny room Amy was very conscious of Stefan. Supposing he touched her, she half wished he would, the magic he had once held for her, was it still there?

He broke in on her thoughts. "You've changed Amy, you look very different".

Amy was aware for the first time since she had arrived, that she was wearing navy slacks and the old sweater she had been wearing all day, moving her stock from the shop. It seemed years ago, the busy morning, the arguement with Charles over the money. When Dinah had phoned she had thrown on a Reefer coat and rushed to catch the train. Amy put up a hand to touch her hair, it would look alright she was sure as only the day before her hairdresser had cut the abundant silver hair into an up-to-date style. What did Stefan think of her being completely grey at thirty six?

He answered her unspoken question. "The hair suits you Amy, it enhances your dark eyes and you have been lucky to keep such a young looking face. I think you appear even more striking, unusual; distinguished is the word I wanted".

"We'll get an early train tomorrow Stefan. You can put us up tonight?"

"The bedroom or the Anderson shelter?".

Becky and Margot looked at Amy, willing her to say that they could sleep out in the garden, an air-raid shelter, almost underground. It would be exciting.

"I think we'll take the bedroom Stefan if it is not putting you out too much".

"Not at all, if the three of you can squeeze into my bed I'll use the sofa in my landlord's sitting room. Mr. Davis is away but he won't mind me taking a liberty", said Stefan.

With a promise to call his guests if an air-raid siren sounded and strict instructions regarding the black-out regulation Stefan said 'goodnight'.

Amy slept soundly and did not hear the wail of the siren. Stefan stood in the doorway and as though from a great distance Amy heard him say, "Come on girls, wake up. Hurry, be as quick as you can, downstairs, out of the back door and into the shelter".

Suddenly Amy was wide awake. Yes it was Stefan telling them to get up, it wasn't a dream, they could be in danger. She shook Becky, Margot was already out of bed and fumbling for her clothes. They stopped to dress, a mistake Amy realized as they searched for their belongings. Stefan shouted from below, he sounded cross, there was the sound of gunfire, the drone of planes above them.

Stefan was at the top of the stairs urging them to get into the shelter and as they reached the bottom of the staircase, the whole house seemed to shudder; a dull thud and the building shook again and this time there was the sound of breaking glass. Amy knew that a bomb had exploded very near. Stefan had pushed the three of them under the stairs and thrown his body on top of them. His beard touched her face, she could feel his breath on her forehead. Amy's heart was thudding, she held, as best she could, the shaking bodies of Margot and Becky. They lay still for a while, Stefan's body shielding them from the plaster that was dropping from the ceiling and the glass that had shattered in the front door.

Amy was aware of a draught and moving her head could see that the front door had been blown open by the blast. Through the dust she could see figures out in the street, hear the voices that were giving instructions, somewhere a dog was whining, a pitiful sound.

Stefan moved and it was a relief to be free of his heavy body. "I think they've gone, we'll soon hear the All-clear", he said. He went out in the street, littered with rubble, A.R.P. workers already assisting the victims of the raid. A house only a few doors away had been hit and Stefan, after a while, came back to report that the occupants had fortunately been found safe in their Anderson shelter.

Amy, her legs shaking went up to Stefan's kitchen to make some strong tea, relieved to find both water and gas available. How calm we all are, observed Amy as she sat with Stefan and the girls sipping the hot tea. We could have been killed or terribly injured and yet here we are joking about the dusty cups. Later she helped Stefan put the house in some kind of order.

"Mr. Davis is in Wales for a few days", said Stefan. "He'll have a shock when he sees all this damage. I'll have to get the door repaired and put on its hinges before tonight. A busy day in front of me and I'm expecting a friend later this morning".

He leaned on the broom, dirty and dishevelled, he looked tired and old, there was blood on his shirt Amy noticed.

"Are you hurt Stefan?", she asked.

"My back feels a bit sore, between the shoulder blades. Maybe a piece of glass cut me".

"Let me look", Amy pulled up his shirt and there were several small cuts and grazes. "I'll clean them up for you", she said.

Later, in the bathroom, washing her hands after bathing Stefan's small wounds, Amy felt his arms go round her waist. She turned to face him. "I was such a fool Amy, to mess things up between us, we were very happy once. Have you forgiven me?".

"Of course Stefan". He was standing very close and Amy knew that she must never be alone with her ex-husband again. He still had the power to charm her, bathing his familiar body and touching his skin had proved it. If he were to kiss her now ... Amy moved away into the kitchen.

"I'll make some toast and then the girls and I must make our way to Paddington".

Breakfast over, Stefan said he would call for a taxi for his guests. "Sorry I can't come to the station but as I said I have a pal on 48 hours leave from the R.A.F. arriving shortly. Must tidy the flat, looks as though it has been hit by a bomb", he joked.

The taxi arrived and Becky clung to her father, making him promise to sleep in the shelter every night. They said their 'goodbyes', neighbours were in the street sweeping up the debris, exchanging details of the raid. A soldier, going back from leave, kissed his wife at his gate and waved as he reluctantly walked away. A tall W.A.A.F., her red hair in a neat roll around her cap, was carefully picking her way through the broken glass.

As Amy turned to give a final wave to Stefan she saw the W.A.A.F. girl in her smart uniform run the last few steps and throw her arms around Stefan. He kissed her and they walked together up the path into the house. His 'pal' on 48 hours leave! 'Poor Anna and Micha' thought Amy.

Becky's behaviour was the cause of some bad feeling between Dinah and Amy. On arrival at Newton Abbot station, Amy and the girls were met by Charles. He took them to Berrycombe and there was a joyful reunion between Margot and her parents. Amy sensed a restraint in Dinah's greeting to herself and Becky. Sitting in the kitchen drinking tea, Margot and Becky enjoying milky cocoa, their latest fad, Amy could feel the tension. Charles and Jim made conversation but Dinah hardly said a word. Just before they left, it all came out. Dinah usually so placid, so gentle, critisized Amy's 'sloppy arrangements' as she put it, for that Saturday morning.

"You should have taken much more care Amy, Margot is precious to us, we would never have left her in charge of some one we hardly knew, as you did with Becky".

"Then Jim shouldn't have let Margot go on to the station without making sure I was there too", retorted a tired Amy. It escalated and it was only Charles' intervention with the remark that they should all be grateful that the runaways were home safe and sound when they could have been maimed or killed in the air-raid, that quietened them down.

Charles had driven back to Hope Lodge with a withdrawn Amy by his side. She was smarting from Dinah's cross words. She never fell out with Dinah and now because of Becky and her headstrong ways, the two friends had said unkind words to each other.

A telephone call the next day found Dinah her old happy, friendly self and the matter was not referred to again.

CHAPTER SIXTEEN

The war touched them all in one way or another. Jim decided to close down his business for the duration and in 1942 he was on war work in Plymouth Docks, secret work that he would not discuss. Dinah saw him only at weekends when he arrived home with a tremendous appetite and went back on Sundays carrying a large bag of his wife's pasties and cakes to sustain him for the week.

Charles had rejoined his old regiment but to his disgust was desk-bound somewhere in Surrey. Amy missed his cheerful presence at home but Charles was lucky to get leave frequently and however short they were, both Amy and Becky ensured that his precious hours with them were enjoyable.

Margot and Becky were now at the same private school near Totnes. Margot stayed at Hope Lodge during the week as Dinah was working at the local hospital and her hours were irregular.

"I love being there Amy", she said. "The staff are so pleased with any extra help they can get. I get some awful jobs sometimes but I never complain and I do so enjoy the company".

Amy felt the need to also contribute some help somewhere. Not nursing though, that did not appeal and she must find something that would not interfere with the journeys to and from the school. The local Billeting Officer was glad of her assistance and Amy was soon involved also in issuing clothing coupons and ration books. It was good to be busy again, to make new friends.

By 1942 Amy had shortened her skirts again, she kept up with the fashion dictated by the war. Plain, tailored clothes, no fussy trimmings, sensible shoes but Amy as always, was her elegant self. Wedding invitations came, sons and daughters of her friends were rushing to the altar before going off to fight. Brides did not wear white any more, a suit with a tiny hat worn to the front of the head, a spray of flowers in place of the bouquet of pre-war days seemed to be the thing. Amy would take Becky and Margot to the service but these days there was no rice to throw, no church bells ringing, no bridesmaids in pretty dresses for the little girls to admire. Margot took it all in, she did not miss a thing. The mother of the bride with a tear or two on her powdered cheek, the expression on the face of the bride. Even the walk back down the aisle was studied, the slight embarrassed look of the parents forced to walk arm in arm with their opposite number from the family into which their offspring was marrying. These days they were often complete strangers to each other.

Margot looked and remembered; she might wish to use this in her future career as an actress. Becky fidgeted, longing to get out of the cold church, she would never get married, she had made up her mind. She wanted to do things her way, a husband might spoil all that.

Amy could see that working was changing Dinah. She had been married for over twenty years, her life had been Berrycombe with its Church Fetes, Women's Institute meetings. A happy family life, nothing exciting but Dinah had been content. Now, in war time Dinah was stimulated by her new friends and their conversations. Nurses who had travelled, who had worked in the London blitz. Nurses who had fallen in love and hadn't waited for marriage before giving themselves to their young men off to war and possible death. Dinah listened and was often amazed at what she heard.

"I sometimes feel I haven't lived Amy", she said one day. "Just existed here in slow old Berrycombe. Do you feel life is passing us by? We shall be thirty eight this year, what have I done with my life? You've worked abroad, had several boyfriends before you married, you've run a business, started one of your own. You've done something with your life, but don't you feel we have got in a rut?"

"No", said Amy. "I am very happy with my life, at least I will be when the war is over and Charles is back with me. You've produced Margot, you have a wonderful marriage and a house that is furnished with the lovely things Jim makes. You are in the right place for you, you're a home-maker. What a great cook you are. Dinah you have done something with your life, believe me".

"I don't know, now Jim has had to go to Scotland to work and I won't see him each weekend I suppose it has made me grumpy", said Dinah in a small, quiet voice.

Amy was worried, this was not like her friend, Dinah was usually bubbling over with enthusiasm for whatever was happening to her, she never complained.

When Dinah, a few weeks later, told Amy that the staff at the hospital had been invited to a dance at Black-Tor Camp and would she go with her, Amy thought it might be a good idea. A neighbour was to look after the girls and Charles and Jim told of their intentions to pretend they were young again.

American troops had been stationed at the camp for a couple of months and had made themselves popular with the locals. The pubs were busy, the young men had plenty of money to spend and certain young ladies now wore sheer stockings with black seams creeping up their legs from their high heeled shoes. Amy and Dinah joined the few nurses and kitchen staff from the hospital for a lift to the dance in a Jeep, a bumpy hilarious ride.

It was a successful evening, the music loud, the dancing fast and furious at first then mellowing into romantic tunes and slow, close dancing. The refreshments were unbelievable, luxuries almost forgotten appeared on the long trestle tables. Amy could see how popular Dinah was with her friends from the hospital and how she hardly ever sat on a chair, someone was always pulling her up and on to the floor to dance. Her chestnut curls danced too and her eyes; Dinah was happy, why did I worry wondered Amy, there's nothing wrong with Dinah.

Their little group was safely delivered home and Amy admitted to her friend it had been just what they needed to make them feel about twenty again.

The R.A.F. was bombing Germany nightly. Amy, listening to the morning news on the wireless, recalled her one night of such an experience; how scared she had been. Those poor civilians in Germany! But this was war, she reminded herself. She thought of Stefan and how he had thrown himself over her and the children. Becky corresponded with her father but Amy did not get involved. She did not want to see Stefan again unless it was strictly necessary.

Amy wrote often to William and Louise, glad that they were far enough away from London to be free from air raids. Sarah and Jack had two little boys billeted on them, evacuees from Silver Town in East London. Mark and John settled in Shearfield amazingly well and Sarah was in her element, a family at last to cook for and to love.

Charles had seven days leave, the weather was warm and dry. "Wish we could have had a holiday in Lynmouth" , he said one morning as they lay in bed. "We will when the war is over. I often think of the many times we have been back. We'll stay at the Lyndale next time, can't you just see it on a morning like this, the trees, the water rushing under the bridge?" Amy snuggled up, it would be heaven to get back to normal. Holidays, shopping together, Charles painting in his studio again. Gentian Interiors making money once more as people again took pride in their houses.

By 1944 the main topic of conversation was of the invasion by the Allies. It would certainly be soon, but where? When? Charles was not getting any leave. Jim was back in Plymouth and home some weekends, not many. Amy and Dinah were still enjoying their work but at their husbands' request did not attend any more dances. "Not dignified for two married ladies to be off dancing all night" , was the joint opinion of Charles and Jim.

Late in May, Amy arranged to meet Charles in London, to see a show and stay overnight. Becky and Margot were staying at the home of a neighbour, a young woman, recently married to John Monk their gardner, at present away in the Navy. Amy made herself comfortable in the carriage that was almost full on arrival at Newton Abbot. Train timetables had become useless, passengers just stood on platforms and hoped a train would arrive in due course. Troops were being moved, large numbers filling the trains.

Amy, as she sat wedged between a sailor and a woman knitting furiously at something in khaki, wondered if she were foolish to be visiting London. Charles had reported that there was a lull in the bombing, it may only be brief but Amy should take the opportunity to spend a few hours with him. Imogen had a day or two free from her ambulance driving and they could meet up. Imogen and Dolly had closed their shops, Dolly was helping in a Forces Canteen and Imogen was a driver for the Red Cross. How all their lives had changed, thought Amy, as she opened her book to read of more pleasant, peaceful times.

The train pulled into Exeter, St. David's; it stood for some while and Amy looked up from her book. The platform was busy, more hustle and bustle than usual, khaki clad figures, British and Americans stood in groups, their kitbags forming small dun coloured hills on the crowded platform. Amy was studying a large poster on the outside wall of the waiting Room. 'Careless Talk Costs Lives', it proclaimed and then she saw them. They stood in front of the poster, the soldier, in the smart uniform of an American officer was holding both of Dinah's hands. Holding her hands! On his face and Dinah's too, was a look of intense sadness. Amy watched as they moved closer to each other and she witnessed their kiss and long embrace. Dinah pulled away, they both turned and walked in opposite directions, never looking back.

The train moved forward and Amy lowered her eyes to the open page of her book. The words were meaningless, she shut out the memory of that embrace, the lingering kiss. The words on the poster became the important thing, 'Careless Talk Costs Lives' as though by concentrating on the poster she could wipe out the two figures who had stood before it.

There would be an explanation of course. Dinah would tell her, he may have been a cousin, passing through, he had called Dinah to meet him in Exeter. Amy knew it was not so. Dinah had no cousins. Who was he that man who had taken her brother Jim's wife in his arms?

The sailor, his head forward on his chest snored gently. The woman clicked away with her needles and Amy practised her delivery of the news of Dinah to Charles. She saw again in her mind the poster, 'Careless Talk ...'

no she would keep this to herself. It was so completely out of character for her friend to act like this but Dinah would tell her, of that Amy was certain.

Dinah never did tell Amy about the incident. For a while after the Allied invasion, Amy noticed that her friend was unusually quiet, wore a worried look. Dinah followed the war news with more interest than before and that was all. Amy often wondered about it, a little mystery, unsolved. 'Oh well', thought Amy, 'I. suppose we all have our little secrets'.

Amy did not visit London again during the war, the VI's and V2's ensured that she stayed safely in Devon. The reports of the damage these new weapons wreaked were frightening, there was no warning given with the V2's and Amy could imagine the horror in the London streets.

The end of hostilities came and Amy's family had all been lucky enough to come through without injury. Imogen would not open her shop in Ilford again because she had found at last 'the most perfect man' as she put it. An Army captain, Henry was a widower and he persuaded Imogen to marry him and share his lovely country house in Hertfordshire. Charles and Amy were delighted that Imogen would be enjoying Henry's retirement with him.

Jim looked older and tired but opened his workshop ready to produce his furniture once more. Dinah joked about having all that sawdust over her floors again but they all knew it was wonderful to get back to normal life. Margot had grown into a most attractive girl and at fifteen was worrying her parents to let her attend a Drama School. She eventually got her own way of course and Becky had to get used to being without her cousin. They had shared most of their young lives at the same school, had the same friends. They would miss each other.

"Had a lovely newsy letter from Sarah this morning", said Amy when Charles came in from his studio for coffee. "You must read it later but I can't wait to tell you this".

Charles smiled at his wife's obvious excitement.

"Come on then, spit it out".

"Sarah has been successful in adopting the boys. I knew when she heard that their parents had been killed in the Blitz, she hoped this would be the outcome. I'm so pleased for her and Jack. Those little evacuees will have plenty of love. I do hope they will appreciate it when they're grown up".

"Your mother and father well?"

"Think so, according to the letter they are fine but at seventy nine and eighty, well who knows", said Amy. She remembered Dinah's sadness when Mrs. Rayne had died, she had yet to cope with losing a parent. She sighed and poured another cup of coffee.

Amy did not mention that Sarah had also written of the death of Hugh's mother, Mrs. Lodge. Amongst Hugh's effects, kept so long by his mother and now kindly forwarded to Sarah by his nephew, had been a half written letter addressed to Amy. A letter the young soldier had been writing when his dug-out had been shelled and he had been killed. His officer, collecting a few personal items to be forwarded to the family, had included the sheet of paper. The letter, as yet unread, was resting in the pocket of Amy's cardigan. She would wait for a quiet moment, when she was alone, unlikely to be disturbed to read those words written so long ago.

Charles was having difficulty in settling down to working alone in his studio. He had been in the company of his fellow officers during the war and as much as he loved Hope Lodge he did find life rather quiet now.

"Have you thought about starting up your business again Amy?" he enquired sneaking another spoonful of sugar into his coffee.

"Mmmmm, I've thought about it and that's as far as I've got".

After a long discussion, Charles and Amy came to a decision to open a shop in Totnes. They would sell fabrics, wallpapers etc. Amy would once again advise and organise interior decoration whilst Charles would sell prints and undertake restoration of oil paintings. He would of course accept commissions for portaits as before and supply a few local landscapes.

"We'll find premises suitable for us both, a gallery upstairs and your Alladin's Cave on the ground floor", teased Charles and he went back into his studio.

It was then that Amy took the mud stained letter out of her pocket. Stained with blood too, she found, as she began to read...

Dear Amy, I have been thinking of you constantly since I returned here. This letter will probably be short as there is a lot of activity at the moment and I may have to make a hasty exit.

It was a wonderful leave, so many happy memories to bring back with me. Our morning in the churchyard is something I shall never forget. I must tell you that I am aware of your feelings for me Amy, dear Amy, You are so young. You must not think of me other than a friend. I could not let you touch my face that morning as we lay in the churchyard, forgive me. In a year or two someone will come along and you will know that what you felt for me was only the beginning, the first stirrings of the deeper, greater feelings of a woman.

There is noise, mud and much more that I do not wish to describe, all around me but Amy in my heart there is the peace and love I found at Shearfield. Your family is a wonderful family, something special, respect them, always. I know you will have your differences with your father but he is a good honest man and means well. I am lucky to have found Sarah, so sweet and gentle. You mustn't be jealous.

I pray that I shall be with you all again before too long. Remember my words to you Amy, make something of your life. Do not be afraid to venture forth. Please do not spoil the love you have to give by thinking only of me, I can never be yours, you know that.

Before I finish this letter I must tell you something that made me laugh...

She read it twice more, trying to imagine the horror of that dug-out, the mud, the noise, the screams of men horribly injured. Tried to see in her mind Hugh killed in the midst of writing a sentence on the paper she now held in her hand. His blood had spattered the page. Amy put the stained paper to her lips, poor, poor Hugh to die so young. He had been right of course, she had been able to love, she had loved Stefan and she loved Charles. The memory of that first love, had, over the years, become fainter but reading the letter, Amy once again saw the churchyard in the October sun and the child who had put out a finger to touch. Yes, he was right, she had begun to experience what it would be like to be a woman, to be stirred by the closeness of a man, to be thrilled by the way in which his hair grew at the nape of his neck or his lashes rested on his cheeks.

Amy's eyes were moist as she folded the letter in two. Yes, it was a love letter. Hugh had loved her, loved her for the little girl she was in 1916.

* * * * *

Amy moved in the narrow hospital bed and came back to the present with a jolt. The pain from her ankle almost made her cry out. How long ago it all seemed when she had been young, when mother and father had still been alive. She was glad they had both lived to see the end of the war and that death for both of them had been quiet and easy. William had died of a heart attack whilst digging the garden and mother, a year or two later, had died in her sleep. They were lucky, thought Amy remembering the later deaths of those she had loved so dearly.

A nurse brought a cup of tea and a newspaper. Amy put on her 'specs, glad to get away from morbid thoughts. She would be glad to get home, to sit in her garden, to have tea in her pretty china. She hated this thick white cup with tea that had a faint taste of disinfectant. She was lucky to have Mrs. Monk to look after her, so many years of service from her and her husband. Margot was good to her too, almost like a daughter. Who would have thought that such a well known actress as Margot Clayden would give up all the glamour that went with her life to marry 'the boy next door' as the papers had put it. Tom, a farmer in Berrycombe, proud of his beautiful wife and the two babies they had so quickly.

If only Becky had married and had children. I would have loved to be a grandmother mused Amy. Becky, clever, astute, energetic but with little imagination had risen to the top and she had no time for romance. There had been one or two affairs and once Becky had brought a man home whom

Amy would have welcomed as a son-in-law but he had gone the way of the others, discarded when Becky wanted to concentrate on her business.

'She can't seem to settle down, just like her father', thought Amy. Thinking of Stefan reminded her that this November that once handsome, charming man would be ninety. Becky would no doubt go over to France to visit him in the residential home near Paris where he was looked after by the gentle nuns. 'He never remembered my eightieth birthday' thought Amy, 'but I'll send him a card'.

She scanned the newspaper. Mrs. Thatcher had promised to look into the cause of the riots that were terrifying various towns. There were more details of the fire damage to York Minster. Amy then turned to her horoscope, something she never read at home. Gemini told of a new man in her life, of an important letter. Amy smiled, folded the paper and placed it on the bedside cabinet.

Letter, of course, there was a letter at home waiting to be opened. Who had written it, where had it come from?

CHAPTER SEVENTEEN

The young doctor who wore an aftershave similar to the one Charles had always used, came to see how his eighty year-old patient was feeling.

"I feel fine, ready to go home", said Amy.

"I think, Mrs. Lambert that whilst you are here it would be sensible to do a few tests".

"Tests?" Amy sat up in bed, her large dark eyes held a questioning look. She didn't like the sound of this.

"Nothing much, check your blood pressure again, see if your heart is behaving normally, that sort of thing. Just for the record, do you know how your parents died?"

Amy had a sudden picture of William and Louise, in their sixties, healthy looking. They were sitting at the kitchen table shelling peas. How silly she was. "Heart, both of them", was her terse reply to the prying doctor.

Amy was allowed home the next day. Mrs. Monk collected the pills from the chemist in Buckfastleigh, drugs that the doctor said would make her feel young again. Silly young man, she always felt young and thought he was mistaken when he reported that Amy's heart needed a little help in functioning.

In the excitement of returning once more to her beloved Hope Lodge, Amy almost forgot to open the letter that had been the reason for her fall. She checked on her treasured possessions; Tessie was in her usual place, Amy touched her cold china face. How lucky the doll was, no wrinkles for her, no heart to worry about. 'After all these years you still look exactly like your portrait' she thought as she studied the pastel hanging in the same room as her own portrait. Oh, the youthfulness of the young! Amy's face, the smooth young skin, the glossy black hair.

The envelope was on the kitchen table and Amy slit it open. The horoscope was correct after all, there was a new man in Amy's life, the writer of this letter. She read it again and again.

Dear Mrs. Lambert,

I have been unable to contact Miss Serovsky (whom I believe is your daughter) recently and as I wish to finalize my business I am writing directly to you. You have seen me on two occasions, at the hotel where you were celebrating a birthday and again when I was admiring your lovely garden. Your house would appear to be exactly what I am looking for and Miss Serovsky agreed my offer would most probably be acceptable to you. I feel the delay may be because you are having difficulty in assessing the value of your costume collection. Perhaps I could help you in that direction having had the experience of purchasing similar collections. Miss Serovsky seems to be delaying my visiting your house to discuss the business and of course to view the interior. I trust you will be able to contact her and make the necessary arrangements.

Yours sincerely,

Maurice Ruston.

So that was what Becky was up to! Her daughter had suggested Amy move into a Residential Home in order that Hope Lodge could be sold and some of the proceeds of the sale could be wheedled out of her mother .and into Becky's pocket. But why the costume collection?

Over the years Amy's wardrobe had continued to grow. She had never lost her interest in fashion and at least one garment a year had been added to a collection which by now must be quite valuable. The 'Mini' of the 'sixties then the 'Midi' and the 'Maxi', clothes worn by Becky and Margot in their younger days. They were housed behind sliding glass doors of the wardrobes which took up all four walls of a large bedroom, a room they called the 'Museum'.

Amy's treasures of the 'Twenties and 'Thirties, the extravagant, luxurious clothes of the pre-war era, complete with shoes, hats and bags. Margot had been allowed to borrow them when at the begining of her career she was appearing in Repertory Theatre. That was before she had been discovered and had achieved fame if not fortune on the London stage and on television. Who would have thought Dinah and Jim's little girl would have become famous?

'I'm wandering', thought Amy, 'I must get in touch with Becky and have this out with her, more important than remembering the past'.

"Miss Serovsky is out of the office", or "Miss Serovsky is with a client", were the answers Amy received when she called Becky's office. A request that the busy lady should contact her mother as soon as possible had no immediate effect but at last Amy was able to talk with her daughter.

It transpired that Mr. Ruston wished to purchase a house in the Torbay or Dartmoor area to house his collection of 'Bygones' and with Amy's collection added he planned to open the house as a Museum and Restaurant. People were begining to take weekend breaks, motoring to Devon in October and even November when the weather could still be warm, when the countryside was vivid with autumn colour. Mr. Ruston anticipated he could capture the tourists on their way to or from visits to Buckfast Abbey or Dartmoor. Lunches or teas would be available at Hope Lodge, beautiful things to look at before they returned to their hotels for dinner and evenings in the bar.

"You really think I would sell my lovely house to a man like that? Hope Lodge to be invaded by hoards of people, feet trampling over the lawns, tourists looking out of my windows, staring at my clothes, the things I have taken years to collect. Did you really think I would agree?"

"Oh Ma, don't take on so. You wouldn't be there to see all the people, you wouldn't know what was happening. Just think, you could be sitting pretty in a super Residential Home. Waited on, cossetted, not a worry in the world".

"I haven't any worries now Becky. I am quite capable of living here on my own. You no doubt envisaged some of the money from the sale coming your way?"

There was a pause before Becky's reply came. "Well Mother, I must admit it would seem sensible to let me have some of the surplus. You would be comfortably off and you no longer need to spend very much. Eventually I would inherit so why not pass some on that I could invest in the business and ensure also that I have enough to enjoy myself whilst I am still young enough to get around?"

The conversation continued but Amy made it quite clear that Becky was to inform Mr. Ruston of her intention not to sell, either the house or the costume collection. Amy would also write a polite but firm letter to the gentleman.

It caused a rift between mother and daughter. The sad feeling she had inside reminded Amy of the time she had almost fallen out with Dinah. It was the afternoon of her return from London, all those years ago after the night of the bombing in Bow. Amy had gone straight to Berrycombe where Charles was waiting with Jim and Dinah. There were cross words that Sunday afternoon and Amy had felt herself unfairly criticised over the arrangements for that Saturday morning. Margot and Becky sat there in Dinah's kitchen drinking cocoa, quite unperturbed, by the ticking off each had received. Charles had driven back to Hope Lodge with a subdued Amy by his side. He did not whistle, did not tap dance up the front steps like Fred Astaire as he usually did to make them laugh. Amy went to bed with a heaviness in her heart and it did not go until she had spoken to Dinah the next day and found that her old school friend was her usual happy self again.

Amy had the same heaviness in her heart. She did not want to fall out with Becky. They loved each other, she knew that, but Becky was like her father, had to have her own way about everything. Money was so important to her, material things meant so much. 'I'm just as bad' thought Amy as she realized that her house and clothes were also only material things. An invitation to come down and spend the weekend together, to get back on a friendly footing was the answer and Amy whilst writing to Mr. Ruston also penned a loving letter to her daughter.

Becky came down, smart and well groomed, every inch the successful business woman. Amy ascertained that Mr. Ruston had been notified of her decision not to sell.

"It doesn't matter about the money Ma", Becky said and she kissed the silver haired old lady on her soft cheek. "I just thought it would enable me to expand the business, another office, in North London this time. More staff and equipment but not to worry, forget the whole thing".

Becky stayed over until Tuesday, a nice long weekend. She drove her mother to favourite beauty spots, so much busier nowadays. So many cars parked on the narrow roads that led over the moors, people crammed into inns whose rooms were too small to cope with the amount of holiday makers demanding lunches. Amy sat next to her daughter, they were happy to be together to recall days long gone when there had been picnics at Dartmeet or Becky Falls, the Falls that Becky as a child thought had been named after her.

They called on Margot at Berrycombe, she lived on the opposite side of the road to the house that had been Dinah and Jim's until their tragic death in 1964. As they sat in the garden near the honeysuckle smelling so sweetly, Amy remembered with a sharp pain the horror of their deaths. Margot, a young mother of two little girls, had been delighted that her mother and father had at last agreed to take a holiday abroad. It was Jim who had decided on Switzerland. "He can't be parted too long from his beloved wood", Dinah had joked. "So we are off to Interlaken from whence we can travel each day to inspect the pretty wooden chalets, the cuckoo clocks and best of all see the wood carvers at work in Brienz".

It was on the very day that Amy and Margot had received colourful postcards of Lake Thun and of a steamer on Lake Brienz that news had also come of the car accident in which both Dinah and Jim had been killed. Looking at Margot and Becky now, Amy recalled how wonderful Becky had proved to be, a tower of strength. It was Becky who had taken charge, made the necessary arrangements, dealt with the paperwork. Amy and Charles had given all their time to Margot, comforting her, looking after Susan and Anne whilst Tom, Margot's caring husband, left his farm to travel to Switzerland. Jim had been sixty-six and Dinah only sixty, too young to die. Looking back on that sad time, knowing their deaths had been quick, Amy was glad it had been that way. She would not have wanted Margot to see her loved ones end their days as her dear Charles had done.

Amy still missed her oldest, her dearest friend. They had told each other everything, well, almost everything, Amy thought. Soon after the tragic accident Amy had been with Margot going through Dinah's possessions. An old chocolate box, similar to the gold one that housed many of Amy's treasured mementos contained a few letters, postcards and photographs. Margot had been studying the faces of long dead relatives when she gave a black and white snapshot to Amy. "Who's this handsome chap Aunt Amy?"

Amy looked at the serious face before her, a young man, good looking, large eyes under straight, dark brows. He was wearing the uniform of an officer in the United States Army. The lie came easily to her lips. "I believe he was a distant cousin of your mother. He took part in the D Day invasion and I think he was killed".

"Never knew we had any relatives in America, she never spoke about them", was all Margot said and put the snap back in the box.

How clear were all the memories of long ago and yet recent events could be forgotten so easily. That was what Amy was thinking as she sat in the garden with the girls.

"Daddy will be ninety in November", Becky was telling Margot. "I shall go over to see him, he's very happy in that Home. Micha and his family visit quite often, it is not too far for them from Paris. I'm afraid Anna never did forgive Daddy his naughty escapades and she refuses to see him".

Margot looked at Amy and gave her a sympathetic look. Amy thought, 'She knows what is in my mind, sensitive Margot. She knows I cannot help feeling just a little bitter that Charles, my kind, loyal Charles, good in every way had such a sad end to his life while Stefan, the habitual womaniser, a selfish charmer lives on in good health, his every need attended to by those nuns'.

Later that day Amy waved her daughter 'goodbye' as she drove off. "Give my good wishes to your father on his birthday", she called. It was useless to bear malice, like herself Stefan was old now. Probably he too suffered from failing eyesight and was hard of hearing and would not admit it. As she went in and closed the door Amy wondered if when she next saw Becky there might be a message of some kind from the man who had once made her so happy.

CHAPTER EIGHTEEN

Becky went back to London and Amy continued her leisurely life. Mrs. Monk put in some more hours and kept a watchful eye on her employer. She knew that the old lady was sometimes a little forgetful and checked each day that the tablets had been pressed out of their foil wrapping.

Autumn came, the lawns littered with leaves of red and gold. John Monk was kept busy sweeping paths and digging up the bedding plants. There were bonfires to give a pleasant smoky aroma to the evening air.

Sometimes, to pass away the afternoons that she found long, Amy looked through her collection, touched the pale, soft crepe-de-chine underclothes, tried on the hats once so fashionable. The coats and dresses still fitted her tall slim figure. Memories of those days as a mannequin, as in those days a model was called, came back vividly. Paris, the flat she had shared with Nicole, the French mannequin. Life had been so exciting, every experience enjoyed to the full. The young Stefan and his blatant admiration of the striking, youthful Amy. Oh, those elegant, carefree days before the war, life would never be like that again.

Tessie still sat on a chair, next to the dressing table. Her wedding dress was quite yellow with age, her one leg chipped and cracked. the result of one of the young Becky's tantrums when the precious doll had been flung across the room. The doll's eyes were still bright, the lashes painted on to the china face over ninety years ago, still black. Amy spoke to her most days, of Imogen and Dolly, sometimes of Sarah and Jim. Mostly though Amy spoke of Charles of how she missed him. She missed them all, they had all gone, left Amy behind, everyone of them. She could hear Imogen's voice quite clearly..... 'Are you free Miss Clayden?' and Dolly's ..... 'Walk slowly, dear, touch the lapel ... ' but Charles' voice, try as she might, Amy could not recall Charles' voice. Could Tessie remember, she asked? No, dear Charles' voice had gone forever.

In 1971 a stroke had robbed Charles of his voice and Amy of the conversations they both so much enjoyed. She had helped him dress and undress, had been there for him to lean on as they walked so slowly around their lovely garden. His right hand had remained useless and if it was imperative to communicate, Charles had scrawled a few words with his left hand. The last three years they had together were happy though in spite of the tragedy. They were together in Hope Lodge, the home they had created between them. Charles never again went into his studio, he could not bear to look upon the portrait, unfinished, of Margot and Becky. He had started it on Margot's fortieth birthday. Margot her dark hair fashionably streaked with gold, large dark eyes so like those of Jim and Amy. Becky, blonde hair and her blue eyes staring out of the canvas looked odd with her nose and mouth not finished. The canvas had remained on the easel and the sitters had aged by more than ten years.

Yes, ten years since Charles had died, Amy could still recall his smile, his whistling as he closed his studio door, finished for the day. She could not remember his voice.

A chest infection had led to pneumonia and Charles, with Amy beside him, died in a little room at the hospital where once Dinah had worked. He was seventy-six, his face twisted and his hair grey but as Amy kissed him goodbye he looked to her, young and defenceless. She had been relieved that he was at rest, the grief and the loneliness came later.

After Charles' death, Becky had tried to persuade her mother to leave Hope Lodge. "A smaller house or even a flat would be so much more suitable", she had said.

Amy stood firm, she loved her home. The years had begun to fly past. Margot was so kind, always telephoning, visiting and regularly inviting her aunt to meals, especially at weekends. Weekends were the lonely times and Margot seemed to understand.

*   *   *   *   *

November came and Becky rang to remind her mother that she was off to Paris to visit Stefan on his ninetieth birthday. "Any messages Ma?"

"No dear, not really, say I hope he is well. I've sent a card and written a few words. Will you be down to see me on the 25th?"

"My birthday! Oh Ma I cannot believe I shall be fifty-three, yes I'll be down, with a friend I hope. Someone you have seen but by now have probably forgotten, it is so long since you met".

"Who Becky?" , asked a curious Amy.

"Wait and see Ma, I really do not want to say too much at the moment, Keep your fingers crossed for me. See you, 'bye", and she was gone.

Becky sounded younger, happier to Amy's ears. Plans were made for Becky's birthday. A table was booked for the Sunday evening at a small restaurant in Bovey Tracey, a favourite meeting place for Becky and Margot. Amy booked a table for five. Margot and Tom were pleased to be invited to join Amy, Becky and her surprise guest.

"See you there around eight o'clock, in the bar", said Amy. "Any idea who Becky may be bringing?"

Margot's reply in the negative somehow didn't ring quite true to Amy.

She had been right to book a table for five; Becky just before the weekend confirmed her friend would be driving her down to Devon.

'I must look my best', thought Amy as she dressed that Saturday morning. A grey, finely pleated wool skirt looked well with the white silk shirt and scarlet jacket she had recently bought on a shopping trip to Exeter. She touched her ears with perfume, 'Jicky' this time, one of the presents she had received on her birthday. The pearls lay in their open box on the dressing table. 'I'll wear them tomorrow, they always look so beautiful in the evenings, gleaming in the soft lights of the restaurant. What a pity Charles and I did not have a son, the tradition will be broken, no heir to pass on the jewellery to his bride'.

It was nearly lunch time when a car drew up, not Becky's car but a larger, more expensive model. Becky jumped out and ran up the steps to her mother. "Happy Birthday darling", said Amy as she kissed her daughter.

The other occupant of the car took his time; he slowly opened his door, stood up and as he raised his head Amy recognised him. It was Graham Harvey, a man to whom at one time Becky had been very close. A man who much to Amy's disappointment had disappeared from the scene.

"How lovely to see you Graham, to see you both", said Amy holding out her hand to the rugged, rather stocky man she remembered with affection.

He kissed her on both cheeks. "Mmmm, you still smell delicious, you always did".

It was a little joke between them. Graham, when he had been seeing Becky regularly was always trying to get her to change her perfume. Becky at that time wore a scent that was rather overpowering. Graham told her to take a leaf out of her mother's book. Had he been too domineering, was that why Becky had dropped him? She was not a lady to be dictated to.

Amy was pleased with the way lunch went. A simple meal of chicken and vegetables but cooked to perfection. Yes, even an old lady could still entertain well with a little thought. Graham went into the garden at Becky's suggestion. Becky and her mother started on the washing up.

"Pleased to see Graham, Ma?", asked Becky.

"Of course, delighted. He's such a pleasant man dear, I was afraid he was right out of the picture".

"Well, Ma, I'm afraid a few years ago he was not free but that has changed now and he has asked me to marry him".

"Marry, you might marry him? Becky that is really wonderful, I can't take it in. Sure you are not joking?"

"It's quite true Ma. We've always kept in touch and recently have been seeing each other. I know I'm rather 'over the hill' as they say. The staff will think I'm mad, my friends will think it a joke but I'm going to say yes".

Becky scraped some left overs into the bin and said, "Ma, what are these tablets in here, in the rubbish?"

Amy answered nonchalantly, "Sometimes when I am trying to get my tablets out of those silly packets they fall on the floor. I'm not going to take them after that, so I sweep them up and throw them away. I found several this morning they must have rolled under the oven".

"But Ma, that's serious isn't it, not to take them each day I mean?"

"Don't fuss Becky. I'm as strong as a horse, no problems with my heart now. Tell me, how was your father?"

Becky put down the tea towel and came to put her arms around her mother. "I know you're changing the subject Ma but that's why I sent Graham out to talk to John. So that I could tell you about my visit. I think talking to Daddy, listening to what he had to say about you and himself brought me up with a jolt".

"What did Stefan say?"

"First of all he was cross with me, for trying to make you sell the house and your collection of clothes. He said he knows just how much you treasure your possessions. He made me promise never to try and persuade you to do anything against your will. Then he told me quite a bit about your marriage. How foolish he had been, how he regretted his arrogant, selfish ways. I could see how, even after all these years, he still cares for you. I also saw that I have been under a misapprehension for years. I had, in my child's mind, a picture of you turning your back on my Daddy, transferring your love to Charles who you had known years before. I loved Daddy so much that I didn't want to believe that he could be cruel to you".

"But ..." Amy tried to interrupt.

"Ma, you never ever painted a black picture of Daddy. You never criticised his behaviour. How stupid I was to always have in the back of my mind the idea that it was Daddy who had been wronged".

Amy, enjoying the feeling of her daughter's warm arms around her also experienced a warm sense of peace, a kind of thankfulness that Stefan understood how much the house and her treasures meant to her. She appreciated him talking to Becky so frankly about their marriage and the reasons for its breakdown.

Margot and Tom were pleased to see Graham at the restaurant on the Sunday evening. "We couldn't be sure who the mystery guest was", said Margot. "We hoped it might be you Graham. Your name has come up quite a lot recently in our chats with Becky".

Becky did not enlarge on the subject but spoke instead of her visit to Stefan. "He looked fine Margot. You would never think he was ninety, still tall and upright. The lucky man has not lost his pride and his hair and beard are immaculately barbered. Between you and me, his eyesight could be better and although he won't admit it, Stefan is very deaf. I told him that he was still 'quite a dish' and he loved that of course, still the same old Stefan!"

"I expect he said that you, like everyone else these days, mumbled instead of speaking clearly", said Amy who, on occasions, used those very words herself.

"Yes Ma, he did. Several times". The talk of speaking clearly reminded Amy of something. She turned to Margot who was engrossed in a battle with the garnish on her pork steak. "1 know this sounds foolish Margot but I've quite forgotten. Can you remember what Charles' voice sounded like?"

"I can Ma", interrupted Becky. "He had a distinctive voice, good enunciation, a low voice and he was always whistling and singing wasn't he".

Margot put down her fork and took Amy's hand in hers. "I know what you mean Aunt Amy" , she said quietly. "Uncle Charles had a lovely voice, as Becky said it was low but when he spoke to you, just you, he changed it in a subtle way. His tone became softer, more gentle, yes that was it. When he spoke to you he had a low, soft, gentle voice and looked at you in a special way. Do you recall it now?"

"Yes dear", lied Amy, with a sigh.

"Just remembered something else Daddy said", Becky informed Amy. "He said I should drive you to Shearfield, to take you to see the church again, walk around the village. We could make a nice weekend of it, in the Spring".

Amy took another sip of wine, wiped her lips on the starched napkin that Graham kept retrieving from the carpet. The silly thing would keep slipping off her silk covered lap. "It was kind of him to suggest that Becky, but I think not. My memory of the place is enough for me. There is no one left there now who means anything to me. I should imagine that like so many villages, many of the cottages have been bought by people outside the area. Colour washed, extended, gardens landscaped and heaven knows what else. They would bear no relation whatsoever to the pictures in my mind of the homes of Sarah, Mrs. Rayne, Mrs. Shepherd and so on. No dear, I shall not trouble you to drive all that way on my account".

Becky then held forth on the prices of country properties and Tom and Graham teased her about how she must have made a pretty packet a few years ago during the property boom. They were a lively party and Amy was happy to be part of it, to listen to as much of the conversation as she could hear.

As she waved to Becky and Graham the next morning as they set out on the journey back to London, Amy fingered the rope of pearls. Bother! She had meant to give them to Becky last night. It was an idea that had come to her when she had watched her daughter and Graham holding hands at the table during the celebratory meal. Becky may like to wear them at her wedding. A Registry Office wedding they had said. The tradition of the Lambert man giving them to his bride had come to an end, it was sad but that was life.

Amy went back into the house, quiet now with only herself. Mrs. Monk moving about upstairs, changing bed linen no doubt. The old lady ran her hands over the William and Mary lowboy that Jim had made. How smooth the wood was, a lovely colour this walnut and polished regularly by her own hands over the years. Amy looked up at the picture of Tessie, the pastel was still as fresh as the day Charles had presented it to his wife.

Amy was glad that her will stated quite clearly that any furniture made by her brother was to go to his family, Margot, Susan and Anne. Tessie was to be given a home by Margot. Amy's jewellery and pictures were for Becky along with the rest of her estate. Amy hoped she would treasure the contents of the old chocolate box. Nothing of value there but foolish little souvenirs of a happy time when Amy Clayden was begining to grow up.

That evening when Becky telephoned to say they had arrived home safely, Amy told her, "one of these days, when I'm no longer here Becky, do as you please about Hope Lodge and my collection. Maybe it is selfish not to share those beautiful things with people who could be interested. I'm getting so forgetful dear, that if you come down again soon please remind me to give you the pearls, for your wedding, I did mean to do so last night".

Christmas had come and gone. Becky was now Mrs. Harvey and soaking up some sun many miles from England. 'What glamorous honeymoons couples have these days' thought Amy as she sat by her fire. She stirred the milky chocolate drink, watched the minute bubbles around the rim of the Coalport cup. A favourite of hers with a border of blue flowers and gold rim. She felt at peace, warm and comfortable after her bath. So tired though, weary and exhausted and Amy knew the milky chocolate, delicious as it was, was not necessary to make her sleep tonight.

Becky came again into Amy's thoughts. This time as a little girl, drinking cocoa, with Margot in Dinah's kitchen, safe after their runaway trip to London. The girls were describing the air raid, sipping at their hot cocoa. How nice it was that she and Becky were such good friends still, and how wonderful that Amy and her daughter now understood each other so well.

She rinsed the delicate cup carefully under the tap and placed it on the draining board. The stairs seemed steeper tonight, it was like climbing a hill; at the top Amy paused for breath. She sat down on the nursing chair that had stood in the same spot since Charles had brought it into the house. Amy looked at the door of the 'Museum' as she and Becky had always called that particular bedroom. Should she have a quick peep at her treasures? Tired as she was Amy could not resist sliding back one or two of the wardrobe doors, touching the garments, revelling in the feel of the smooth silks and soft velvets. Her hands as they explored the contents of the wardrobes looked old, the fingers bent, crooked with rheumatism.

In her own bedroom Amy removed her dressing gown, turned down the bed clothes. Through the uncurtained window the moon shone down on Tessie's perfect face, the light giving her dress an unearthly, silvery hue. Amy smiled at her and got into bed.

The dream that Amy was experiencing in the early hours of the morning was a long one, it seemed to go on forever. She was on holiday, in a hotel and part of the country she did not recognise. Amy stood in the hotel's kitchen, a round table held a large amount of blue and white china that seemed familiar and Dinah and Jim were preparing vegetables. Then Amy found herself walking in the country, she was lost, knew she had to find Charles that they may get back to the hotel for dinner. In the distance, at the top of a hill stood three people; they waved to Amy, beckoned to her. Her legs felt heavy, she was short of breath and the hill was steep. Amy toiled on, ever upwards, her chest hurt and there was pain in her arms but she must go on. Surely that was mother and father standing behind Charles; they all looked so young. Were they on holiday too?

The hill was so steep but at last Amy was closer to Charles; he put out his hands and she ignored the pain to take one more step to touch his fingers. Amy saw to her amazement her fingers were straight, her skin smooth and of course that was Charles' voice, how could she have forgotten. "Amy , sweetheart, at last". She gave a long deep sigh.

Only the doll, sitting there in the moonlight heard Amy's last, long drawn out breath. The curtains moved slightly in a sudden small breeze and then the night was still.

ACKNOWLEDGEMENTS

Publishing this novel at long last has been the greatest pleasure for me. It is the realisation of a long-held ambition, and there are a number of key people to whom I am greatly indebted for the vital parts they played in supporting and encouraging me over the years.

First and foremost I wish to thank my dear Father who was himself a born storyteller. He encouraged me to to write from an early age and he was my chief inspiration.

My sincere gratitude also goes to publisher and writer Anthony Grey, and his Lovemore Books colleague Sonja Haggett for their help and editorial guidance which enabled me finally to realize my dream. Marian Baker – a good friend, expert secretary and typist – has also played an important continuing role, and I am very grateful to another dear friend Dinah Goom, an expert photographer who provided the author portraits for the covers of the novel and other pictures for the promotion and publicity stages of publication.

My especial thanks also go finally to Sally Warboyes and Pamela Cleaver, tutors at Fen Farm Residential Writing Course in Norfolk, whom I met in 1991. They recommended and introduced me to the Romantic Novelist Association, a most important step forward, and as a result 'Portrait of Amy' was written in 1992.

For further information about Lovemore Books authors, e-books, DVDs and audio CDs see www.lovemorebooks.co.uk
To order Lovemore Books titles direct contact:
Sonja Haggett, Lovemore House, Layer Hall Farm,
Layer de la Haye, Colchester CO2 0ET.
t. 0845 6444186 e. tagmandistribute@btinternet.com

This Is Dorothy

Head held high in an elegant jaunt
Dark eyes flash, entice, then taunt.
Fashionable clothes, hair style of today,
Charming, vivacious with her own certain play.
This is Dorothy.

Sadness as memories drift from the past,
Quiet voice, now sad, she seems so overcast.
New friends, someone to listen, someone to heed
She's started to climb and with a will, can succeed.
This is Dorothy.

Grand with style, entertaining a flair,
She takes what life offers with hardly a care.
Luxury enfolds her like a cluster of dreams,
Serenity, understanding and friendship she beams.
This is Dorothy.

tribute to the author by a late friend, Doreen James